P.E.N.
New Fiction I

P.E.N.
New Fiction I

Edited by Peter Ackroyd

Quartet Books
London Melbourne New York

First published by Quartet Books Limited 1984
A member of the Namara Group
27/29 Goodge Street, London W1P 1FD

Copyright © 1984 by Peter Ackroyd

British Library Cataloguing in Publication Data

P.E.N. new fiction I.
  1. Short stories, English   2. English
  fiction—20th century
  I. Ackroyd, Peter
  823'.01'08[FS]   PR1309.S5

  ISBN 0-7043-2453-9

Typeset by MC Typeset, Chatham, Kent
  Printed and bound in Great Britain
  by Mackays of Chatham Ltd, Kent

62373

Published with the financial assistance
of the Arts Council of Great Britain.

Contents

Introduction   Peter Ackroyd   vii

Ties   Desmond Hogan   1

At the Beach   Robert Mullen   9

Pleasure Trips   John Greening   18

Mammy's Boy   Thomas McCarthy   25

Dark Steps   S.R. Wallace   38

Proletarian Zen   Deborah Levy   46

Visit   Mark Harding   54

Brides of the Pleiades   Iain Sinclair   62

Villa Marta   Clare Boylan   67

Confession of a Catamite   Bryan Allan   76

Disparities   Ben Okri   83

Dead Flower   Patricia Connolly   96

African Story   G.P. Davis   99

My Other Grandmother   T. Walsh   104

The Gift of Sunday   Meira Chand   115

What's Eating You?   Anthony Edkins   131

Stella Artois   Deborah Singmaster   139

SF   Andy Soutter   147

Urchins   Ronald Hayman   161

Book Review   Pat Revill   169

Dreams of Leaving   D. J. Taylor   174

The Silver Fish   Eric Slayter   183

Ratón Ladrón   Penelope Shuttle   195

The Priest   Alex Auswaks   203
Splices   Manny Draycott   213
Crossing Demon   J. New   222
The Licences to Eat Meat   Rosalind Belben   232
The Present   Cheryl Moskowitz   234
Children's Games   Gabriel Josipovici   243

Introduction

There is really no need to speculate on the nature of the short story, either in explanation or in justification of this anthology; the writers gathered here have performed that task already, and the variety of styles and themes which they have chosen provides the best commentary upon a bewilderingly diverse form. There are those who used to think of the short story as somehow 'like' the novel, although more truncated; most of the contributors to this volume prove that to be far from the case: Iain Sinclair's 'Brides of the Pleiades' and Deborah Levy's 'Proletarian Zen', for example, show that short narratives are established on quite different principles of tone and organization. And although this collection is in no way representative of contemporary English fiction – you cannot represent that which still remains undefined – it does at least provide some evidence of the vitality and inventiveness which the best of that fiction still possesses. More than four hundred stories were submitted, and the task of selecting only a handful of that number was a difficult one; clearly it would have been absurd, were it not also impossible, to choose examples only of a certain type or style, but, if there is one common feature among those finally selected, it is the presence of a sustained and convincing 'voice' which is able to create its own world – from the objective and recognizable setting of John Greening's 'Pleasure Trips' to the dispossessed consciousness of Ben Okri's 'Disparities'; from the ironic fantasies of Andy Soutter's 'SF' to the comic realism of Thomas McCarthy's 'Mammy's Boy'. Some of the writers in this anthology are well-known, others are not; but the distinction, in writing of this quality, is not an important one. All of them provide something gratifyingly unique – I hope, and believe, that the pleasure they have afforded me will be shared by other readers.

Peter Ackroyd

P.E.N.
New Fiction I

DESMOND HOGAN

Ties

I

The Forty Steps led nowhere. They were grey and wide, shadowed at the sides by creeper and bush. In fact it was officially declared by Patsy Fogarthy that there were forty-four steps. These steps were erected by an English landlord as a memorial to some doubtful subject. A greyhound, a wife? If you climbed them you had a view of the recesses of the woods and the places where Patsy Fogarthy practised with his trombone. Besides playing – in a navy uniform – in the brass band, Patsy Fogarthy was my father's shop assistant. While the steps were dark-grey the counter in my father's shop was a dark and fathomless brown. We lived where the town men's Protestant society had once been and that was where our shop was too. And still is. Despite the fact my father is dead. My father bought the house, built the shop from nothing after a row with a brother with whom he shared the traditional family grocery-cum-bar business. Patsy Fogarthy was my father's first shop assistant. They navigated waters together. They sold silk ties, demonstrating them carefully to country farmers. (Now the shop sells acrylic sports shorts and burdensome suits.)

Patsy Fogarthy was from the country and had a tremendous welter of tragedy in his family – which always was a point of distinction – deranged aunts, a paralytic mother. We knew that Patsy's house – cottage – was in the country. We never went there. It was just a picture. And in my mind, in the cottage in its turn were many pictures – paintings, embroideries by a prolific local artist who took to embroidery when she was told she was destined to die from leukaemia. Even my mother had one of

1

her works. A bowl of flowers on a firescreen. From his inception as part of our household it seemed that Patsy had allied himself towards me. In fact he'd been my father's assistant from before I was born. But he dragged me on walks, he described linnets to me, he indicated ragwort, he seated me on wooden benches in the hall outside town opposite a line of sycamores as he puffed into his trombone, as his fat stomach heaved into it. Patsy had not always been fat. That was obvious. He'd been corpulent, not fat.

'Look,' he said one day on the avenue leading to the Forty Steps – I was seven – 'a blackbird about to burst into song.'

Patsy had burst into song once. At a Saint Patrick's night concert. He sang 'Patsy Fagan'. Beside a calendar photograph of a woman at the back of our shop he did not sing for me but recited poetry: 'The Ballad of Athlone'. The taking of the bridge at Athlone by the Williamites in 1691 had dire consequences for this area. It implanted it for evermore with Williamites. It directly caused the Irish defeat at Aughrim. Patsy lived in the shadow of the hills of Aughrim. Poppies were the consequences of battle. There were balloons of defeat in the air. Patsy Fogarthy brought me a gift of mushrooms once from the fields of Aughrim.

Patsy had a bedding of blackberry curls about his cherubic face; he had cherubic lips that smiled often; there was a snowy sparkle in his deep blue eyes. Once he'd have been exceedingly good-looking. When I was nine his buttocks slouched obesely. Once he'd have been as the man in the cigarette advertisements. When I was nine on top of the Forty Steps he pulled down his jaded trousers as if to pee, opened up his knickers and exposed his gargantuan balls. Delicately I turned away. The same year he tried to put the same penis in the backside of a drummer in the brass band, or so trembling, thin members of the Legion of Mary vouched. Without the murmur of a court case Patsy was expelled from town. The boy hadn't complained. He'd been caught in the act by a postman who was one of the church's most faithful members in town. Patsy Fogarthy crossed the Irish Sea, leaving a trail of mucus after him.

I left Ireland for good and all 11 October 1977. There'd been many explanations for Patsy's behaviour: an aunt who used to have fits, throwing her arms about like seven snakes; the fact he might really have been of implanted Williamite stock. One way or the other he'd never been quite forgotten, unmentioned for a while, yes, but meanwhile the ecumenical movement had revived thoughts of him. My mother attended a Protestant service in Saint John's church in 1976. As I left home she pressed a white, skeletal piece of paper into my hands. The address of a hospital where Patsy Fogarthy was now incarcerated. The message was this: 'Visit him. We are now Christian (we go to Protestant services) and if not forgiven he can have some alms.' It was the fact that one could now go back that made people accept him a little. He'd sung so well once. He smiled so cheerily. And sure wasn't there the time he gave purple Michaelmas daisies to the dying and octogenarian and well nigh crippled Mrs Connaughton (she whose husband left her and went to America in 1927).

I did not bring Patsy Fogarthy purple Michaelmas daisies. In the house I was staying in in Battersea there were marigolds. Brought there regularly by myself. Patsy was nearby in a Catholic hospital in Wandsworth. Old clay was dug up. Had my mother recently been speaking to a relative of his? A casual conversation on the street with a country woman. Anyway this was the task I was given. There was an amber, welcoming light in Battersea. Young deer talked to children in Battersea Park. I crept around Soho like an escaped prisoner. I knew there was something connecting then and now, yes, a piece of paper, connecting the far-off, starched days of childhood to an adulthood which was confused, desperate, but determined to make a niche away from family and all the friends that had ensued from a middle-class Irish upbringing. I tiptoed up bare wooden stairs at night, scared of waking those who'd given me lodging. I tried to write to my mother and then I remembered the guilty conscience on her face. Gas works burgeoned into the honey-coloured sky, oblivious of the landscape inside me, the dirty avenue cascading on the Forty Steps.

'Why do you think they built it?'

'To hide something.'

'Why did they want to hide something?'

'Because people don't want to know about some things.'

'What things?'

Patsy had shrugged, a fawn coat draped on his shoulders that day.

'Patsy, I'll never hide anything.'

There'd been many things I'd hidden. A girlfriend's abortion. An image of a little boy inside myself, a blue and white striped tee shirt on him. The mortal end of a relationship with a girl. Desire for my own sex. Loneliness. I'd tried to hide loneliness, but Dublin, city of my youth, had exposed loneliness like neon at evening. I'd hidden a whole part of my childhood, the 1950s, but hitting London took them out of the bag. Irish pubs in London, their jukeboxes, united the 1950s with the 1970s with the kiss of a song. 'Patsy Fagin'. Murky waters wheezed under a mirror in a pub lavatory. A young man in an Italian-style duffel coat, standing erect, eddied into a little boy being tugged along by a small fat man.

'Patsy, what is beauty?'

'Beauty is in the eye of the beholder.'

'But what is it?'

He looked at me. 'Pretending we're father and son now.'

I brought Patsy Fogarthy white carnations. It was a sunny afternoon early in November. I'd followed instructions on a piece of paper. Walking into the demesne of the hospital I perceived light playing in a bush. He was not surprised to see me. He was a small, fat, bald man in pyjamas. His face and his baldness were a carnage of reds and purples. Little wriggles of grey hair stood out. He wore maroon and red striped pyjamas. He gorged me with a look. 'You're . . .'

I did not want him to say my name. He took my hand. There was death in the intimacy. He was in a hospital for the mad. He made a fuss of being grateful for the flowers. 'How's Georgina?'

He called my mother by her first name. 'And Bert?' My father was not yet dead. It was as if he was charging them with something. Patsy Fogarthy, our small-town Oscar Wilde, reclined in pyjamas on a chair against the shimmering citadels of Wandsworth. A white nun infrequently scurried in to see to some man in the corridor. 'You made a fine young man.' 'It was the band I missed most.' 'Them were the days.' In the middle of snippets of conversation – he sounded not unlike an Irish bank clerk, aged though and more graven-voiced – I imagined the tableau of love, Patsy with a young boy. 'It was a great old band. Sure you've been years out of the place now. What age are ye?'

'Twenty-six.'

'Do you have a girlfriend? The English girls will be out to grab you now.'

A plane noisily slid over Wandsworth. We simultaneously looked to it. An old, swede-faced man bent over a bedside dresser. 'Do ya remember me? I used bring you on walks.' Of course I said. Of course. 'It's not true what they said about us. Not true. They're all mad. They're all lunatics. How's Bert?' Suddenly he started shouting at me: 'You never wrote back. You never wrote back to my letters. And all the ones I sent you.' More easy-voiced, he was about to return the flowers until he suddenly avowed: 'They'll be all right for Our Lady. They'll be all right for Our Lady.' Our Lady was a white statue, over bananas and pears, by his bed.

III

It is hot summer in London. Tiger lilies have come to my door. I'd never known Patsy had written to me. I'd never received his letters of course. They'd curdled in my mother's hand. All through my adolescence I imagined them filing in, never to be answered. I was Patsy's boy. More than the drummer lad. He had betrothed himself to me. The week after seeing him, after being virtually chased out of the ward by him, I took a week's holiday in Italy with money I'd saved up in Dublin. The trattorias of Florence in November illumined the face of a young man who'd been Patsy Fogarthy before I'd been born. It's now six years on and that face still puzzles me, the face I saw in Florence, a young man with black hair, and it makes a story that solves a lot of mystery for me. There's a young man with black hair in a scarlet tie but it's not Patsy. It's a young man my father met in London in 1939, the year he came to study tailoring. Perhaps now it's the summer and the heat and the picture of my father on the wall – a red and yellow striped tie on him – and my illimitable estrangement from family, but this summer this city creates a series of icons. Patsy is one of them. But the sequence begins in the summer of 1939.

Bert ended up on the wide pavements of London in the early summer of 1939. He came from a town in the Western Midlands of Ireland whose wide river had scintillated at the back of town before he left and whose handsome façades radiated with sunshine. There were girls left behind that summer and cricket matches. Bert had decided on the tailoring course after a row with an older brother with whom he'd shared the family grocery-cum-bar business. The family house was one of the most sizeable on the street. Bert had his eye on another house to buy now. He'd come to London to forge a little bit of independence from family for himself and in so doing he forwent some of the pleasures of the summer. Not only had he left the green cricket fields by the river but he had come to a city that exhaled news bulletins. He was not staying long. He'd strolled into a cavern of death, for behind the cheery faces of London that summer was death. Bert would do his course in Cheapside and not linger. Badges pressed against military lapels, old dishonours to Ireland. Once Bert had taken a Protestant girl out. They sailed in the bumpers at the October fair together. That was the height of his forgiveness for England. He did not consider playing cricket a leaning to England. Cricket was an Irish game, pure and simple, as could be seen from its popularity in his small, Protestant-built town.

Living was not easy for Bert in London: an Irish landlady –
she was from Armagh, a mangy woman – had him. Otherwise
the broth of his accent was rebuffed. He stooped a little under
English disdain but his hair was still orange and his face ruddy
in fragments. By day Bert travelled; a dusty, dark cubicle. At
evening he walked. It was the midsummer which made him
raise his head a little. Twilight rushing over the tops of the trees
at the edge of Hyde Park made him think of his dead parents,
Galway people. He was suddenly both proud of and abstracted
by his lineage. A hat was vaunted by his red hands on his waist.
One evening, as perfumes and colours floated by, he thought of
his mother, her tallness, her military posture, the black clothes
she had always been stuffed into. In marrying her husband she
declared she'd married a bucket. Her face looked a bit like a
bucket itself. Bert had recovered his poise. The width of his
shoulders breathed again. His chest was out. It was that evening
a young man wearing a scarlet tie stopped and talked to him
under a particularly dusky tree by Hyde Park. 'You're Irish,'
the young man had said.

'How do you know?'

'Those sparkling blue eyes.'

The young man had worn a kind of perfume himself. 'You
know,' he said – his accent was very posh – 'there's going to be a
war. You would be better off in Ireland.'

Bert considered the information. 'I'm here on a course.'

Between that remark and a London hotel there was an island
of nothing. Masculine things for Bert had always been brothers
pissing, the spray and the smell of their piss, smelly Protestants
in the cricket changing-rooms. That night Bert – how he
became one he did not know – was a body. His youth was in the
hands of an Englishman from Devon. The creaminess of his
skin and the red curls of his hair had attained a new state for
one night, that of an angel at the side of the Gothic steeple at
home. There was beauty in Bert's chest. His penis was in the fist
of another young man.

Marriage, children, a drapery business in Ireland virtually
eliminated it all, but they could not quite eliminate the choice

7

colours of sin, red of handkerchiefs in men's pockets in a smoky hotel lounge, red of claret wine, red of blood on sheets where lovemaking was too violent. In the morning there was a single thread of a red hair on a pillow autographed in pink.

When my father opened his drapery business he ran it by himself for a while, but on his marriage he felt the need for an assistant and Patsy was the first person who presented himself for the job. It was Patsy's black hair, his child's lips, his Roman sky-blue eyes that struck a resonance in my father. Patsy came on an autumn day. My father was reminded of a night in London. His partnership with Patsy was a marital one. When I came along it was me Patsy chose over my brothers. He was passing on a night in London. The young man in London? He'd worn a scarlet tie. My father specialized in ties. Patsy wore blue and emerald ones to town dos. He was photographed for the *Connaught Tribune* in a broad, blue, black speckled one. His shy smile hung over the tie. Long years ago my mother knew there was something missing from her marriage to my father – all the earnest hot-water jars in the world could not obliterate this knowledge – she was snidely suspicious of Patsy (she too had blackberry hair) and when Patsy's dénouement came along it was she who expelled him from the shop, afraid for the part of her husband he had taken, afraid for the parcel of her child's emotions he would abduct now that adolescence was near. But the damage, the violation, had been done. Patsy had twined my neck in a scarlet tie one sunny autumn afternoon in the shop, tied it decorously and smudged a patient, fat, wet kiss on my lips.

ROBERT MULLEN

At the Beach

I

'I really don't believe this,' she's saying, coming down the walk
with her arms full of Kleenex boxes and stuffed toys. 'I don't
believe it's still the middle of the night.'

He says nothing, she's up and she's dressed, he has already
won his point.

'Just don't expect me to read any maps,' she warns, 'or make
brilliant conversation.'

She opens the car door gently, gets in, kicks off her shoes,
tucks her feet up under her, and then twists around in the seat
to check on Kitty.

What he most looks forward to is the leaving, the slipping away
in the dark, like thieves, before anyone else has budged. Or if
not leaving early then leaving late, at lunchtime, leaving early
or leaving late just so long as it isn't anywhere near the time he
normally goes to work.

If it were up to her she wouldn't plan anything, not on a
vacation, especially not what time to wake up.

Stretch out if you want to, he says, and put your head in
my lap.

Another thing she wouldn't do if she were him is stop at
stoplights when there's no one else around.

What he used to do before he was married was just drive,
sometimes hundreds of miles, for no reason at all, with the car
radio turned up full blast. What he used to do was pick out

some town at random on the map, drive there, turn around,
without even getting out of the car, and then drive back home.

She watches as Kitty begins to stir. Some days she can watch her
for hours, just watch her, watch her and try to imagine what
must be going through her mind.

She watches as Kitty blinks.

She watches as a look of alarm appears on the child's face but
then quickly disappears again as she works out where she is.

He offers to give a nickel to the first person to see the
mountains.

'What do mountains look like?' asks Kitty.

'Surely,' he laughs, 'you must have seen enough television by
now to know what mountains look like.'

'I think I'm about to see one,' warns Mommy.

The car has begun to pull.

'Who can feel it pull?' he asks.

The car has begun to pull and the trucks which they are
passing now are moving at little better than a crawl. She tucks
her skirt down over her knees and watches, over her shoulder,
as Kitty does the same.

At the filling station a family of Indians is squatting together in
the dust, just beside the concrete, and one of them, the
grandfather by the look of him, comes over while the tank is
being filled to ask for a ride.

'Friend' he calls them.

'Could you give us a lift, friend?'

'What's wrong with their car,' she asks, 'is it broken?'

'Couldn't they see that there wasn't room?' says Daddy.

'They don't have a car, sweetheart,' says Mommy. 'Not
everyone has a car.'

'Why not?' she wonders.

'They must have thought they could squeeze in,' says Mommy.

'I spy something white,' says Kitty.
'A cowboy hat?' he guesses.

The highway begins to descend. She feels better, she would be willing to spell him at the wheel, she's fully awake now, but she doesn't offer. He knows that she can drive.

He knows that she can drive but he's not tired. His shoulder muscles ache and his back is stiff but he's not sleepy and once he starts something he likes to finish it. That's one way in which they are different. She has at any given moment perhaps two dozen half-completed projects under way. He was greatly surprised, he teased her at the time, that she carried Kitty for the full nine months.

Once they reach the last flat stretch of desert there are four lanes headed toward the coast and only two lanes coming back.

II

It's roasting out. Inside the car, even with the windows open, as the traffic slows, it's becoming stifling. No wonder the women out here, he's thinking, don't wear underwear.
  'Who can smell the sea? he says.

They pass a giant billboard advertising suntan lotion: Baste Don't Burn.

They've made it. They promised Kitty months ago what they would see first and she hasn't forgotten so he leaves the highway short of the sea and turns into a parking lot which must be half as big again as the two they live in. His muscles ache and his shirt and trousers are sticking to the seat but they've made it.

'Where Wishes Are Horses,' reads the motto above the gates.

'It means,' he paraphrases, 'out here all you've got to do is wish for something and you've got it.'

She scrunches down in the seat. If someone sees her then they see her but she's not going anywhere until she changes her blouse.

'All I wish,' says Kitty, 'is that we had a bigger car.'

'Why?' they ask.

'So the Indians would fit in,' says Kitty.

They stand in line first, two adults and one child, for the Jungle Riverboat. The line moves slowly, through a maze of metal railings and then out on to a wooden jetty and up a gently sloping ramp to where a young man, handsome, intelligent-looking, in a spotless white uniform, a would-be actor in all probability, is waiting to help them climb aboard.

There wouldn't happen to be, would there, he asks, looking right down at Kitty, a little girl on board who would like to help the captain blow the whistle?

She nods her permission. She doesn't want Kitty to grow up being afraid of anything. Whenever in life there are whistles to be blown she wants Kitty to be the one who blows them.

He accepts the rifle solemnly and kneels down at the rail beside the other men and begins scanning the wall of trees for danger.

When the attack does come, she at first refuses to take cover. Your mother's not afraid of cannibals, she tells Kitty, cannibals eat people only when they're really really hungry and these look well fed enough to me. But then glancing around and seeing that everyone else has ducked she begins to feel a little foolish.

In one direction, when they disembark, great stonelike ramparts rise. In another direction the shell of a silver rocket gleams, almost incandescent. In yet a third direction lie the gaily-coloured awnings of cafés along what purports to be the Champs Elysées.

One place Kitty definitely has to go, she has already promised herself, before she gets married or cohabits or whatever, is Paris.

Paris, France.

She knows, Kitty insists indignantly, that it's only make-believe, she knows *that*, but he can see that she is starting to get scared and so he lifts her up on to his shoulders. Scared and sleepy. Perhaps she's still a little young yet for Space Shot.

'Who can see Saturn?' he says. 'Who can see the rings?'

Afterwards, in the shop, they buy her a locket, a small locket on a fine silver chain, containing a tiny speck of moondust.

III

The clouds are tinted pink, the palm trees are tinted pink, it's as if even the seagulls have been tinted pink. She holds Kitty, asleep now, in her lap. He has put on the radio to hear the news. Every now and then a police squad car pulls out, siren screaming, and forces its way ahead through the oncoming traffic in pursuit of some distant evil which has nothing to do, thank God, with them.

At the motel, in the bathroom, the first thing she does is take off her blouse and wash it out in the sink. Through the half-open door she can hear the sound of an electric razor and Kitty laughing. She turns on the shower well before she's ready for it because at home it takes for ever for the hot water to reach the upstairs taps.

How it works is that first she has to get into her pyjamas and then she has to sit quietly and watch until he has done everything except his neck. Then it's her turn. He turns to face

her, kneels down, tips his head back, and she takes hold of the
razor with both hands.

Mowing the grass, they call it.

She has already got, she can see, some sun. She has to keep
wiping the glass free of steam. Sometimes she can go for months
on end without looking at herself in a mirror, sometimes not, it
all depends on the mood she's in. She lifts her breasts for
inspection, by first throwing back her shoulders and then using
her hands.

Tomorrow he promises as he tucks her in, tomorrow early they
will go down to the beach.

'When it's still dark?' she asks apprehensively.

The babysitter arranged for by the motel is a Mexican woman,
Amalia, a middle-aged, heavy-set woman, with a roll of
love-story comic books tucked under her arm.

IV

She sits a little closer to him this time, feeling clean, feeling
refreshed, feeling relaxed, though not so close as to be accused
of interfering with his driving. There were more police out here
than at home. There were more minorities. People out here
used their horns more. When they find a place to park, it's
between, she notices, two sports cars.

He makes a real song and dance out of coming around to open
the door for her. Would madame care to leave her coach now?
He used to drive to places but not even get out of the car for
fear of appearing foolish, a stranger, on his own, for fear of
someone asking him what he wanted there.

'Amalia,' she repeats to herself, having memorized the

14

woman's name in the same way as, back home, she would have memorized the licence-plate number of an out-of-state car parked near the bank.

They take their time. They look at things. They inadvertently look a panhandler in the eye.

They turn a corner.
   'Well!' she laughs.
   FLAGELLATIONS!
   PIN PALS!
   For five bucks you can watch men watch women masturbate.

'What do you suppose they do in a Sex Academy,' she wants to know, 'that we don't do?'
   'Listen to the sexperts,' he says. 'Go on sexcursions.'

They stop to watch a smokecharmer, wondering whether it's incense or marijuana that they're smelling. They stop to watch a pickpocket being arrested. They pass a man in a business suit; he could be a lawyer or an accountant, a stockbroker, a well-dressed man standing in the middle of the crowded sidewalk holding up a placard.
   'Come home, Sheila,' it reads. 'We love you.'

In the elevator, on the way up to the restaurant, though there are other people around, she presses herself close up against him.
   'You don't think,' she starts to ask, 'that Kitty would ever. . .?'
   'Kitty?' he laughs, ruffling her hair. 'Kitty would be the last one.'
   'But don't you think,' she argues, 'that that's what that man thought as well?'

It has something to do with a trip, with a long trip, it has to do with looking out of a window and suddenly seeing that the

15

earth, where she lives, is getting further and further away.

She wakes up screaming.

Tomorrow they'll spend on the beach, he promises her, tomorrow they'll be all three together.

V

There are no police cars, there are no fire engines, there are no ambulances, everything at the motel is exactly as it was when they left, with yellow light streaming out through the curtains of the rooms and a softer, blue light, seeping up from the pool.

'Just a dream,' says the woman, Amalia, gathering up her reading, 'she had a little dream, that was all.'

She checks just to make sure. She turns down the sheets just to make certain that it really is Kitty and not some other child that they have substituted. She gently lifts Kitty's head off the pillow and unfastens the chain of the locket and removes it from around her neck and lays it on the dresser.

She believes that it really is a speck of moondust.

She doesn't believe that they would be allowed to lie about a thing like that.

A dream. A nightmare, the woman meant. He sees the locket lying on the dresser. He wouldn't be surprised to find out that it was nothing but an ordinary grain of sand. Or salt. Or even talcum powder.

She watches him, from bed, the way she sometimes watches Kitty. She watches him double-lock the door and check the windows and then fold his robe just so before placing it over the back of a chair.

She smiles.

'Do I get my wish now?' she smiles.

'I want it,' she whispers.

'You got it,' he says.

'I want it,' she whispers. 'I want it like there's no tomorrow.'

'You got it, babe,' says Daddy.

JOHN GREENING

Pleasure Trips

Vin Tan was in difficulties. Not twenty feet from his face sat a naked girl; in his hand, a damp stick of charcoal was slowly disintegrating. And he was being expected somehow to connect the two. Every now and then during the three-hour session, the tutor would come and lean over him, grunt, and point out some minor improvement that could be made. Yet it was obvious Vin Tan lacked that instinct the weakest of his colleagues possessed – the instinct to copy from life.

'Hmm,' grunted the tutor. He was genial enough, and sympathetic, although with that manner that Vin Tan was beginning to recognize, where you could almost hear the tutting, 'poor devil. . .'

No hint had been given of what was likely to be required of him at the art college, and he was totally unprepared for such mountains of flesh. How could they be copied, those sugar-loaf peaks, hogs' backs, ridges running in all directions? It was impossible – not in a few hours, and not with charcoal!

'Hmm. . .' His tutor was taking a long draw on a panatella, perhaps wondering what more he could say about the strangely spiky and two-dimensional sketch before him.

In China, where Vin Tan had first studied art, you begin not with the human form, but with the characters of the Chinese language. Using a fine brush, you learn to express the meaning of the ideogram through a subtle and refined representation. After months and years of practice in this area, you may move on to landscapes; but still everything you paint is dominated by your training as a calligrapher. He could not bear this crumbling lump of black they had given him. What did this have to do with art?

'In Vietnam, we use this for cook!'

And the tutor smiled back, relieved to get away from the sketch and on to another subject even closer to his heart.

'What sort of things do you cook?'

'Fish! A lot fish!'

'Over charcoal?'

'Yes!'

The tutor's eyes gleamed through the cigar smoke, and he leant on a chair.

'I'm something of a fish freak myself. Have you been down to the harbour here?'

Vin Tan laughed – a slightly cynical chuckle – and pursued his drawing.

At home, he had found good work reproducing American film posters for local cinemas, but here, almost before anything else, they were told at the reception centre how unlikely it was that anyone would offer them a job. Then they were given the choice between Northern Ireland or the north of Scotland.

It hadn't even occurred to Vin Tan how cold it might be, and when he first saw snow it seemed more like some kind of entertainment than anything hostile. He didn't need to go out in it, unless he felt like an English lesson, or had to buy noodles, or sign on. He consumed mugfuls of a chrysanthemum infusion and felt satisfied that he would be able to face a Scottish winter. The family assigned to look after him kept saying he ought to switch on his storage heaters, since he spent so much time at home. But he had heard about electricity bills, how they lay in wait for you on the doormat, and sprung their demands on you for money you did not have. So they brought him some old winter clothes, and from October through to December Vin Tan spent his time either gazing out of the window contemplating snowscapes, or huddled in front of the television in a coat, scarf, gloves, and skiing hat.

By January, the chrysanthemum infusion had become cheap whisky. But he didn't enjoy drinking alone. The others had their wives and children, their parents or grandparents; they all visited each other regularly, and laughed and joked together during the English lessons. Vin Tan disdained to join in any of this. He had never visited any of the other refugees. They were, after all, only common fishing people. He was of Chinese stock. His father had been a doctor.

Painting became impossible once the cold weather set in. Once he did try, and by the end of the day his hand was so blue and swollen that he abandoned the attempt. For six months nobody even knew he was an artist, and it wasn't until his teacher called on him and asked about the paper cut-out dragon in his window that he produced the copies from biscuit tins and sweet boxes. Her husband taught at the art college, and so these life classes were arranged for the spring.

How inexplicable he found it, how distasteful, to have to inspect this woman. If she were wearing just some loose garment he knew he would be able to cope with those lines, but these seemed to change as he looked at them, and confuse themselves in his head with all kinds of unpleasant memories.

His companions in the class were friendly, but he found it difficult to relax when they began questioning him, obviously curious about his experiences as one of the 'boat people', and they, in turn, had difficulty understanding him. So he had ceased trying to communicate. They offered him cigarettes still. And their sketches remained a nagging rebuke to his own inability to draw in the required way. He had noticed that some of them were reading glossy magazines during the coffee break, so be bought one in an attempt to train his eye, but the curious shapes and grotesque poses bore so little resemblance to anything he saw in the class that he decided he would do better to save his money. The charcoal and sugar-paper were expensive enough, and he was trying to save as much as he could to send back to his mother.

He lived for her letters, although they were scarce and gave frightening hints of the life she was having to endure. It pleased her, of course, that one of her family was in a free country, and she said she would do her best to join him, but had not yet received the visa-promise letter. Vin Tan had been warned there would be difficulties because of tightening immigration laws, but he persuaded his support family and his teacher to write to the Home Office and the UNHCR asking if her application could be in any way speeded up. Their letters were designed to stress how his mother was suffering at the hands of the Communists, how important it was that she should be allowed to come quickly. But in reality he knew what numerous delays there could be at the Vietnamese end, and he was more than once on the point of suggesting to his mother that she buy herself a boat ticket.

The house in Ho Chi Minh City was in a notoriously rough area, and his mother was quite on her own except for the three young children. They were his brother's, but he had been killed in the war and his wife had disappeared leaving a house full of babies. In her last letter, Vin Tan's mother complained that she couldn't even go out to search for food as there was nobody left she could ask to babysit. As for her own children, those that had survived the war were scattered throughout the world. Some she heard from, others she knew nothing about. She was quite alone.

Then why, as Vin Tan's English teacher kept asking him, did he abandon her and come to Britain? Couldn't he have waited? They could have travelled together. What was the advantage in coming on his own?

In fact, he hadn't come on his own. He had left with his wife.

It is hard to rationalize your behaviour when you are the citizen of a country like Vietnam. Vin Tan couldn't begin to explain what it meant. To live somewhere your children are taught to despise their parents and grandparents, and to love only the state. Where you never know what next you will be called on to perform in the name of 'the people', yet where you have seen those same people kicked out of their homes, their life savings reduced at a blow to small change, all hope of a livelihood wrenched out of their control. It is more than enough to split a family. It is enough to make winter seas a favourable alternative.

21

For most, it was a matter of saving up for a year, perhaps longer – borrowing, selling, bargaining – then surrendering every last scrap to some reprobate boat owner, fixing a date, waiting. The date would come; and most probably the boat owner has been gone six weeks. And it all starts over again. Or if the boat is there, it turns out to be so grossly overcrowded that it never even leaves the harbour. Or it gets just outside only to be intercepted by the police. Or it gets further, and springs a leak, and has to be escorted back to Vietnam – and, if you can't afford the bribe, a prison sentence. Or if there's nobody at hand to escort you, you grab what you can and start to bail out. . .

Stories of the sufferings of refugees are commonplace. Everyone knows refugees have a hard time.

Hearing all these accounts, Vin Tan's mother had at first sworn she would never leave, and she forbade any of her children to go. But slowly she began to weaken. And when the family medicine shop was outlawed, along with thousands of others, as a 'bourgeois trade', she had no choice but to let her children take the initiative. She knew that her neighbour's eldest had endured a boat to Hong Kong and reached West Germany, that a letter had come one day and soon after the entire household had been able to leave by plane. So she decided Vin Tan and his wife must in the same way attempt to reach Hong Kong and then some other country.

Their boat was by no means as bad as some. It at least had an engine, and rode quite high in the water. Since the seas weren't too rough, they were never in any serious danger of capsizing. There was even occasionally room to lie down. The captain, however, proved to be a crook. He had demanded large sums of money for their provisions, but continually refused to hand out food. Halfway through the crossing there was a mutiny and he was murdered. That ended the food problems, but since he had been the only one to understand the whims of the engine, they now had to spend a lot of time drifting, trying to coax life into it.

During one of these becalmed periods, some days after the captain's death, a powerful motor launch was seen coming swiftly towards them. It stopped alongside. The first thought was that somebody had come to give them a hand, and a cheer went up, but the seven men on board were all heavily armed and their expressions tight and hard. They stripped the refugees of whatever they could find, and then demanded a girl. The Vietnamese all pointed at Vin Tan and his attractive Chinese wife. She was taken and sent over to the launch. Afterwards they threw her into the sea, and began ramming the refugee boat, then drove full throttle at the heads in the water. The boat survived, and even reached Hong Kong; and there was certainly no welcome or commiseration there.

'How about coming with me to the harbour after the class?'

The tutor was still leaning on the chair, sucking at his cigar.

Vin Tan shrugged, 'OK. . .'

He couldn't understand anything of what was being said round about him, although he was the subject of a lot of the banter, that was certain. As more boxes full of haddock were heaved on to the scales, his tutor hailed some of the men, who replied with sudden nods. One of them pointed to a large yellow fish that nobody else seemed to be bidding for. The tutor looked interested, and pushed through to examine it, abandoning Vin Tan on the harbour wall.

He wasn't at all sure why they had come here. It wasn't pleasant. The smell of fish. The shouting and clatter of crates on scales. Gulls shrieking. The waves in successive thunderclaps behind him. And then, this bitter wind off the sea. Vin Tan's head ached. He wished he had brought his scarf with him. Did winter really always last so long?

When his tutor had bought the fish, he returned to the wall and sat down beside Vin Tan, holding it up and laughing.

'Do you think it's edible?'

'Eat?'

'I don't know. What do you think? Anyway, I felt sorry for it.'

And he threw the fish aside and proceeded to set up an easel. It was to paint, rather than to shop for fish, that they had come.

On the easel he placed a large and incomplete painting – a watercolour, a minutely detailed copy of this forgotten corner of the harbour. An upturned boat was rotting among some old iron girders in front of a disused hut. And on the side of the hut (the painted hut, not the real one) was a sign, the words in faded red. Vin Tan stared at the words. They fascinated him. He had begun to assume that no one ever copied anything but naked women. Here was something very different, the imagery appearing to embrace the actual characters of the language, as in a Chinese painting. Why a hut, those heaps of iron, that boat, he couldn't imagine – such ordinary, uninteresting subjects. But those words. That was something he could appreciate.

His tutor was already at work, bent on reproducing everything exactly, his fine brush barely flickering on the paper as it attended to that scrap of rust on the rudder.

Vin Tan stared at the words. Of course, they would have some particular significance. He asked his tutor what they meant.

'Pleasure Trips? Well, it's when you have a boat out.'

'Why?'

'Just for fun. By the hour or for a day. For a trip.'

'Is this very fun?'

'Well . . . you can fish.'

'Ah, for fish men.'

'No, anyone. You can look at the cliffs. Go out to the Bell Rock. The lighthouse.'

'In *that*?'

'No, no, that's an old one, but only in the season of course. That's why the sign's been taken down.'

He dipped his fine brush into a small jar of water. 'Pleasure trips,' he repeated.

Vin Tan was quiet for a while, trying to make sense of this, and of the fish-auctioneer's broad Scots. Why did they teach him a language that nobody seemed to use? There was so much here that remained indecipherable. He tried to concentrate on what his tutor must be seeing as he copied each exact patch on the upturned boat.

THOMAS McCARTHY

Mammy's Boy

'You'll never believe it,' Harry Murphy said in the sneering, world-weary tone he affected, 'but the Mammy's Boy is running his own station today.'

'Jesus, you're jokin' me,' I said, but I was amused too.

'That's what the man said.'

We were changing for lunch in the bowels of the hotel, next to the boiler-room, in fact, in the room with the old tin lockers that was grandly known as the Waiters' and Commis' Staff-room. It was a dusty dump and you left anything of value there with the certain knowledge that it would be fecked before you got back to reclaim it.

'Today's the big day, Johnny,' Harry half-sneered as Johnny Berry brushed his spiky hair into some sort of order, aided by a generous dollop of Brylcreem.

'Ah, don't be going on at me, youse are always picking on me, Harry Murphy,' Johnny said plaintively.

'My dear fellow,' Harry said in his posh English accent – he was very good at accents – 'nothing could be further from the truth, I wish you well.' He bowed from the waist, as Mr O'Connell, the staff head waiter, called us from the corridor and we filed out through the labyrinth of passages, past the kitchen, then up the stairs to the still-room before entering the restaurant for the morning inspection.

Through the windows I could see Stephen's Green. The flowers were out, so were the girls, and I resented being at work, trussed up in a wing collar, a heavy dinner-jacket and the long white apron that was worn to just below the knee by all commis waiters.

'Right, commis on the left, station waiters on the right.' Mr O'Connell was small and round; he had a rather high-pitched voice and a Kerry accent that twenty-five years in Dublin had not altered, despite his zealous efforts to shed it. There was a rumour that he had gone so far as to take elocution lessons, but like so many of the rumours about Mr O'Connell, nobody knew for certain.

'HANDS!' Mr O'Connell said, as we dutifully held our hands out before turning them over. 'SOCKS!' he said next. He lifted our trousers up to reveal the colour of our socks.

'Where's the football match, Murphy?' he all but screamed at Harry.

'Sorry, sir, I forgot to change.'

'Fined half a crown, and be sure you're changed tonight, and get a clean collar on you, that one's a disgrace, I'd say your ould wan hasn't seen it to wash for a month.'

I was next and as I waited I saw Johnny Berry shuffle over to the waiters' line, a self-conscious grin on his face as he stood in his tails for the first time.

'Jesus, he's had those tails for two years,' Harry said, as we moved to our positions around the restaurant and as Monsieur Lafoy, the restaurant manager, opened the doors. It was 12.15 p.m. exactly.

I watched Johnny as he settled in at his station to wait. It's the worst part of the job, the waiting, not on people, but standing around, waiting for them to come to the restaurant so that you can so some work. But Johnny Berry, who had waited so long for this day, was far too nervous to stand still. He was fidgeting with the cutlery in the station sideboard, he turned the knob on the lamp, sending a blue flame up to the ceiling before turning it down so quickly that the flame went out and he had to light the lamp again.

Johnny was an odd-ball. Clumsy, awkward in appearance and actions, he was the last person you would expect to be training as a waiter, for he was also extremely shy and blushed to the roots of his hair when spoken to by any female. His widowed mother had been responsible for getting him a job as a commis when he was fifteen, mainly because of her friendship with Mr O'Connell, who was known to spend Christmas Day and St Patrick's Day at the little house the Berrys lived in just off Capel Street. Mr O'Connell was a bachelor, and Harry Murphy had at first suggested that there was a sexual relationship between Mrs Berry and Mr O'Connell, but that theory had long been discounted: if Mr O'Connell had any sexual relationships they tended to be with other men, for he had been seen from time to time in a pub in Donnybrook where effeminate-sounding men gathered. It was, of course, all rumour and speculation, nobody really knew, and I suspect that Mr O'Connell was glad to have a house to visit from time to time simply as a break from his digs on the Pembroke Road. But what was undeniable was that without Mr O'Connell's patron-age and protection Johnny would not have lasted long. It would have made no difference the fact that Johnny was always turned out immaculately: hair cut regularly, even if it was spiky and needed a lot of Brylcreem to keep it in place; his wing collar was clean every day; his dinner-jacket and trousers were pressed every week on his day off and dry-cleaned once a month; his shoes were always highly polished and never down at heel, and needless to say he always wore black socks, which endeared him to Mr O'Connell who was paranoid about the wearing of black socks. We used to say that Johnny always wore black socks, even on his days off.

The hotel was renowned for its cuisine. Mr Delahunty, the proprietor, employed only Frenchmen in the key jobs, head chef, restaurant manager and general manager. The menus were in French, the language in the kitchen was French; and the standards demanded of the waiters were extremely high. It had been known for a waiter to be dismissed for dropping a particle of food from a plate as he took it to the station sideboard; and given such rigorous rules, Johnny Berry's continuing presence was a constant mystery, and the idea that he was today running his own station as a waiter seemed absurd. But there he was, large red face beneath the slicked-down hair that fought through the congealed glue of hair cream to reassert its spiky nature, nervously trying to look busy and occupied.

Harry and I decided during a quick conference in the still-room that Mr O'Connell had probably done it to give Johnny a bit of confidence. Johnny Berry had been a commis waiter for well over four years as opposed to the normal three; he had not been made up to improver, which was the next stage before becoming a station waiter, and as lunchtime on Saturday was generally the quietest time of the week, we decided Johnny was being given a chance. And yet as I loaded ice into wine buckets, and checked that the bottle and half-bottle wine baskets were in place and not full of old corks and foil, I still found it hard to imagine Johnny running a station. Tales about Johnny's clumsiness were legion. He had turned the sweet trolley over on its side once as he had attempted to round a table at speed; the hors d'oeuvre trolly had been rammed into the still-room door: the number of plates and glasses that he had smashed were innumerable, and yet he had survived. Partly it was Mr O'Connell's protection, another part of it was the devotion of his mother to his appearance, but mostly it was sympathy. Everybody felt sorry for Johnny, even the French did, which was amazing for they seemed heartless about human folly in every other respect, but Johnny tried and tried, and he was endlessly willing. Any errand that needed doing, Johnny was available. Obliging and quick, he would run to fetch Monsieur Lafoy's dry-cleaning or his shoes, or take his letters to France to the GPO to post. He was the same for all the staff, and in that way we all sort of protected him, for to us commis he was a soft touch for a loan, or a few fags, or a clean collar, or standing in for you if you wanted to change your day off. We knew that he told Mr O'Connell all the tittle-tattle, but so did others and at least there was nothing mean or vindictive about Johnny.

It was one before we had our first customer, Judge D'Arcy, who came to lunch every Saturday and sat in the corner to read the law reports in the London *Times*. I stood respectfully behind Con Nolan, the wine waiter, who said: 'Will it be the usual, sir?' and the judge replied brusquely as he always did: 'Large gin, Gilbey's gin and tonic, no ice.' I went to the dispense bar, which served only the restaurant.

'Gilbey's gin for the judge.'

'Oh, feck him and his Gilbey's gin,' Mrs Cunningham, the dispense bar manageress, said crossly, 'why can't he have Cork gin or even Gordon's?'

'Because he has shares in Gilbey's,' I replied. 'He told me once.'

'He's a fecking nuisance,' she grumbled, reaching up to the top shelf for the Gilbey's bottle, and exposing for a tantalizing moment the top of her stocking.

'Thanks,' I said, handing her the docket that Con Nolan had written the order on. 'I suppose he'll have the usual half-bottle of Côtes du Rhone.'

The judge was often grumpy and forgot to order his wine until the last moment, then he attempted to blame the wine waiter if the wine was not at room temperature, so we always got a half-bottle from the bar and kept it in the restaurant in the hope of stopping his complaint. But when I returned to the restaurant with his gin and tonic, he growled: 'Bring me half a bottle of Côtes du Rhone, there's a good man.'

There were two other tables occupied, one of them on Johnny's station. Mr O'Connell had given him the smallest station in the room, just five tables as against the more usual six, and four of the tables were in the middle of the restaurant and not against the wall. These tables were not very popular and were used by the head waiter of the day to seat those who had little money to spend, usually American matrons with blue hair who were doing Europe on a shoestring and ate either the table d'hôte menu, or in the case of the more canny ones, lunched or dined off the hors d'oeuvre trolley and rolls and a pot of tea, thereby saving themselves six shillings. The only other people who sat at these tables were the culchies, which is Dublin slang for all those who are from outside the city and do not possess that city smartness; or else there were young men with little money trying to impress their girlfriends. There was, therefore, little chance of Johnny causing damage to anybody of importance, and I reckoned that Mr O'Connell felt he could handle any likely complaints.

The time seemed to pass slowly; there was little to do, yet I had to stand and look attentive. Mr Delahunty stalked into the restaurant to cast his (literally) beady eyes on the place, and stopped to say a few words with the judge. It was 1.30 and I began to hope that we would have no further customers so that I might get away early and sit in a deck chair in the Green to watch the girls go by. I had already noted from the diary on Monsieur Lafoy's desk that we were fully booked for tonight, which meant it would be midnight at the earliest before I got home.

'Good-day, Lady Mary, good-day to you, sir,' Mr O'Connell said in his ridiculous voice to the couple in the doorway, and any hopes I had of finishing early went like leaves on a windy day.

'Good morning, Michael,' Lady Mary said, giving Mr O'Connell a searchlight of a smile. 'You seem quiet today.'

'Ah, Saturdays is always a quiet time, madame.' He attempted to lead her to a table by the window, one of the most favoured in the restaurant, but Lady Mary pointed to a table along the wall.

'No, I think I'd like to sit over there, Michael.' And she made her way towards Johnny Berry, who stood blushing by the sideboard.

'You've been promoted, I see, Johnny,' she smiled, as Johnny pulled the table out and Lady Mary and her companion sat side by side with their backs to the wall.

'Campari and soda, large Power's Gold Label,' said the Honourable Desmond Morrissy as Mr O'Connell handed them the menus.

'See to it,' he snapped at me, for Con Nolan had gone for a smoke.

'That's done it,' I grumbled to Mrs Cunningham. 'The Hon. Des and Lady Mary have just arrived, we'll be here all afternoon now.'

'Jesus, Mary and Joseph, have they nothing better to do than to sit and gorge themselves? God they make me sick, don't they you?'

When I got back with the drinks, Con Nolan was standing by the table offering advice to the Honourable Desmond as he consulted the wine list.

'Oh thank you,' Lady Mary always gushed with enthusiasm, and she gave me that wonderful smile, her deep-blue eyes twinkled, her dark, red hair, which she wore cut short, gave her an added sensuousness, as well as the low-cut dress which exposed a nice rounded cleavage. Despite my best efforts to remain polite but aloof – as all the best waiters do – I found myself smiling back at her. Lady Mary was a great favourite with all the staff: the object of unbridled sexual fantasy amongst the waiters and commis, yet very popular also because of her obvious niceness. Which contrasted greatly with her long-time companion, the Honourable Desmond, who had a short, brutish temper and was known by the female staff as the Horrible Desmond. We could never understand why somebody like Lady Mary should be the regular companion of somebody so nasty, but of course the Hon. (as the waiters referred to him) was very wealthy and quite good-looking in a florid way. He was separated from his wife, which was why he and Lady Mary could not marry.

'Hmm, that's nice,' said Lady Mary appreciatively, 'but do you think I could have a little more ice, please?'

'Certainly, madame.'

She smiled again then leaned forward to sniff at the small

bouquet of roses on the table, and for a fleeting moment I caught sight of a black, lacy brassiere. I hurried away with her Campari to add the extra ice, and found myself shaking. God, I thought, she really was some woman.

I busied myself with the ice bucket, I put the half-bottle of Chablis in before I carried it to their table, then retreated as Con Nolan went through the ritual of showing the label, opening the bottle and the Hon. went through his part of the ritual by sniffing, then swilling the wine around the glass before he tasted it, looked at the ceiling, and finally pronounced it to his satisfaction.

Johnny Berry waited as his commis waiter wheeled the hors d'oeuvre trolley alongside the table. Lady Mary asked him about some of the dishes, then indicated what she wanted as Johnny began carefully to spoon the food on to a plate. He worked attentively, yet somehow managed to give the impression that he was digging a ditch. When Lady Mary had enough, he put the plate before her.

'Sardine, madame?' Johnny stood with the tin of sardines on a plate.

'Please.' Lady Mary liked her food. She looked a little greedily at the heaped plate, as Johnny, in the prescribed manner, began, with the aid of a fork, to slide the sardine from the top of the tin to the top of the pile of food. It was something he had done thousands of times without mishap but at that moment his touch deserted him. Perhaps it was his nervousness, or perhaps – as Harry Murphy claimed later – it was lust, but he contrived to send the sardine not on to the food, but with unerring accuracy straight down the cleavage of Lady Mary's ample bosom.

For a moment there was a stillness as if the three people around the table were a tableau, so transfixed did they seem. No one spoke, no one moved. I can see it now, the look of puzzlement on the Hon.'s face, the amused smile on Lady Mary's face, and the beetroot features of Johnny Berry, who was the first to move. He put the plate with the sardine can on the table, as if it were a slow-motion film, then he began to move his hand towards Lady Mary as though he intended to retrieve the sardine with his hand. Mr O'Connell could move very rapidly for someone of his bulk and he did so now, inserting his body between Johnny Berry and the table.

'May I suggest that madame goes to the head housekeeper's room where she can be assisted?' He waited for a moment until Lady Mary nodded her assent, then he pulled the table away and escorted her to the housekeeper.

It was all over very quickly, for apart from Mr O'Connell and myself the only other witnesses had been Con Nolan and Harry Murphy, and between us we moved to cover up the accident. Con appeared to talk to the Hon. about the wine, Harry wheeled the hors d'oeuvre trolley away and I brought the carafe of the house red wine to the sideboard. Johnny had gone to the still-room, where I found him in tears by the sink.

'What'll I do?' he cried, 'I'll be fired, me Mammy's heart will be broken, I'll never get another job! I swear to Jesus it was an accident.' It was piteous; even old Mary who was in charge of the still-room softened enough to come from behind her water urn and put a motherly arm around him.

'What's the matter with you, Berry?' Mr O'Connell screeched, his Kerry accent so thick I was barely able to understand him. 'Have you never seen a pair of tits before in your life? Where else would you put the bloody sardine but down her dress; by Christ you're for the high jump this time, boyo, I'll tell you that! I give you your chance and you disgrace me! Disgrace me and the hotel! I could lose my job as well and all because of your lecherous mind. When did you last go to confession? And what do you think your mother's going to say when I tell her? Is that what you do all day, go around thinking about women's bodies? My God no wonder the country is going to the dogs if it's the likes of ye who're the next generation. By Jesus, Berry, in all my thirty years in the business I never saw *that* happen before, I can tell you!'

'Honest to God, Mr O'Connell, it was an accident, I never even saw her. . .' Johnny was in tears. 'And I was at confession last night and I went to communion this morning, you can ask me Mammy, we went to seven Mass in the Jesuits in Clarendon Street.'

Mr O'Connell softened. He spoke quietly. 'This is your last chance, Berry. You're a lucky man 'twas Lady Mary and not one of those other bitches we get in here. Now go and wash your face, smarten yourself up and for the love of Christ don't make any more mistakes or you're for the hop! Got that?'

'Oh, thank you Mr O'Connell, I won't let you down, I promise you that,' Johnny gabbled, rubbing his eyes with a handkerchief before he went off to the staff toilets to wash his face.

I was amazed that Johnny had survived, but also pleased. Mr O'Connell, I thought, wasn't such a bastard after all; he was taking a big risk for Johnny Berry.

'What's so shagging funny?' Mr O'Connell screeched. 'I'll put that grin on the other side of your mouth, bucko, laughing at that misfortunate, you can stay on as duty commis this afternoon. That might learn you some manners. Ye jackeens think ye knows everything.'

It was useless to protest, I knew, and to try and even explain that it was his humanity I had been smiling at, would simply be wasted on Mr O'Connell. I knew from past experience that the best thing to do was to stay silent and accept my punishment.

Back in the restaurant I watched as Johnny slid the sardine on to the hors d'oeuvre before Lady Mary, who laughed and said something to Johnny, who went scarlet before he moved to serve the Hon. with a plate of smoked salmon.

'Jesus, did you see what I've seen?' Harry and I were sharing a cigarette in the still-room, using the steam from the hot water to disguise the smoke.

'What?'

'Lady Mary coming down the stairs from the housekeeper's with no bra on. They were bouncing beautifully! What a pair! Jesus I could play with them for a month and never get tired.'

'Are you sure?' I was dubious.

'I'll betcha ten bob, that's how sure I am,' Harry said, and as he was known to be cute about money, I shut up.

The time went by with grinding slowness. Johnny served Lady Mary and the Honourable Desmond with their main course without mishap. I went to pour the carafe of red wine and in straining to see if Lady Mary was or wasn't wearing a bra, very nearly filled her glass to overflowing.

'This beef is tough,' the Hon. said truculently.

'I'll get Mr O'Connell, sir,' I replied.

'Oh, don't bother, just pour the bloody wine,' he snapped. Lady Mary leaned across to whisper in his ear, putting her hand on his thigh, and I caught a glimpse of a rosy pink nipple. My hand started to shake and I don't know how I managed not to spill any wine. Fortunately whatever Lady Mary has said caused the Hon. to roar with laughter, otherwise I am sure he must have noticed.

The judge dozed at the table, the decanter of port in front of him three glasses emptier than when it had been served; he would have a fourth when he woke, which could be in five minutes or in half an hour. The clock over the cashier's desk was showing 2.30, and there was only the judge at one table, Lady Mary and the Hon. at the other. All the staff had gone apart from Mr O'Connell, Johnny Berry, and thanks to Mr O'Connell, me. I sighed; it could be at least half-past three before I got away.

I brought brandy for Lady Mary and green Chartreuse for the Hon. They were sitting very closely together, holding hands (or something, I thought cynically) beneath the tablecloth. As usual Lady Mary gave me a radiant smile, and as I remembered her bra-less breasts, I blushed. The Hon., as was his wont, said nothing. Johnny Berry poured coffee, the judge poured himself port; in the still-room Mr O'Connell poured himself a cup of tea and chatted to Mary, and the interminable boredom of waiting continued.

I wandered through the lounge and the cocktail bar to the reception area, but they were all deserted, save for the solitary receptionist huddled over her bills, and Cormack, the head porter, studying the *Sporting Life* at his desk in the front hall. Even Mrs Cunningham in the dispense bar was engrossed in her knitting. So back I went and stood by the cashier's empty desk, for on a Saturday all the bills were made up by the reception staff.

Eventually the judge began to move. I pressed the bell on the cashier's desk and Mr O'Connell hurried in from the still-room. The judge was drunk, as he usually was whenever he lunched or dined at the restaurant. He staggered slightly, bumping against the next table and rattling the cutlery.

'So sorry, so sorry,' he muttered, as Mr O'Connell and I took an arm each and escorted him to the hall where he talked about horses to Cormack as he waited for a taxi.

'They want another round of liqueurs,' Johnny Berry said apologetically, as he handed me the order he had written.

'We'll be here all afternoon now,' I said to Mrs Cunningham, for it was not unknown for the Hon. and Lady Mary and their friends to stay on drinking all afternoon and through the night.

'Bloody bastards,' Mrs Cunningham said darkly, 'and half the city of Dublin hasn't enough to eat. No wonder there's Communists, when you see the likes of the Lady Marys behaving themselves.' She poured brandy into a measure then transferred it to the brandy glass and poured the green Chartreuse directly into the liqueur glass. 'There, and I hope it bloody chokes them!'

Lady Mary rested her head on the Hon.'s shoulder. They were as close together as could be, their hands beneath the tablecloth were moving as if they were tickling each other, but their flushed faces told me otherwise. I hated them at that moment, flaunting their money and their indifference to the waiters, as if we were as inanimate as the tables or chairs.

I stood by the desk hoping that they might notice me and take the hint that we too would like to go home, but of course they were so wrapped up in their own games – for that, I thought, was what it was – they had no time to notice anything else. Johnny Berry stood statue-like by the sideboard, looking at them every few seconds so as not to miss their smallest wish. It was 3.30 and the sun had gone behind the clouds, it looked like rain, and I would have to be back at the hotel by six if I wanted my evening meal before work.

I walked slowly around the restaurant hoping to stir them. I wondered if I dare turn out the lights. Why the hell could they not go to their house and play around there? Nothing changed. I went back to the doorway and stood there looking along the wall to their table. Lady Mary started to laugh, the Hon. shifted in his seat and Johnny Berry rushed across and yanked the table away.

'You stupid bastard!' the Hon. said viciously, while Lady Mary smiled but did not remove her hand from the Hon.'s trousers, nor did he remove his hand from under her dress, as Johnny slammed the table back into place before fleeing from the restaurant.

'Where is Mr O'Connell?' Mr Delahunty demanded in a harsh whisper. 'Tell him to fire that stupid boy and I want to see him in my office as soon as the restaurant is closed. Got it?'

'Yes, sir.'

The Honourable Desmond and Lady Mary waited for five minutes before they left – just long enough, Harry said that evening, to let the bloody thing go down – and the Hon. shoved a ten-shilling note into my hand, hoping no doubt to bribe me to silence. Lady Mary smiled sweetly, but it was a smile of treachery I thought, for that was the end of Johnny Berry's career and of his mother's hopes. I stood stony-faced and let the note slip to the floor. The Hon. looked at me in puzzled anger. Only when they were gone did I pick it up. It wasn't much, but it was the best I could do.

S.R. WALLACE

Dark Steps

It will not mean anything to you, but last week I went back to Grindlay Street – just to see how it is now, rattle the doors of the past – no more. I would be satisfied to look the wrong way through peep-holes and see a colour. I did not care. I would register willingly the little changes, but I will admit that I hoped there would be no big transformations – nothing which slipped the noose of memory entirely.

The only difference in the solid street door was that the names of the staircase occupants, some neatly printed, some in scrawled handwriting – but all on little strips of card – had been pressed under a metal grate at about shoulder level. I did not read them. It would have meant putting spectacles on.

Inside. The familiar gloom. I let my eyes become accustomed to the light. Far above me the sloping, dirty skylight filtered no more of the day than it was possible to see by. It was economical, my father used to say with a grin, 'like the miser switch on a gas fire'.

I hauled my old body up the four stone flights, leaning forward and counting each step as I went, and reached the top with a strange number in my mind. Erskin's sonorous edict was 'Woe betide the man who knows the number of steps to his own dwelling.'

But Erskin is dead long since, and no one but I shared his superstitions. It was the only time that he sounded like a minister of the church, and it put the fear of God into me.

My lungs wheezed and I clutched the top rail and peered down into the stairwell. Erskin was sitting on a step at the foot, looking up. He seemed dispirited and full of grief.

'One hundred and three,' I shouted down. There was a faint echo and he vanished. One hundred and three. I kept tight hold of the railing and the number.

You have heard and laughed often at my word 'whorling' when I mean to say 'hurrying'. The years have flattened out its meaning, but its origins are here. It came into existence at 8.30 one dark morning after the clocks had been put forward. I was late for school and discovered in my haste that my legs and feet were capable of working autonomously – I no longer needed to think about each step. It was as though the stairs themselves tipped me down, and if once I tried to regain control, I lost balance. I would borrow my father's watch, check the second hand and trust my feet to propel me headlong to the street door. There I would leave the watch behind the door for my father to pick up on his way to work. Erskin usually beat me, his legs being longer and able to take the steps in pairs. I whorled on the inner side, with two hands on the rail – the left buttoning the right cuff – and Erskin shadowed me on the outside of the spiral. Two dark figures overtook us both at the end of each flight, glancing off the green and white walls, the larger catching up with the smaller in the end.

I often wished that there was a word which would make the long and difficult journey *up* the stairs easier. If I began to count, Erskin would say, 'Stop counting', in a whisper, like the wind rushing under doors.

'What if I *guess* the right number – like the sweet jar at the jumble sale?'

Erskin always shook his head at this and smiled: 'Who ever wins the sweet jar?'

Nevertheless it used to worry me, and I can clearly remember letting as many things as I could tumble into my head, in an attempt to stop my mind from alighting on random numbers – just in case. It was because of this that I could no longer recite my tables to fend off the boredom on the way up each day. Instead I sang the psalms I had been taught at school, and as I grew older, conjugated Latin nouns, or told Erskin about the day's lessons. I recalled those conversations which were as one-sided as prayers. I was wishing that I could tell him then about the *years'* lessons, when I realized that he was sitting on the step beside me staring at my face.

'Have you forgotten your key again?' he said. I nodded. I'm sixty years older than he is now, but when he first came to live on the stair, I was his junior by many years, and when he died, we were about ages with each other.

'Your mother's shopping, she won't be long.'

'I wish she'd hurry up, it's cold.' The stone step was as chilling as it had always been, and a draught curled up the stairwell, stealthily, two steps at a time.

'She's fetching some messages for Mrs MaClaverty, she won't be long,' he reassured me.

A door slammed below and Erskin shouted out desperately: 'Hurry, Mother, hurry.'

The emergency ladder hung down from the skylight on the wall opposite. I counted the rungs – there was no harm in that unless your dwelling place was the heavens. The first step was too high up the wall for even a fully-grown man to reach, and I remember my father saying, 'Economical, but a mighty lot of good if the house was ablaze.' I used to tell him that if the house *was* on fire, we could trust Erskin to let the three of us climb up on to his shoulders and reach the ladder.

If one person had had to be left behind, I would have left Mrs MaClaverty. She didn't have much to live for. My mother used to say: 'Run in and see Mrs MaClaverty – she likes you sitting with her, she doesn't have much to live for these days.' Mrs MaClaverty had silver-grey hair tied back in ornate braids. She would give me a chocolate biscuit if I played noughts and crosses with her. To begin with I used to go in every day after school, but afterwards I preferred to speak to Erskin on the stair. My mother suggested that I take Erskin in with me. Three people cannot play noughts and crosses, so I would draw up a grid of dots and we took it turn about to join them, gaining a point each time we completed a square. Mrs MaClaverty often told me that Erskin had been in to visit her during the day – and

I was glad of that. I remember that once she said he had gone with her when she went to her sister's funeral.

Mrs MaClaverty used to take in washing. Not because she had to – she wasn't as pinched as the rest of us – but because she was the only one with a washing machine. 'Cleanliness is next to godliness.' On Monday mornings she would stand on her landing and shout up and down the stairwell: 'Washing, washing', and my mother and the other women brought out brown paper parcels marked with their names. She agreed to do Erskin's clothes too, and after that every Monday she would call out 'Erskin, Erskin' instead of 'Washing'. Both she and the other women preferred it that way. I pictured those women, aproned, all thin and worn with dark straggly hair, taking their parcels to the second landing. The only door which did not open at the shout of 'Erskin' was on the third landing. The house belonged to the art school, and six girl-students used to live their. They changed from year to year, but my mother always said they were hussies and should be ashamed. She said it was a midden in there.

I looked down through the railings at that door. I heard a tap being turned on in our old house. There was a slight screech above the water as it twisted into the bath just as it used to on Saturday afternoons when my father did his ablutions. He would spend two full hours filling the bathroom with steam, flooding the floor (despite two layers of cork mats), splashing, and scraping the paint of the windowsill with his fingers, and finally emerge red-faced and warm and happy.

At that moment a young man came out of old Mr Marshall's door, looking as lank and limp as his predecessor had looked starched and spruce. I startled him slightly, and it made me uncomfortable to have been caught inactive, dallying. But he made my excuse for me: 'Are they no in? You'll catch your death – away in tae my missus – wait on them in the warm.'

Erskin and I moved apart quickly to let him pass by, and I leant tight against the railings for a few seconds like a paper bag blown by the wind and pinned unnaturally against a wall. He ran down the stairs with his knees and feet turned out, saying until he reached the street door: 'Away on in.'

The lights went on as the street door slammed shut and Erskin voiced my thoughts: 'Hurry, Mother, hurry.' Forty watts. The light above me swung at the end of its long flex, and Erskin swayed and shivered in the cold. Mr Marshall's wireless used to blare out at this time – the news, the news, always the news. He hoarded facts and information. He prided himself on it. He used to staple pound notes together in threes, separating the Scottish loaning notes from the legal tender. A good union man, my father said of him: 'That man can tell you what happened in any week in any year like. . .'

'. . .a card sharp with a full pack,' Erskin reminded me.

Mr Marshall couldn't tolerate Erskin. He said that he was 'a filament', and spoke it with conviction although he used the wrong word. A filament. My father had made the baffling comment that 'Mr Marshall had never put his milk teeth under the pillow'.

I could not help smiling as these piecemeal memories rose up in my mind. I looked about me. The dim lights cast only a dinginess in the stairwell. In the past there were those who had been grateful for that: 'If we were all candelabras and luminescence,' my father used to say, 'where would Shona and Andrew do their courting and kissing?' Andrew was an apprentice to a printer. He was doing well for himself. Shona was one of the art students. They were sweethearts. More than anything, I wanted her to be *my* sweetheart. I knew it was possible, because she was faithless. She beguiled me. I would have perpetrated crimes for her. I would have lied myself to the caverns of hell for her.

Erskin looked at me, and then at the art-school door, and then back at me again, with sadness and reproach.

'She's gone too, Erskin.'

He put his head in his hands and wept. I picked up a red milk token which lay beside two milk bottles, and flipped it into the air. It slipped through my fingers as I tried to catch it and rolled down to the art-school door. From this height I could see the top of the ledge above that door. It was still grimy, and still had fingermarks where someone had jumped up.

'How is Old Tam?' I asked Erskin, trying to cheer him up. My mother used to say that Old Tam, our milkman, was as frail and rickety as the cuddy which pulled his cart, and it beat her how he managed the stairs, and my father said: 'Must needs keep in trim – there's a ladder to heaven, isn't there?' I often tried to picture him climbing the steps, but despite every effort of imagination, I could only envisage him stooped over the banister at the third step. There could be no other explanation – it was *Erskin* who delivered the milk in our staircase. Tam had once been offered a little van to take the milk round, but he had said: 'Och, Tam's too old to drive onything but a 'orse an' cart.' My mother had said that you couldn't call it *driving* at all – the old nag could do the milk round with its blinkers tied across its nose, and its head deep in its food bag.

Erskin still stared at the art-school door.

'Did you do the milk this morning, Erskin?' I insisted.

'Aye,' he said.

'And Mr Marshall isn't still saying that it's you that steals the tokens?'

'No, but he told your mother that I wasn't a rightfully paying tenant, and that I should go back to my mansions in the sky – and they laughed together.'

'My mother scrimps to pay the rent too,' I offered. And then to get off the subject: 'You *have* seen Mrs MaClaverty today, haven't you? She's got nothing to live for.'

'Aye,' he said.

I suddenly felt better, stretched my legs and took a whisky bottle from my pocket.

'How did she die, Erskin? In her sleep like she said she was going to – with you sitting beside her?'

There were sounds below: squabbling voices; a light tread and a heavy tread; a door opening and clicking shut; a chain link being drawn across.

'Who are they, Erskin? Or who *were* they?' I was no longer sure where the present divided from the past. Erskin's face was all screwed up – he hated argy-bargying.

'They live below – down there,' he replied, stuttering slightly, and it seemed like a cord tightened around the sentence. I leant back on my elbows and arched my foot. The walls were the colour of carnation stalks. Suddenly a slate slipped from the roof and clattered on to the thick glass skylight and Erskin's foot slid down a step. It must be very windy out there. 'Hurry, Mother, hurry.' I heard rain on the roof. 'The best fire brigade there is.' A drop fell on to my forehead, christening me. I used a handkerchief. Erskin still looked cheerless.

'It was those two little tykes over the way who stole the milk tokens,' I told him. 'They were the thieves.' I remembered how everyone said that they should be hung – 'little tykes'. Erskin still looked at the art-school door. I thought about Shona. In those days she had been bonny and dark. And *how often* I had sat here just waiting to see her. Sometimes she would look up quickly and wink when I thought she hadn't noticed me – and then she would walk away looking beautiful. I wanted to touch her. Erskin had always disapproved. He would look away when he saw her – but I stared and sometimes made signs, handcuffed gestures.

Erskin held vigil in our staircase for ten years, but he seemed unable to secure my safety against her attractions. She never came near me when Erskin was with me – silently shunning him as Mr Marshall vocally shunned him. I thought of her dressed in her grey coat and stockings, red lipstick and a hat perched side-on on her head. In time I became angry that Erskin didn't make himself scarce when Shona was there. I told him so, but he did not desist from his vigilance. He was *always* there, always there, always with me. I kicked him, I girned; the stones I threw at him bounded down the stairs. I evicted him, I pulled my father's penknife on him, I told him to go and bother someone else. I wanted to touch her and no one was going to stop me. I ignored him, I tripped him up – I cursed him.

'I'm old enough to look after myself,' I had said, quoting my mother. But he stayed and Shona never spoke to me. I was enthralled by her.

Erskin slithered along the step, crablike, and looked at me with terror. I remembered how, unable to approach her because of Erskin, I had spoken to my father. He was in the bathroom, standing in front of the mirror. He was filling the large sink with water, cold water – it was Sunday. I told him about Shona, asked him what I should do, how I could get to know her – if it was all right to get to know her. He plunged his arms in the sink, almost to his shoulders, and then completely immersed his face. I shivered. When he came up out of the water, he said: 'You know what I think of the art-school door – den of iniquity in there, son. Leave her to Andrew – the devil loves his own. Don't let her go tempting you in the wilderness.' He laughed and then was serious. 'D'ye hear me?' He brushed his teeth, looking at me in the mirror, swilled his mouth out, and laughed again as he said: 'That's my "spittle" sermon over.'

But within three days – a traitor's time – I had found a rope, slipped the noose around Erskin's neck and hung him from the topmost rail. He had hung into the stairwell, his head forwards, and his feet a slight distance apart, but as even as a spirit-level. I had pushed my hand through the railing and butted them so that they swung slightly, in time with the light above me – and I had thought that perhaps Mr Marshall was right, Erskin *was* a filament.

I felt the guilt again and turned to thank Erskin for meeting me here after so many years, but he was no longer on the step beside me. I stood up slowly and buried my chin in my scarf. I am eighty years of age and world-weary. There is not long to wait.

The stairs gently tipped me down – with respect for an old man, friendless – and my shadow caught up with me four times and four times sped away.

DEBORAH LEVY

Proletarian Zen

A Domesticated Short Story
for All the Family

How Zen master change sister life?

First sister play many hour with silk worm. She wash saké cup
when saké cup clean. She arrange flower till flower open mouth
lose youth. She become very strict housekeeper. Every day she
make health food. Other sister feel pale moon so much health
food. Today she make beancurd seaweed carrot small portion
rice. Take to sister in garden. She give each chopstick tell chew
very slow. First sister often get migraine. She lie on futon dim
light, try make sense disturbance behind eye and in heart. She
image hand of Zen master place lightly small of back. This
make feel better. Sometime she read book increase understanding of life.
Book often confuse sister.

Second sister no like beancurd. She image prawnburger and cola.
This sister modern. In morning she buy roller-skate at market,
tuck dress in knicker practise motion on wheel, concentrate
keep weight forward; haiku make itself. She careful not scuff
knee. Zen master no like scab knee he want woman smooth like
melon. Second sister write many poem. She read at small
gathering to Very Big clap. Zen master approve. Sometime he
slip holy arm in sister arm walk across flat grass where she speak
new idea. He like sister be excited. In head. But sister also get

46

excited in flesh. When this happen master make cold eye, give sister koan solve.

Sister write very sad poem.

Third sister like beancurd very much. She eat all second sister beancurd. She have many chin. On ear very many jewel, see no ear only jewel. Black eye much fire. Third sister dream of Zen mistress all sun all moon. She want put jewel ear on dark belly Zen mistress listen woman secret. Zen mistress very secret woman. She crush lemon verbena leaf on skin. Third sister intoxicate. She eat way through thousand plan catch heart Zen mistress.

New chin grow, new jewel on ear.

Under lemon tree Zen master and first sister make love. It happen once month because Zen master swear celibacy vow. He break vow but jade stem need friend. It citrus affair. He silent. She satisfy. After, drink lemon kill thirst.

Much juice.

Second sister smell Zen sex on first sister and write more sad poem. Rainstorm run down cheek. Why why why why why why second sister want know, Zen master choose illiterate one? Such clever man. Why he choose one with evil headache, who measure bowel movement in morning, check tongue for white sickness, who think haiku mean sound cock crow? Why not she with almond eye, shoulder like dancer? She ask him. Yes. Fed up. She make contraceptive. Very clever. From lychee skin. Aaaah.

She want taste Zen master.

'Thigh glorious plump,' whisper Zen mistress in jewel ear third Zuki sister.

'Body smell make deeelirious,' third sister take red pearl from ear thread pubic hair Zen mistress.

'We meet often?' Zen mistress moan.

'Often.'

Under lime nylon duvet swap story and sister introduce Zen mistress pork scratching and beer.

'Pig wonderful beast,' Zen mistress say, mouth full.

'Woman more wonderful.'

Third sister switch on TV. Watch election result.

'We see nation massacre itself,' Zen mistress sigh.

Advert come. Many kiss.

Zen master drink wine with disciple in garden many stone. Wrist quiet for sundown teaching. He smoke thin cigarette. New gold ring on finger. He make loud laugh. Second Zuki sister hear before see. Colour fry in cheek. She curse body tell tale. I GLIDE TO HIM she say. Curious beetle watch. She glide to him. She arrive. She very very close. Zen disciple disappear. Master lift eyebrow high on holy forehead. Curious beetle turn on back.

Sister improvise scenario.

First Zuki sister lie on hard floorboard. She exercise weak muscle small of back. Breathe in deep hold, lift leg breath out, lower leg back hard floorboard. She make note go dentist next rice harvest. She feel good humour. Why? No tell why!

She decide prepare small treat for sister.

'What can do for second sister?' ask Zen master.

'I want speak with you.'

'Speak.' He make magnificent gesture.

'I would like offer non-literary experience.'

'Ah.' Zen master put hand to lip. He make thinking sculpture.

Then he say: 'You offer buy me sweet plum wine?'

'I do not.'

'What then might you offer me?' He smile. Second sister say no word.

'You will sing for me?'

'I will not.'

'ENLIGHTEN ME.' He cross arm and wait.

48

'I would like fuck with you.' Sister cheek go berserk. She wait answer. Will he give riddle first to solve?

'Where?'

Sister surprise. Master answer very quick.

'Perhaps in car park? Cloud very discreet tonight.'

Zen master stand up. 'Come on then,' he say.

They walk. No look each other. Straight ahead.

'You very forward woman.' Master catch moth.

'I no cherry petal exotic.'

Master laugh and squash moth.

First Zuki sister put three plum in bowl soak maple syrup. Then she wash hand open newspaper election result. It very bloody massacre. Ballot box full 40% poison.

'Good evening sister,' third sister say. She smell of beer. Eye shine like new computer. She put hand in bowl, take out plum, put in mouth. Lick finger.

'Beautiful first sister. I will give massage and then you grow supple like plum tree.'

She stretch out arm. Yawn very deep.

'You drink too much grain liquid to forget massacre?' First sister put lid on bowl plum. Third sister shake chin.

'You choose new jewel for ear?'

'I commune with Goddess.'

First sister find life very big puzzle.

Door open. Second sister enter. Hair hang like oil rag.

First sister smile buddha smile.

'Good evening second sister. You mend third sister motor-bike?'

'No.' Second sister sit. She have grease on leg.

Third sister know answer.

'You put oil on body forget massacre?'

'No.' Second sister light small pipe make smoke.

'What then you do?' First sister dare ask, in case sister talk long long time about poem she write.

'I commune with Mini Metro.' Sister make more smoke.

First sister think . . . aaah . . . sister artist, she make word with spirit of ancestor.

Third sister understand too. Zen mistress tell many tale jade stem in car park.

'Then I must give you massage also. Make much lead poison come out body.'

First sister despair life pass her by like small butterfly.

Outside bird cry. Foot step in garden. Close. Twig snap. Zen master stand by window. Shadow make two Zen master. First and second sister look each other. Heart flutter like calculator go wrong. Third sister take more plum. Open newspaper on Woman page. Wind blow. Blossom fall soft drift on master. First sister open window. Vein in long neck throb like baby thunder. Zen master speak.

'Like petal scatter in wind . . . I also make journey.'

'You leave us master?' Second sister hold breath.

'They call me back Tokyo.' Zen master wear new straw sandal.

'You make new temple?' First sister touch pulse.

'One way yes other way no.'

Third sister spit out plum stone.

'You take wife?'

Master walk two hard footstep. Worm break on grass.

'No. YOU take wife.' Master close hand. 'I have gift.' Master open hand. Red pearl centre of lifeline.

'Take.'

Third sister take. She smile new moon smile. Put red pearl in mouth. First and second sister no understand. Why master give sister gift?

'What do you do Tokyo?' Second sister ask. Already she make sad poem.

'Now we hear election result it very good time for all master. They make me manager big car factory.'

'You Zen capitalist.' Third sister scoff.

Master blink.

First sister take bowl plum.

'Master like sweet plum?' she say make voice like lute.

'I like very much.' Master bow head.

First sister open lid. No plum. She choke dragon.

'I grow plum so I eat plum.' Third sister put out fire. She look master very fierce eye.

'Master no make car so why master make much gold lotus?'

Master make wind with hand.

'First sister. You already have small gift from master.'

First sister drop head. Tear fall on kimono.

Second and third sister feel much pain hit breast. Third sister wipe away tear with chin. Second sister stroke first sister hair. She feel much noise in sister head.

'Second sister.' Master voice like emperor now he manager big car factory.

'You speak me master?'

'Second sister. It true you no cherry petal exotic. Lychee skin like razor. It take off skin jade stem. But master forgive.'

Second sister make two strawberry in cheek. Master speak more.

'Zen is radical philosophy. Church of England no make woman priest . . . I make you mistress to disciple here.'

Second sister forget sad poem. She feel light bulb in chest. On off on off on off.

'It very great medal master.'

Master click tongue.

'First task. Burn one perfume. Then two perfume. Then three perfume. Disciple must say what material go into perfume and write apposite poem. What aim of task sister?'

Sister think three second.

'Aim of task understand civilization master.'

'WRONG second sister. Aim of task banish intellect.'

Master make three bow. He have much little white snow in hair. Take five step back, make more bow, turn half moon, leave sister.

For Ever.

Second and third sister look at first sister. Sun dip in cloud. Concorde aeroplane fly above house.

'What your gift first sister?'

First sister make no speak. She put hand on belly and make many weeping.

Four year pass. Very hard year. New government commit much poverty.

Second sister sit in garden of many stone. She smoke small pipe make much subversive smoke. She famous teacher. In beginning sister find no intellect with disciple to banish. She teach complete work Mao Tse-tung, Marx, Lenin, Alexandra Kollontai, Rosa Luxemburg. Three disciple become barefoot doctor.

New government censor sister poem. Italy like sister poem very much. Peasant and worker take turn read. Whole family listen and nod head.

First sister enter garden with young daughter. Often second sister teach first sister and now sister find life not so big puzzle and teach small daughter. Small sister wave Auntie, small hand much love. 'We go roller-skate?'

Sister look each other.

'I do lesson solo,' first sister say. She glad have break. Head full ant. When she say this second sister, sister say not ant, dialectic.

They go. Big hand in small hand. Young daughter will scuff knee many many time.

Sound of motorbike in garden. Snail tuck head in shell. Third sister speak through helmet. She have four new chin.

'Dearest first sister. I must go give speech for new election victory. On new mountain we sing new song.'

She rev motorbike.

'Are you scare sister?'

'Only seventh chin scare. For what scientific never fear criticism.'

First sister feel much proud.

'We grow ourself new orchard sister.'

Tree in garden listen. It resolve grow two inch.

'I have message. Zen mistress make seaweed chestnut duck prawn thick noodle beancurd beef and rice. She use whole month social-security cheque. So when you and sister and small sister want eat, you come.'

First sister no longer get migraine.

'Tell Zen mistress we thank her. And tell Zen mistress tonight I oil and coil long black hair make perfect. We eat soon.'

'Righteo.'

Third sister whizz off. Snail come out of shell. Motorbike have sticker say: 'BIG SISTER HAVE BIG VISION.'

Cricket make song in grass. Sky make blush. Tree try very hard grow centimetre. Sound of roller-skate far distance. Blossom make radical juice. First sister shut eyelid. Make very quiet in centre of belly. She think of holiday for daughter sister and Zen mistress. Plan make itself.

Package Tour, Five, Moscow.

END IS BEGINNING.

Visit

John, between two casual jobs, and having nowhere else to go, returned home a few days before his twenty-second birthday.

The house was empty (his father had had to move afield to get even temporary work and his mother had gone away to visit a distant friend she had made during her stay in hospital) and so on the evening of his arrival John decided to visit his only and younger sister.

He thought it best to catch the bus rather than walk as each time he returned to the streets of his youth they had again been developed; into traffic islands, or shopping precincts, or sometimes roads would abruptly end in newly-created hills of sandy-coloured earth and clay, or new roads would stretch to their destinations like black arrows, but without providing pavements, and without actually joining together mere houses but skirting them behind wire-mesh fences and half-green embankments. A bus would be better than the tiring business of travelling open unsheltered roads, climbing fences, and avoiding cars.

He had to wait at the bus stop for quite a time. Twice he took a few steps in the direction of his sister's but twice he returned – made indecisive by the thought that the longer he had waited, the more chance there was of the bus turning up.

Eventually it did. The fare for the slight distance used up all of John's small change. The bus travelled past the familiar green iron railings with red berries of spiked Coca-Cola tins; picking up, in the early dusk, the odd passenger or two – youths to the pubs, or giggling girls; then past the familiar shopping arcade via a new road and unfamiliar route, then bringing John to the block of flats in which his sister lived.

There were a few moments of worry as John tried to remember in which particular flat she lived. Luckily, through one of the black windows he caught sight of the silver mirror he had bought her some Christmasses ago; for this he headed.

The hallway and stairs were clean and airy. His footsteps sharply echoed from the quarry tiled floor and then loudly shuffled up the stairs. Slightly nervous, he noisily banged the letter box of her door.

Dark hair. White face. Wide smile. A smile between them of affection and the hidden recall of forgotten fond moments. Rather battered corduroys. A pullover she had owned the last time he was home.

In the living-room was the carpet from his bedroom. Familiar curtains too. Her domestic clutter – pointless ornaments, hairclips, brushes, make-up, used glasses, tissues, handker-chiefs, socks – everywhere. Odours of make-up and perfume in the warm air.

Steve was watching telly.

'Oh! It's Spike,' John said, failing to achieve the right tone of casual friendliness.

Steve grunted.

His sister continued showing John around the flat, her girlfriend Maureen now in tow. The bedroom (''E 'asn't even made the bed an' Orve bin at work all day'); the bathroom ('Ov bin doing some washin''); back quickly, through the living-room and to the kitchen for a cup of tea and a chat.

A small kitchen. Weak electric light. Against the wall a blue formica-topped table with white-painted metal chairs; vaguely cushioned.

John sat beside one of the smaller edges of the table. Maureen sat opposite, disconcertingly staring into John's face. Greasy black hair. From the top of her cheekbones to her chin a sharp triangle. Skinny dark lip.

The sink and cooker were adjacent. Jan, his sister, stood, looking older than she should in the dim yellow light.

'I see you've got the same water heater as Mom's,' John said, as the tea and biscuits came. Thus the talk got under way: fast, monotonous, incessant.

'Yea an' it's just as bad,' Jan said, 'that's what the bucket's for – it's dripping water all the time – Ov bin to the council loads of times – in the end two men came to fix it – I 'ad to 'ave a day off work to let 'em in an' all. They just messed about with it – yo' know? O couldn't be bothered goin' back to the council – anyow it's stopped drippin' na'.'

'Yeahmmm,' Maureen interposed.

'What work was that?' John asked.

'I got a work experience job in the clothes shop off Highborn Road opposite Woolies – yo' know?'

'No.'

'Ya know the Swan pub,' Maureen began . . .

'Oh! It doesn't marrer. What about it anyow?'

'Yea, it's this 'orrible woman – 'er an' the shop assistant were *awful*. I 'ad to go in an' clean 'er car out. An' I 'ad to clean the windows wi' Windolene an' when Ard finished 'er'd come up you know an' look at it every square inch – an' if there was just a tiny bit o' streak of dirt or Windolene or somethin' 'er'd go *mad*! An' then I'm supposed to clean the floor an' 'er keeps forgettin' to bring the vacuum cleaner in from 'ome – or sayin' 'er's forgotten – an' I 'ave to clean it by pickin' up the bits an' sweepin' the floor.'

'An' they were always sending you out when ya were gonna sell somethin' wor they?' Maureen almost shouted in her enthusiasm.

'Yea, when a customer comes in who was goin' to buy a lot the assistant always sent me out on some made up errand to make sure 'er gets the commission. An' they wouldn' really talk to me, just look down on me. An' anathin' they didn't want to do they'd just get me to do an' then it turns out the shop was goin' to close down an' all the time 'er was sayin' "do this an' you'll get a real job 'ere" an' all this.'

John could imagine it. The war of looks and silences. His sister making strategic retreats into sullen manners.

'O work at Brookside now at the greengrocer's on the parade by the railway crossing. It's much better, I really like the woman who runs that an' when I was ill those times an' 'ad some time off 'er was really good about it none of the "oh and what was wrong with you?"! Once when O was ill 'er sent me 'ome.'

'There's some right people shop there,' Maureen said.

'Yea,' Jan began, 'there's one woman comes in 'ose a nymphomaniac. 'Er 'ad all the blokes around there. 'Er's married too.'

'Once 'er 'usband came 'ome and found 'er in bed wi' two men – 'e just carries on and pretends it dou 'appen.' (Laughter.)

'Gina lives down there.' (Maureen and Jan go into squeals of delight.)

'Yea,' Jan said, 'remember Gina. Gina at school.' (Squeals.)

'Gina was arh, Gina was ooo! 'Er was terrible!'

'Terrible,' Maureen agreed.

'Ya know 'er used to 'ave scragglin' 'orrible 'air.'

'Greasy.'

'Yea. An' old clothes. The same stainey ones all the time ya know. 'Er used to pick 'er nose, and leave it on the edges of desk.'

'Remember that once – '

'Yeaah! Remember once. What we did. 'Er left this urgh! Huge bogey he! Great green urgh! On this desk. An', an' Maureen picked it up on a bit o' tape.'

'Yeahmmhee.'

'An' we put it in 'er 'air!'

'Yeah!' said Maureen, by now snorting with excitement.

'An' 'er went round all day – ' (Snort) ' – and didn't even know it was there! Oh dear it was funny!' (Squeals.)

'An', an' 'er mother,' Maureen urged.

'Oh, yea. . .' (Serious now), ''er mother 'ates 'er. 'Er's always 'ad te, ya know, look after the younger kids an' cook the dinners an' everythin' 'erself. 'Er mother was separated from 'er dad. They're divorced now proper. Yo know why?'

'Yeahmm.'

' 'Er dad left 'er 'cos 'e was homosexual.'

'Yea.'

'– Ye know. 'Er went round after five years or somethin' of not seein' 'im. She went to visit 'im. An' ya know – 'e was married again. 'Er was *amazed* ya know. 'Er knocked the door and a blonde woman answered – 'is wife. An' then 'er met the two sons 'erd already got. 'Er met um. 'Er ses one was twenty the other was seventeen.'

'Does 'er still live with 'er mother?' John asked.

'Yeaaa. Yeah. 'Er – 'er mother – is living with this 'ippy –'

'Yeahmm. Long 'air. I've seen 'im.'

'An' 'e 'ates 'er. If 'er goes in the living-room to watch telly or somethin' an' 'e's there 'er's told to go into the kitchen an' stay there.'

'Yeahmm.'

' 'Er used to 'ave to get up about quarter-past five ya know to walk five miles to the bus stop to get to work.'

'Yeahmm. That was when 'er worked at Dison's.'

'Yea, it's not so bad now – 'er's changed jobs.'

(Pause.)

Maureen licked out the last remaining drops of biscuited supersaturated cold tea and gently moved the green mug to make the liquid adhering to its bottom rim splash milky yellow drops into the pool on the table.

' 'Ow are things at 'ome?'

'Oh, yo know. The usual. Yo know Dad. . . Ohhh! Yeah! Lena came up. Dad and Mom were both away. Ya know Mom's gone to Eileen's. An' Lena came up on 'er own – Paula next door said. But Dad was in Anglesey and Paula didn't know my address so Lena just had to go back 'ome. Paula says 'er was pale and seemed, ya know, upset. I want to write to 'er but when they moved I lost the card they sent with the new address on it. Dad reckons 'er's pregnant.'

John pulled a face, 'Tut! Yuagh!'

' 'E's just got the idea. It's what 'e reckons. 'Er came on 'er own. An' was upset. O wish I 'ad the address. Yo' dou 'ave it do ya? No.'

'I'll tell you what,' John said, 'I'll look up some directories. They're rich. They'll be on the phone. I'll get the one for the area and get their number. OK?'

'Yeahmm.'

'An' Mom?' John asked.

''E's gettin' worse. Ya know 'er was given a job at Dison's?'

'No, I dai.'

'Yea, but 'e wouldn't let 'er do it 'cos the only way 'er could get in on time would be to 'ave a lift with Jack next door. An' 'e wouldn't 'ave it: "It's too eeearly," 'e ses, "What if 'e misses a day?" An', "I dou like bein' in debt." Ya know why 'e wouldn't let 'er dou ya?'

'Yeahmm.'

''E's *jealous*. That's why. 'E dou want 'er to go in to work with Jack every mornin' that's all.'

'An' he wouldn't let Ted an' Bess come up to stay. Mom 'ad arranged it all but 'e reckoned 'e'd be neglected if they cum. "I'll come 'ome an' me tea wou be ready," 'e ses. 'E's never there anyway 'e's always at the pub. I dou know 'ow 'e'd be neglected! – An' 'e day want 'er to go to Eileen's either – an' *'e's* in Wales! "I dou like the 'ouse empty," 'e ses. Burrrr!'

'Well, 'e wasn't there so 'er went 'cos 'e couldn't stop 'er.'

'An' the fuss now 'er's learnt to drive! I do feel sorry for 'er. 'E gus all over the place ya know, but now, "Petrol's so expensive." 'E moans all day if Mom uses the car to see me an' we go out shoppin' or somethin'.'

''E's got worse 'as 'e?'

'Yeahh, she's sick of 'im. An' I am. . .'

Maureen leaves to catch the quarter-past bus which also went through John's estate. John didn't particularly wish to stay, but as a rarely-seen brother he felt he ought to remain a little longer. And anyway, he didn't particularly want to share a seat with Maureen on the way home.

John followed his sister to the living-room. After more tea and biscuits, a few minutes of 'News at Ten' and a discussion of the Blakes' plan to holiday with long overlooked moneyed relatives ('Well ya never know'), John said goodbye, promised to call in before he went back to London, and left.

The night had brought a chill air with it and John pushed in his hands in his coat pockets towards each other against the pull of the cloth. It occurred to him that Jan hadn't mentioned his birthday which was on Thursday. But he knew she couldn't afford to buy him a present, and he knew he always forgot hers.

Maureen was at the bus stop, she had missed the quarter-past. Leaning against the shelter, twitching leg muscles to relieve the boredom of the wait, John listened, occasionally attempting to raise some real interest in the conversation.

'Yea, O put four pound a week in the box at work so that O leave it alone and I use that for mi driving lessons. I'll be havin' mi test soon. It'll be good when I've passed 'cos then I wou need to spend mi money on driving lessons. I'll try an' save it. It must be good in London. There's nowhere to go 'ere – bet there are lots of discos in London.'

'Yea, but to be honest I dou really like discos much. I've got a temporary job in London startin' next week but other than that I've got to look for a job and somewhere to live.'

'A' ya goin' to try an' get a job 'ere?'

'Not especially, I've only been 'ere a few hours and I can't wait to leave – I 'ate this place.'

'Yeahmm.' (Pause.)

'It's bad 'ere,' Maureen began. 'There's nowhere to go. The bus cost thirty p just to Chesdon, an' the last bus is quarter-to eleven anyway which dou give you time to go anywhere. An' a taxi just from Chesdon to the Western Road cost one pound thirty.'

Undirected thoughts like discrete frames clicked through John's mind; no countryside really – no way to get there anyway, and nowhere else worth going to. Just hot concrete with patches of sandy earth in the heat, or when cold, cold concrete with patches of dark frozen earth.

A scarecrow, loosened. Blown with the winds, teased by dogs.

The bus stop was green, made of corrugated fibreglass and

metal. Someone had succeeded in kicking out one of the transparent plastic panels that began at knee height. John might have kicked one out himself except for the whimpering fear of possible consequences, but more, because behind the chilling, sapping darkness, within the burning cold air enclosing him and stripping him and piercing his body – came a deadening, bone wearing, stunning and absolute weariness.

IAIN SINCLAIR

Brides of the Pleiades

Gathering coins in a pint pot, clink of copper among the nickel, rolled tubes of notes . . . arching, the spine bow, cased in brown fat, unsweating, hair scarf dropping behind her, swung rhythmic; back on her heels, compasses, pseudo-caressing, stroking her own thighs, faking, a skin'd nylon bundle, as if a child's heat was being born into a net. The long mirror behind her repeating and distorting the act.

A riff of workers their backs to her. And loafers at the tables: out of the brewery in boiler suits, overalls, tee-shirts spilling belly hair, dead eye and rigid neck muscles. She is smoking, talking, with one man; rotating, thin shoulders, in and out of a black transparent shirt.

The surrounding streets: a mosque, a school, curry clip joints, white potato stones drying to powder, grasses, ferns breaking the pavings. Lit shop fronts. Butchers. All night bagels. Headache reds.

'It is remarkable that the skin of the penis and scrotum was perfectly normal in every respect.'

Into the here, off the street, but carrying it across the shoulders, nodding forward into the heat zone: each face, facing up, giving off, bars of mutant colour. Across the floor, heightened expectancy lifting the noise. The man is at the corner table, others mostly standing up at the bar, dull denim, jackets and turbans, whores ignored, barman rolling, looming, tall glass seeping with piss-coloured liquid. A meeting place. The girl, barelegged on the stage, reading a paperback.

Merrick allows the room to perform its cellular function. The evening. Slides across. Nurse adjusting the coals in the grate. The moment holds breath like a studio oil; darkens into its frame. Sitting-room. The silver tongs. Hairs stroked across his wrist. Indenting the skin. Brushing up the magnetic channels. Mirrorless, senses the doorspace, now, filled by his protector. 'A little excursion.' Curtain'd. Theatre lights. Lifting the eyebrows. Demonic masks of glittering paint. Hell poses. The heavy-limb'd dancers. Low flame. The coach summoned.

A wall of glass flattens the dancer. They put up a rim of coins along the edge of the stage for her to pluck, suck up the tribute, with dried lips.

Arcadian wall design. A harbour. Ritual figures arranged as if to load a cargo, so that the poses they strike will convert into an alphabet of secret interpretations. The man in the cap tools his pipe stem, comfortable within his stubble.

'By this stage Treves was beginning to take a positive relish in introducing Joseph to new experiences. . . Pleasure to be derived from watching.'

Bathed, assisted by nurses, the tub dragged before the fire, Treves hovering, hand on hip, toying with watch-chains. Assisted into the evening, not knowing if he would return, the purpose of his journey a mystery. To make this a routine, merely. On his stick, the coachman's arm around his shoulders.

Across Bedstead Square, the gardens, and out, lifted into the sealed cab. A flick at the horses. Treves, arms folded, smiling.

Reassuring, the first evenings of autumn: mildness. Hay in the streets from the bales brought in on carts for the market. Horsedung. Groups in the doorways of public houses. The route varied, the duration seemingly fixed. No conversation. The interval between these excursions was not to be anticipated.

Joseph's fear then was caged. It must have been later, there was the pantomime at Drury Lane. In a box, shaded by nurses in evening dress from the curiosity of the crowd.

'He was awed. He was enthralled. The spectacle left him speechless, so that if he was spoken to he took no heed. He often seemed to be panting for breath . . . thrilled by a vision that was almost beyond his contemplation.'

By carriage across Whitechapel Road and into Brady Street, west then, between the Jews' Burial Ground and the station, across Bakers Row and into Hanbury Street, south now: the moon speared on the great church tower.

In the room Treves is consulting, mixing authority with jocular good humour. Merrick carried up and put in a rug-covered armchair, heavily cushioned. Treves with his back to the window. The coachman settled in the frame of the doorway, ushers in the women: the old one and the girl.

Merrick half-rises, the left hand, gloved, held out. A bubble of address gobbing his throat, mucoid leer. Is he here as witness or participant? Oilcloth across the window. Cobbles in the street. Men wrestling over a bottle, mud dance, keeping it delicately between them, keeping their balance, over the curb, into the gutter. A head wound, mouths slowly: blood-soaked hair. A fire in the market square.

Around the brazier the vegetable refuse is burnt, torn up with palsied hands, crammed into the mouth. Teeth stumps champing and gumming the shells. Waste water boiling in the can. The bottle passing between the window and the moon.

From above it is a feast. Of feathers. Boots on earth. Visions of the dream. Of the century snake dying. Ghost dance messiahs. White clouds boiling slow like cauliflower scum.

It is the Strange Case of Dr Jekyll and Mr Hyde written by Stevenson, after a series of hideous nightmares, published 1885–6. Received and transmitted by those tuned to accept the hot currency of image that both masks and reveals his appalling message.

Treves was determined to reverse this process. He had found his Caliban, his Hyde, his natural man: needed now to absorb him, to give fire to his own nature, to the hidden being within, swimming back out of the mirror of deformity into the urbane and politic surgeon. To reclaim the aboriginal, the green, the skin of fruits and scales, the mineral cloak. To manifest his true consciousness. To seal the journey within the boundary of expectation.

In the Seven Stars the whole side of vision is filled with mirror glass and heats, the dancer on her back on the platform, spreading legs to the smoke. Coins in the pot. Illusions of grace and angelhood. Exit in wallpaper.

The old woman on the bed appears to be eating her way into the other, a witch, Merrick shrinking back, black mouth towards the head of the unborn child: the apprehension and creation of his own deformity, he pushes back into the chair. Treves has shed his jacket, sleeves rolled, no water, pulls the old woman back and will lift his creature up into her place. The coachman taking her out into the courtyard. Treves blocking the window, facing the room. The coachman lifting and banging the woman against the wall, repeatedly driving against her, her head almost broken from her neck, shaking loose, a dried-up orange in a torn stocking. Tongue lolling and dribbling. Dead eyes. Finishing with her, letting her fall into the doorway of the house; returning to the carriage, seeing to, petting the restless horse.

The room. Holding Merrick above the body of the girl so that he stares directly into her face. And sees what Treves cannot see. Whatever else is happening he is insensible to all motions and urgencies, whatever else is merely automatic, electricity jolted through dead meat. Staring deep at what the surgeon cannot see: who is behind him, supporting his weight, supporting him wholly, back to the window, into the tumourous mat of hair and flesh, and they are, all, just then, entirely, one being.

CLARE BOYLAN

Villa Marta

The sun rose gently over Villa Marta, like a little half-baked madeleine, but by nine o'clock it was a giant lobster, squeezing the pretty *pension* in its red claws. Honeysuckle and rose tumbled over the walls of the villa, the petals forced apart, dismembered blossom dangling in the probing heat. Sally and Rose stumbled down to the patio and ate their hard rolls called *bocadillos*, and drank bowls of scummy coffee, feeling faintly sick because of the heat and the coffee. The tables on the terrace had been arranged under a filigree of vine and splashes of sun came through, burning them in patches. Through a cascade of leaves, which made a dividing curtain, a group of Swedish boys watched them with pale, intelligent eyes. 'You come out with us,' they hissed solemnly through the vines; 'you come fucky-fuckies.'

They had come away together because they needed time to think about the future. Sally had been to bed with a boy she did not much like and imagined she might be pregnant. Rose had a boyfriend who was pressing for an engagement and she required a time in the sun to arrange her feelings.

They stretched out beside the pool and talked about food and records and clothes and sex. They did not like sex very much but it was 1967 and you'd get yourself laughed off the face of the earth if you said you were a virgin. They understood that sex was an acquired taste and you had to learn to like it or you might turn out like your mother. Already they had learnt a thing or two. Sally had discovered, from a survey in *Time* magazine, that smoking added fifty per cent more sex appeal to a girl. Both thought that men's things were awful-looking and they wondered if you were hopelessly, truly in love, would you know because you would even think the man's thing was nice-looking. This was a mystery and also a risk because if such a love did not exist and you spent your life waiting for it, you would be on the shelf, an old maid and hairy.

Built into their contempt for old maids was the knowledge that marriage meant an end to office life and it was so pleasant to lie by the pool, barely disturbed by the prowling vigil of the Swedish boys and the sun rolling over them in bales of heat, that both were firmly resolved to a domestic solution.

It was merely a question of finding the right man or finding the right feelings for some sort of a man.

When they spoke of their married lives, Sally detailed a red sofa and Japanese paper lanterns. Rose was going to have a television in the bedroom.

Sometimes they fetched a guitar and went and sat among the cacti and sang: 'Sally free and easy, that should be her name – took a sailor's loving for a nursery game.'

In the afternoons they went for a walk around the streets of Palma. Sally wore a dress of turquoise frills. Rose's frock was white linen. It was the beginning of the minis but they had turned up the hems several times over so that the twitch of their buttocks showed a glimpse of flower-patterned panty. Men followed them up and down the hot narrow lanes walking so close to them that their furiously imprisoned penises could have lifted the hems of the brief dresses had they been flashers or mashers or maniacs. 'See how they look at you!' Sally exclaimed. 'Their eyes go down and up as if they can look right up inside you.'

'Why would they want to do that?' Rose said.

In fact she was very aware of their pursuers, of the tense silence in the street behind them as if the air itself was choked with excitement – the stalking whisper of plimsolled feet on cobbles – the hot, shocked breath on the back of the neck. One day one of them captured her as she rounded a corner, caught her by the waist with a hand as brown as a glove and gazed into her face with puzzled eyes and then he kissed her, moaning as he did so as if in protest. She slapped his face and ran on giggling to catch up with her friend but all day little shuddering fingers of excitement crept up and twisted inside her.

In the evenings they grew despondent for the heat of the day made them lethargic and they did not enjoy the foreign food. 'Drunk-man's-vomit-on-a-Saturday-night,' Sally would sigh, spooning through a thick yellow bean soup. After dinner there began a long ritual of preparation, of painting eyes and nails, of pinning little flowers and jewelled clips in their hair before going out dancing. They did not bother much with washing because they had dipped in the pool during the day and the showers at the Villa Marta were violent and boiling, but they sprayed recklessly with *L'Air du Temps*.

The dances were not, actually, fun. The boys were young and modern and although their sexual needs were, if anything, more urgent than those of the men in the lane their desire was not skilfully mounted. They yapped and scrabbled like puppies. They did not know how to make sex without touching so that it hung in heavy droplets on the air. They did not know how to make fire from sticks.

One day on the beach they met a group of Americans, schoolgirls from a convent in Valencia, tall and beautiful although they were only fifteen. They had come to the island for a holiday and the girls pitied them because they still seemed bound by school regulations, crunching the white-hot sand in leather shoes that were the colour of dried blood. The shoes were taken off only when they went into the water and tried to drown one of their companions. The girls joined in splashing the victim who was blonde and tanned and identical in appearance to the others, until they realized that she was terrified and in genuine danger of drowning. 'Stop!' Sally commanded nervously. 'She's afraid.'

'She's a creep,' an ethereal clone justified.

'Why?' Rose pulled the sodden beauty from the floor of the ocean.

'*She* hasn't got ox-blood loafers.'

A few days later the Americans came running along the beach, their heavy golden hair and breasts bouncing, their feet like aubergines in the shiny purple shoes. 'Hey!' they called out to Rose and Sally who were bathing grittily in the sand. 'There's sailors.'

An American ship had docked in Palma. The girls watched silently as the sailors were strewn along the quay, wonderful in uniforms that were crisp as money. They whistled at the girls and the girls ran after them, their knees shivering on the sweet seductive note. 'Come on, honey,' one boy called to them. 'Where d'you wanna go? You wanna go to a bullfight?' 'Sure!' the American girls called, and their leather shoes squeaked and their rumps muscled prettily under little shorts as they ran to catch up.

Sally and Rose had been hoping for something more attractive than a bullfight. Given the opportunity they might have pressed for lunch in one of the glass-fronted restaurants in Palma, where lobsters and pineapples were displayed in the window; but the Americans moved in a tide, scrambling for a bus, juggling with coins and they had to concentrate or get left behind.

Following the example of the giant schoolgirls they pressed themselves down beside the loose forms of two of the young men. 'I'm Will,' the boy beside Sally said, showing wonderful teeth and something small and grey and lumpy like a tiny sheep, which was endlessly ground between them. 'I'm Bob,' Rose's sailor said and laughed to show that names were not to be taken seriously.

The bullring smelled like a cardboard box that had got damp and been left to dry in the sun. It was constructed as a circus with benches arranged in giant circles on many different levels and all of these spaces were crammed with human beings who were waiting for a death. They were pungent with heat and the tension of this expectation. This dire communion wrought a huge hot communal breath which had a little echo in the men who had followed the girls through the lanes of Palma, but here the fear was not exciting and pleasant. Saly and Rose did not believe in death. They sat clammy with dismay, waiting for the animals to be saved. No matter that it was an honourable sport, that the dead bulls' meat fed the island's orphans; they were unimpressed by the series of little fancy men who pranced around the bewildered animals which lurched and pawed at bubbles of their own blood that bulged brilliantly and then shrank back shabbily into the sand.

How many orphans could so small a city support, Rose wondered as one animal died and then two? She saw the orphans as the left luggage of tourists who had stayed too long in the lanes. She sympathized with this; she too had wanted, in an awful way, to go back alone, without Sally, to exploit her helplessness in those strong brown hands. Her only distaste was for the huge animals crumbling down one by one with hot dribbles and the sides all lacquered red by a pile of little sticks jammed in, like knitting needles stuck in a ball of wool.

'He's dead!' Sally accused Will. A third animal folded up its slender legs and rolled in the sticky sawdust.

'Sure is, honey,' Will said eagerly and squeezed her fingers. He seemed radiantly happy. 'Say, can I come on back to your hotel?'

Sally gave Rose a careful look. Rose's sailor, Bob, was watching Will for a clue.

Rose thought it couldn't matter much what happened to Sally since she was probably pregnant and that for herself, anything was better than death by starvation.

'We're late for our dinner,' she said. 'We'd have to have a hamburger.'

'Sure thing,' Bob said amiably.

'With lettuce and tomato,' she bargained.

The girls ate with the speed and concentration of thieving dogs. Their pocket money did not run to delicacies. The sailors treated them to banana splits which they ate with the taint of fish in their minds, for both were thinking of the prawn cocktails which they might have had to start since these men were so rich and so foolish with their money.

On the way back to the hotel after supper they were wreathed in virtue. It was thick around them, like scent over the honeysuckle. Both of them felt like sacrificial virgins although they were not, actually, virgins. In the terms of the understanding, they were going to lie down beside Will and Bob and let them do, within reason, what they wanted. They walked together, no longer feeling a need to be sociable. The sailors were playful in their wake.

When they got to the hotel they let the men into their room and sat with cold invitation on each bed. The sailors took cigarettes from their pockets and asked if there was anything to drink. Rose grudgingly brought a bottle of Bacardi from the wardrobe. 'I gotta girl like you at home,' Bob said. He rubbed her hand and drew up a linty patch on her burnt skin.

He kissed her then and she could feel his dry lips stretched in a smile even as they sought her mouth. He was the most amiable man she had ever met. She had no notion how to treat or be treated by a man as an equal. Sexual excitement grew out of fear or power. She could only regard him with contempt. 'You like to see my girl?' he said. He brought out his wallet and withdrew some coloured snapshots of a girl with a rounded face and baby curls.

Will had pictures too. Chapters of American life were spread out on the woven bedspreads and soon the girls were lulled into yawns by the multitude of brothers and sisters, moms and dads, *dawgs* and faithful girlfriends. The sailors spoke of the lives they would have, the houses and children. They had joined the navy to see the world but it seemed that their ship had been in a bottle. Soon they would settle down, have families, mow the grass at weekends. The lives ahead of them were as familiar and wholesome as family serials on the television.

Catching Sally's eye, which was hard under the watering of boredom, Rose suddenly suffered an enlightenment. It was herelf that she saw in the balding Polaroids – at the barbecue, at the bake sale – squinting into the faded glare of the sky. She was looking at her future.

She gathered in her mind from the assorted periods of films she had seen, a white convertible with a rug and a radio in the back seat, a beach house with a verandah, an orchestra playing round the pool in the moonlight. All Americans had television in the bedroom.

'Bob,' she warned. 'Put your arms around me.' She swept the photographs into a neat pile and put them prissily face down. Bob's arms fell on her languidly. She drew them back and arranged them with efficiency, one on a breast and one on a hard, brown leg. He gave her a swift look of inquiry but she closed her eyes to avoid it and offered him her open mouth. 'You're as ripe as a little berry. You sure are,' Bob sighed, and for once his smile faded and his languor forsook him. He began kissing her in a heavy rhythmic way and his hands pursued the same rhythm on her spine, on her breasts, on her thighs. Rose had a moment of pure panic. She could not think. Her good shrewd plotting mind deserted her. Clothes, body, common sense seemed to be slipping away and she was fading into his grasp, the touch of his tongue and fingertips, the velvety, masterly, liquid magical rhythm that had melted through bone and muscle and was now singing inside her body.

She opened her eyes to gaze at him and saw his goodness in the chestnut sweep of his eyebrows and his hair. 'I love you,' was the first thought to return to her head. She reached out to touch his hair and thought of reproducing his features in a child.

Bob felt her stillness. He opened his eyes. He found himself staring into blue eyes that were huge with discovery but all that he saw there was fear. He pushed her away harshly. 'Now don't you go round doing that sort of thing with all the guys,' he said. 'You're a nice girl.'

Rose did not know what to do. Bob shook his head and stood up. He fetched his cigarettes from the dressing-table and went to tap the pack on his palm to release one, but he hit it with such violence that all the cigarettes were bent. He lit one anyway and went to the window, opening the shutters and leaning out to sigh long and deeply. Rose, watching the indifferently entwined bodies on the other bed, felt very close to tears.

'Jesus Christmas!' Bob let out a whoop. 'Would you look at that pool!'

In a second, Will had leaped from the disarrayed Sally and joined his friend, his buddy, at the window.

'Holy shit!' Will said with reverence.

'Mind your mouth.' Bob cuffed him good-humouredly. 'Last man in is a holy shit.'

The Villa Marta was constructed on a single storey so the young men were able to let themselves out with a soft thump on to the cactussy lawn beneath. They breathed muffled swear-words as the cacti grazed their ankles and then ran to the pool, tearing off their beautiful uniforms as they went.

The girls stood at the window watching them playing like small boys in the water. They splashed each other and pulled at one another's shorts. Will jumped from the water, waving his friend's underpants. 'Hey, come back here,' Bob yelled. 'I've lost my drawers. I got a bare ass.'

'Don't worry,' his friend hollered back. 'It's a small thing.'

Bob scrambled from the pool and they tussled on the edge of the prickly lawn. With a cold pang Rose noted that his body was beautiful, every part of it, golden and beautiful. She beat on the shutters savagely with her knuckles. 'Hey you out there! You better go now,' she said.

'Sure thing!' the sailors laughed with soft amusement as they pulled on their clothes.

They came to the window to kiss the girls goodnight and then leaped at the flower-covered wall to scramble on to the street.

'Bob!' Rose howled out softly to the vanishing figure. Bob dropped back lightly to the ground. He came back to where she was huddled at the window. 'What's up, honey?'

'Don't you have a pool at home?' she said. She was troubled by the way he had reacted to the pool at the Villa Marta. All Americans had swimming pools.

'What kind of a question is that?' Bob said. 'We don't have no pool! We live in the hills. We gotta few cows and hens and sheep. We gotta a few acres but we ain't got no pool.'

He ran off again but before making his effortless jump at the wall he paused and cried out, 'Wait for me!' and she thought of his chestnut hair and the wild echoes of his touch and for a moment she imagined that she might, but then she saw the bleak snowfall of blossoms from the wall and she realized that he had been calling out to his buddy. He was gone.

In a panic she ran from the room and out into the dark, polish-smelling hall of the villa. As she stood trying to contain herself, the front door opened and two of the Swedish boys entered the hotel, back from their evening's pursuit. They were immaculately attired in evening dress and carried half-filled bottles of whisky but both seemed as sober as Mormons. They paused to acknowledge her hesitation.

'Good evening,' one said.

'You like to fuck sailors?' the other inquired respectfully. He had watched the visitors emerging from the wall.

Rose hurled herself at him, slapping his face with both hands in a fury of frustration. He delivered his bottle for safe keeping to his friend and calmly trapped her hands with his. 'You act like the little wolf' – he spoke with scholarly detachment – 'but you are really the grandmother in disguise.'

He let her go and she fled through the carved entrance, tearing along the street, down one alley, through the next. At last she emerged into a long, tree-lined street and there were the sailors. She stood and watched them until the young men had disappeared and only the hipswing of their little buttocks was picked out by the moon like ghostly butterflies in their tight white pants.

'Creeps,' she hissed after them.

BRYAN ALLAN

Confession of a Catamite

The profession of a catamite is not new, nor is it of real time. This is an old and honourable institution which is feared and despised by many. Indeed by almost all at this present time. But this is neither here nor there. Much more importantly it is not even in question. As in facts of facts, I was chosen to be a catamite and it chose me.

It could be said that it was the influence of cold, spartan, northern nights. Of such isolation and soul-poverty that the way out could only be intrigue. Value and worthy this may be, but this is not the way, nor should it be trusted. To rely on the presence of memories and contingent recollections is to be stopped. Is stopped.

One-two-three-four. One-two-three-four-

Is everything here is everything remembered. I was hoping so very much indeed. I was at the station and I wasn't sure whether I had told the address properly. As if the newness and strangeness wasn't really me. Met at the platform and my heart was thumping, very quickly immersed in pleasant surrounds and comforts, which pleased me greatly and animated chatting and talking that enticed and delighted me.

Axiom 1 – this could not last

Indeed it did not. It came to a swift and lasting conclusion, I was not wanted and was made to feel so. I could feel much fragmentation and hopelessness in my despair, my breath caught tight with my lips dry and parching. This was a glimpse of an end.

Scurrying scurrying and made my way laden with such grief of burdens that this was seen to be pity and readily taken as such. Only living as a life could be allowed to live.

Such haste and unseemly kindness rapidly became a reality tenaciously clung to. I lived in a green room with a close view of the stars.

To be as close to those stars as indeed I was, gave me a worldly and clear vision of the works of the heavens. In return I guess, I was blessed with much visitation and insight that is rarely given to one as unworthy. This did not take place in real time however, which made the coming months of autumn more special and precious than indeed I could realize. I was much taken by the movements of events, such changing hues of golden and pale reds intoxicated and defied me. And was my gaze so humble and adoring that frequently my attentions were given wholeheartedly from my bed, for periods of two-three-four day stretches. In thralls of ecstasy akin to an experience, was perfectly awe-inspiring and complete. This did not lend itself to accepted norms of social behaviour, which admittedly I grant to be true. When it is a question of beatitude v clearing rotten food-ends, practicality loses always.

This is the moment of my revelation.

I know such accuracy.

I could see such dancing patterns of beauty and delight, that this could not be sustained.

Axiom 2 – a catamite is a religious calling

Indeed the confusion of magic numbers and magic light worsened and I sought independent advice. This advice was cool, and of great authority, and after a short induction the nature of my visits was revealed and invoked long, and lifetime deepest, gratitude. She granted a weekly audience which after some indifference on my part became such a popular event that this was increased to twice-weekly visiting.

And towards the middle of this period it may be revealed, that I began to pay for this privilege and pleasure. Release from such pressure and worry suited me so. I began a job and I began my nightly vigils to the thanks of receiving such benign notification. Washing plates and glasses, dirty and used, collecting, drying and issue. All was my domain. If I kept showing a modicum of interest then indeed the reward could be judged at a manifest level. Judged and not found to be greatly lacking in kind. But this was only a start and I took it to be so.

Every evening I would look forward with eager anticipation and expectation. On the stroke of the night hour I would rush the streets of London and be stalking and preying would I begin my visitation. Such darkness and dark times. Such promise. Wrapped well and usually in a sitting position. I would cast my gaze leftwards and to the right, hither and thither. Shadows fleeting but in shape form, and by a slow seductive process of transference would I conjure up my beloved of the hour.

Oh light of lights accept my deepest gratitude.

Often on bended knees, often in a revealing manner, often in the inner sanctums would I display my devotion. This frenzy of fervour was benign and acclaimed. I was not one to be secretive about such bounty. Indeed I was most generous in the giving of favours. And so began my initiation to a world not previously recognized. It was with great fortune that I could use my time and opportunity to investigate all most thoroughly. Downstairs and in closed rooms. Open spaces and at traffic-light halts. It was during this time, a time of long long vision and of extreme separatedness that two matters became apparent.

– Such nocturnal happenings spawn the catamite.

– A catamite is of a dual nature.

Not at all obvious but so much in evidence.

Time began to split and move.

I was seeing so many benevolences that I took to return to the stars in the green room for confirmation. I reported all such events to the lady who began a process of deep, deeper discovery and identification. It confused some that the white light which could be seen in turn and for some few moments even together, was of a different time and place than that observed by the stars.

I was not to worry.

I knew my calling.

Axiom 3 – the gods are of a jealous nature and demand revenge

Having my room well and squarely pegged gave rise to several aspects of incipient delinquent behaviour. I began to yearn, at first merely for humble artefacts. But with time and in increasing demand, the scale and scope of my wishes multiplied and grew.

From most modest and uncluttered beginnings at first one, then three to one new fitted room was supplied and admired. I could now contemplate and design with a most comfortable view of the stars. Shiny and glittery and most becoming. Yet I grew less, not more hospitable. Give me more thundered the insatiable child. A most difficult and dangerous roused part of the self. Once summoned and then encouraged its hold is most grasping and firm. I was struggling and in ferment. Much of my life and in myself was in revolt and denied being judged. Hidden conspiracies existed extant. The gods have their way and smite the deceivers, the heretics and the deluded. I was spirited away to begin a new calling which would take place in quiet times, in sanctioned houses with most refined views.

Axiom 4 – to imprison a catamite is to adjust the inevitable

A false consciousness reigned. In this most high and very respected part of London, England, anything magical or light-enhancing was severely excluded. By this time the nature of my commitments and responsibilities was widening greatly. A new employment, given as a gift and gratefully mistreated. A new house.

This womb of entombment with which to struggle and feign death. But being positioned close to the womb is to face the wrath of the provider. And the wrath is of a spitting anger, an end reserved for hooked aborted notices, spurned and neglected.

I decanted often.

When I did not do so, I would retreat to a corner of a small room with all necessary luxuries and sit and reflect. A favourite thought would be of foreign travel, but this could not be so, as it is a question of financial matters. And does not suffer any close investigation. On fine evenings in a suitable area with a fine view of the main thoroughfare, I would seek the night food. Of such a rare and defined quality in these parts of such quality! And given with much good intention.

This holy food is most essential for the passages to the next life, such tortuous journeys need a residual token to fortify the soul. A devout and a zealot as myself could recognize this fact, take note, and seek celestial sustenance. This is a most precarious profession and is seen as such. This search could take me far and wide if the angles of the stars and constellations were in their necessary conjunctions. It reminded me at that time of the earlier hunts and goings-on in secluded parts of the country and in my younger years.

Axiom 5 – the path of a catamite is narrow and danger-fraught

It was at this time when I discovered the area of nighttime and diurnal bliss. The woodlands. It is a mystery to me, how large grey and dull cities manage to retain part of an earlier age in their midst. Secluded and shaded, yet tempting and inviting. I had been unaware completely of this pastoral and contented being. One night I followed the smells of the night air, with the jingles and jangling of the darkness as my guide. Such blackness and fear stroke deeply, but I was an initiate with a purity of purpose and I persevered.

Rewards were rewards were rewards were mine.

Leaving quickly I marked a path to serve as my mentor and guide. It was written very personally and would light for the single few. Because of my newly world views, I took to deception. This disguise proved to be easy and suitable to my complexion and general temperament. Shortly it became second nature and with consummate skill could I dip and weave through many a harsh and one-sided winter's evening. Sadly my vision grew weaker, it dimmed and became strained.

I took to the medical profession.

Axiom 6 – a catamite seeks compensation at every turning

I was booked in solidly and my days dwindled to nought. It was a nightmare. Tense, tortuous, aching, wild wide colour-shifts to blue. Every day was becoming a graduated scale of a drive to desperation.

I despaired.

I cried.

I died.

In states of un-recognition did I devour whole streets.

Pacing, prowling, ever-ready until at least 3 a.m. did my life distort and bend to geometric shapes of pattern and design. I thought out many diversions and delayings. My favourite was an escape to foreign climes. Lying on rock shores for instant daytimes, cocooned in coconut oils and balms.

Nothing could halt this onrush of doom.

I climbed to the skylight each evening, wailing the fall of the sun through the sky. I huddled and crouched beneath the feet of many saints, offerings given but patently refused.

Gradually my spirits were tended.

Softly retrieved from my innermost parts. Carefully nurtured and cultured. I began to invest in household shrines and would deliver and offer fresh incense each day. My free times were spent collecting paints and discarded utensils to construct mobile icons, which were completed and sold.

Such maturity and independence grew marked and was noted.
I no longer needed to consult the holy books.
I no longer needed to avoid the staring of the onlookers.
The cycle is over and was complete.

Axiom 7 – a catamite is marked by circadian rhythms

BEN OKRI

Disparities

I do not know what season it is. It might be spring, summer or
winter for all anyone cares. Autumn always misses me for some
reason. It probably is winter. It always seems to be winter in
this damn poxy place. When the sun is up and people make a
nuisance of themselves, revealing flaccid and shapeless bodies,
I am always aware of a ceaseless chill in my marrow. My fingers
tremble. My toes squash together. And my teeth chatter. That
is the worst; there is more. And when the severity of the grey
weather returns, when the seasons run into one another, and
when advertisements everywhere irritate the eye and spirit –
depicting vivid roses, family togetherness and laughter mouth-
deep – I cannot help feeling that civilizations are based on an
uneasy yoking of lies; and that is precisely when the sight of
flowers and pubs and massive white houses and people
depresses me most; when, in fact, I am most nauseated. Then I
have constant fits of puking, nervous tremulation and withdrawal symptoms so merciless that I cannot separate the world
from the sharp exultant pangs in my chest. My resistance is low.
The only season I know from this side of the battering days is
starvation. I know it is warm when I have filled my stomach
with a tin of baked beans; it is limpid when I must have had a
piece of toast; and it is cold and grey when I have bloated my
stomach on a pint of milk some idiots left standing at their
doorstep. When an individual learns to cope with the absurdity
of seasons without changing trivial externalities – THEN, in my
estimation, THEY have acquired the most vital trappings of

culture. All else is just overlaid loneliness and desperation and group brutality.

The trouble is I lived in a house for a few days. My first house. It was all peaceful and full of the curls of dogshit and totally decrepit. The walls had been broken down, cushions torn, the windows fitted with gashed rubbish-bin linings. It was a lovely place; I had never before found such serenity. To have a house, that is the journey of our solitude. Then of all the horrible things that can happen to disrupt so miraculous a discovery – a bunch of undergraduates moved in upstairs. They made a hell of a lot of noise, had long drinking and smoking parties, talked tediously about books and forties clothes and turbans and dope from exotic places and the vice chancellor. They brought with them a large tape-recorder and played reggae and post-punk sort of music. Then they brought in mattresses, pillows, food, lampshades, silk screens and large lurid posters and BOOKS. It is impossible to imagine my revulsion. They talked about Marx and Lévi-Strauss and Sartre and now and then one of the girls would say how easy it was to appreciate those BASTARDS (she said this laughingly) when one is sufficiently stoned. That was it. Definitely. It was enough that one had to hold oneself in a single frame but to add to that a bunch of idiots who were playing holiday games with broken and empty houses was more than any sane person could swallow without going berserk. A genocidal mood gripped me. I got my bundle together and stormed upstairs. The house was in a far worse state of devastation than I imagined. The banisters had all been knocked down and attempts had been made to wreck the stairs. The rooms were bad. I banged around up into the higher reaches of the house and finally found the students. The door to their room had been broken down. There were about six of them. Group desolation. They were all variations of a type: their hair dyed red or blue or purple; they wore tight-fitting trousers, and the girls wore desperate short dresses, and their eyelids were painted with varied iridescent sheen. I found it impossible to see one for the other; they seemed so interchangeable. The room had been cleared up, it was almost – a ROOM. There were mirrors all over the place and their interchangeability, reflecting back and forth, compounded my confusion. When I banged in they were lying down, coupled, women to women, men to men, women to men. They jerked their heads, moderately stoned, responding with awkward gestures to the reggae music. For a long moment words escaped me. One of them said something about going home and returning shortly; another replied, saying that this was a good SCENE and forget home and CHECK IT OUT, YEAH. Another said: 'YEAH PASS THE JOINT' and for some group reason they all LAUGHED. Two things happened inside me: I was angry; and I instantly became aware of a low point in my season. I didn't want to eat or anything like that; I was simply possessed with the desire to retch. Instead I kicked one of the mirrors and foamed. They LAUGHED. One of them said: 'Hey man, are you the LANDLORD?' and another said: 'Pass the joint' and another: 'Join the party' and another one (laughingly): 'I tell you, right; WE ARE LANDLORDS.' The voices merged and became cluttered: 'WE ARE COMMUN- ISTS. ANARCHO-COMMUNISTS.' My toes felt squashed. 'GET IT, RIGHT: WE ARE COMFEMISTS.' My throat began a curious process of strangling me and my head grew livid with twitches: 'WE ARE WHITE. BUT WE ARE FUCK- TOGETHERNESS, RIGHT.' There was a diminutive black girl with them. She was cradled by a white girl with a pinched face, and whose elaborate gestures and accentuation were frankly repulsive. They were giggling. The music stopped. The girl with the pinched face stood up: 'WE STAND FOR FREEDOM.' I turned around, tripped over some stupid fitting and fumbled my way down the beautiful death-trap that was the stairs. When I came out into the street I could still hear them laughing.

Well. So. I was yet again unhoused. Landlords have the queerest ways. Anyway. That was that. And who denies that the system (monster invisible) has the capacity of absorbing all its blighted offshoots. And so I took to the streets. The long endless streets. Plane trees growing from cement. I walked and walked and I inspected the houses as I went along. Houses. I avoided taking in the eyesores that were human beings and stuck my eyes to the pavement in front of me. This was highly rewarding for I was continually entertained with the shapes of dogshit. Pavements and pavements patterned with dogshit. Do THEY ever walk the streets? This is the height of civilization. This is what to look out for when everything else seems a nightmare. Following these patterns, and where they seem to lead, I came to a park.

The park was all right as parks in this place go. All the usual greenery and undulations and grey statues and run-down cafés and playgrounds. And, of course, there were people. I saw old men and women with dogs. Children playing about in all the sorts of games with which they are for ever trapped as children. They ran about, shouted, cried, called names, laughed, were sweet; they formed little groups and kept the brutality intact; they pretended they were adults, calling the different names of animals and birds and flowers. The older people were no different: they trundled around, looked wistfully at the sky, pretended to enjoy their isolation, called to their dogs, looked on fondly and complacently when their dogs urinated; they smiled at the children, sat stiffly on benches, meditating. When the children's football rolled towards them they sometimes kicked it back with a crotchety grace. I saw the young couples nestled together near a tree or in the open fields; they too looked complacent – the whole of nature as a lover's dream. They laughed, nice little laughs without any depth and without any pain. Insipid love; cultured laughter. Or they threw balls at one another, stiffly mimicking the children; or they walked slowly along, hair fingered by the wind, their faces pale pink on blue-white. They, too, must enjoy their isolation.
So I followed my compass. Away from the wreckful siege. It pointed north, to the furthest part where there were no landscaped undulations and no lovers and no children of any

sort; where only nobbled and ugly trees consorted and where the earth was slashed in the beginnings of some building project recently liberated from red tape. I first of all eased myself comfortably on one of these trees and then I searched for an area of unattractive grass. Not far from where I was going to sit there was a bird. Maggots crawled out of its beak. I stared at it for a while, all sorts of temptations going through my mind. It was upturned in a grotesque enchantment and for a while I experienced a cluttered remembrance of all those fairy tales that were bludgeoned into us when young. The memories irritated me. I spat, generously, and then I lay down. There seemed no distance between me and the sky. I hate skies. They seem to me a sentimental creation. Skies are another thing that have been bludgeoned into us. They are everywhere: in adverts, on window panes, reflected in patches of dog piss. Hardly a conversation takes place without someone mentioning the sky: you hardly open a novel without the author attempting some sort of description. Honestly. Skies are quite boring. Anyway. I entertained the thought, and I am ashamed of it, and my shame is my business, of how it would be like to be able to leave this body and become part of the sky. The relentless visitations. The upending of myths and the tremendous reversals and the creating of new myths to enable people to become complacent again. Foul thoughts.

I was about to explore the true foulness of the fantasy when, of all visitations, a bunch of children led by a schoolteacher went past. If they had just tramped past and gone on, and on, it would have been fine. But no. Every sweet solitude had to be destroyed. And they lingered. The teacher told them the names of trees (elm, plane, horse-chestnuts, etc), asked them the names of the cloud formations, told them not to fight, asked them to pay attention, and so on. If it had been just a little educational trip it would have been fine. Horrors – the children began to prowl around. They brought back mushrooms, worms skewered on twigs, butterflies cupped in hands; they had a PICNIC. Then at one point the most annoying thing happened:

they saw THE ENCHANTED BIRD. If there is anything more annoying than the self-conscious giggles of lovers it is the cacophony of inquisitive children. This is what happened. Three of the kids were running about, chasing one another. They saw me and stopped. They looked at me and looked at each other and then they laughed. They whispered amongst themselves. Their interest soon vanished. They had seen the bird.

'What is it?'

'It's a bird.'

They stood around the bird. One of them kicked it over and ran away. The others ran with her. They soon came back.

'What is it?'

'It's a dead pigeon.'

'It's a dead pigeon – ooooooh.'

They ran away again and came back.

'What is it?'

'I thought it was a dead duck.'

'A DEAD DUCK!'

'IT'S A DEAD PIGEON. CAN'T YOU SEE?'

They poked at the bird again. One of them lifted it up delicately with the tip of her fingers as though it were the most diseased thing imaginable. Then she dropped it.

'Uuuuuuhhhh. It's got maggots all over it.'

They regarded the bird for a moment. There was a morbid fascination in their eyes. I had seen adult mutations of that look several times. It is a look that is perched between the power for terror and the possibility of inflicting that terror. I have seen it highly concentrated, and hidden, when a policeman regards me at night, a moment before he grabs me by the collar and shoves me out of the tube station where he knows I have to spend the night. I have seen it frustrated and sly when I encounter bands of youths. I have seen it in the men when they think I am more than eyeing their women. And when I saw it then in the eyes of those children I could not restrain myself from yelling. They looked at me. Shocked. I looked at them. Their teacher said: 'Jane leave the bird alone. Come on, come along girls.'

The girls regarded me with utmost suspicion. They stared at me and stared at the bird. I think they must have imagined the most profound and intriguing relationship between me and that bird. Fear trembled in their eyes. Fear and eternal curiosity. They waited for one of them to make the first movement. One of them did and the next minute they all fled. I watched them. The teacher moved them on. They talked among themselves and kept looking back at me. Maybe they expected me to turn into a huge black bird and take off into the air. Their teacher, who eyed me with iron severity, soon mercifully herded them away. I tried to recover my reverie about some sort of room in the sky where lies and illusions and self-deceptions are debunked; and where humanity can recover its very basic sense of terror and compassion. But nothing is allowed me. A dachshund came towards me from across the fields. It stopped at the tree where I had earlier on eased myself; it raised a hind leg and had a piss. Then it too saw me. Sniffed me out. Barked and barked; and then discovered the bird. It sniffed the bird, carried it off in its mouth, and brought it back again. The dog's owner, an old man with an absurd sense of self-dignity, trundled past me, saw me, but, thanks to decorum, pretended not to see me. He stopped, whistled, and said as if to a child: 'Come on, Jimmy.'

The dog raced off, and the old man followed. Dogs and their owners always make such a pair. That, again, was that. I got up. Made my way through the park and hugged the streets again.

It really does pay to avoid sight of human beings. I had a windfall; I found a pound note. There it was wet and stuck to the ground amongst the leaves that had fallen from the plane trees. Plane trees grow from cement. That was that. And it called for a celebration of another minor season. I decided to make my way to a favourite pub in town. When I arrived, pushing aggressively through the door, the barman instantly recognized me and that morbid fascination leaped into his eyes. He licked his lips. He had a fierce bullying face with a wild growth of beard. He was tall. He had that angry and grumpy air of one who had kicked himself out of a rebellious and idealistic generation. I suspected that running the pub was for him an act of masochistically guttering the dreams that had abandoned him. The pub stank thoroughly. It had as its clientele the very cream of left-overs, kicked-outs, eternal trendies, hoboes, wierdos, addicts, pedlars, in other words, the carousing scrum of discontent. The foulest exhalations of humanity were nowhere so pungent. The pub and its depressing decor, having soaked the infinitely varied stinks of its customers, recycled its pollutions free of charge with the drinks. And this is precisely what the pub celebrates. I didn't mind: I had been entangled in enough fights and had uttered enough that was blasphemous to enable me to buy drinks on credit. After all, having a credit is one of the finer things of life.

So the barman watched me. His face twitched. He moved towards me: 'WHAT WILL IT BE? PAYING UP? OR MORE CREDIT?'

Before I could make up my mind, an old man rushed at me. The wheels grind; and one has to take the grindings as they come. The old man offered to buy me a drink. We had an unstated pact; it had been going on, silently, and with no attention drawn to it, for weeks. Whenever I came in he would rush to buy me a drink and then I was supposed to listen to the accumulation of his problems. He told me everything. He told me about how he had hated going to the war. He told me of his first wife, who had made several attempts to kill him, his second wife, who didn't like sex, and his third wife; how he gave up wives and discovered prostitution. He told about his overdrafts, how he contracted VD, his suicide attempts, his varicose veins and how they throbbed and about the cat he bought and was forced to kill one wintry night. It was the way it purred, he said, the way it shivered. He simply inundated me with the grimiest details of his condition. I didn't mind; I had my drinks paid for; and besides, listening just as carelessly to his recitals of woe, of being trapped in his own miserable and entangled fate, I found the most staggering and healthy account of an individual's suffering. Whenever I saw him I knew that my dose of participation in humanity was assured. Then I could go away, search for a place for the night, and dream of huge varicose veins and strangled kittens.

He was holding a newspaper. He trembled as if in the grip of a curious sexual fever. His fingers twitched. He stuttered and slavered. The barman looked on, his mouth twisted in a peculiar dream of sadism. I ordered two drinks: a half for the old man and a pint for me. The barman licked his lips. The old man stuttered and brought out his crinkled wallet. I fingered my windfall; I laughed. Someone put a coin into the jukebox and plunged that human cesspit into perfect unmelodious gloom. The barman plonked the drinks on the counter, and scowled. I plonked my windfall on the counter, hugged the drinks, and edged the old man into one of the grimy seats.

I tasted my drink and then took a mouthful. The old man smiled. He put his newspaper down on the table and then struggled with his pocket. He was always doing things like that. Grey with decrepit mystery, he bought out a packet of razor-blades from the side pocket of his coat.

'I am going to have a shave,' he said.

'Here?'

'No. Later.'

I drank some more. The bar filled out, became crowded, and all the groups that fought for supremacy made their loud noises in the dull lights of the pub. He drank as well. He looked around, from one group to the next, from one spaced-out hippy to another hash-pedlar. He was uncertain. He struggled with his pockets again and brought out a handkerchief. It was stained beyond description.

'You should be a magician,' I said.

He smiled, but his face made it into a mask of unredeemable anguish. That bilious face! He coughed, looked at me, coughed again. He scraped his throat with the cough, out flew his phlegm. The phlegm, thick, green, and sludgy, was trapped between his mouth and the handkerchief. Then it dribbled down his chin. He rescued it with the handkerchief. I could see how the handkerchief got its colour. He smiled again, a perfect mask. He was not satisfied: with another sharp and deep-grinding cough he dragged up more phlegm; the same thing happened. I caught myself watching. I could no longer taste my drink; everything soon seemed to be composed of the old man's phlegm. Then he began to talk. Uncertain. He did not know if the pact was still operative; he rambled. He told me of the foxes he saw along the desolate railway tracks at night. He told me of the old woman who died downstairs. At some point when my disgust had begun to turn upon itself, I told him to stop.

'What's the matter?'

That bilious face!

'I want you to listen to me.'

He nodded. Then without knowing why I began to talk. That's how we do it sometimes. We talk ourselves into the inescapable heart of our predicament. I told him about the number of times I had been beaten up outside tube stations at night. I told him where I have to sleep, unmentionable places that leave a dampness in your soul. I told him how I lived from one day to another, which is too long and too terrifying for me to contemplate. I told him how I wander around the city inspecting the houses with only a tubful of yoghurt in my stomach. I am on hunger strike, I said. I can't strike and I'm hungry. When I had a fever, the streets saw me through it. I just went on and on till I got so confused in the heart of what I was saying that all I wanted to do was fall asleep. I was tired; I had drained myself; I stopped. When I looked up, the old man was crying. He sobbed and puckered his lips and scratched his hands. I was irritated. I picked up the newspaper and read the news story of a Nigerian who had left a quarter of a million pounds in the back of a taxi-cab. The old man still wept and kicked on the seat. Everyone looked at us; they didn't really care; it was the common run of the place. The old man suddenly stopped crying. He picked up the packet of razor-blades and made for the toilet. It occurred to me, as he stumbled against the table and spilled some of our drink, that I NEEDED razor-blades. I went after him and after a scuffle disarmed the decrepit magician of the packet. He went back to his chair and I got fed up with the whole farce. I felt dizzy. I recognized the dizziness: it was the mark of a low season. When it first happened to me I thought it was the first sign that I was going mad. Then I learned that all I really needed was a pint of some idiot's milk and a can of baked beans.

I got up; I told the old man to have my drink and asked him for some cigarettes. He threw his well-fingered packet at me. I went out, avoiding the bullying glance of the barman, glad to be rid of that insistent sound of weeping, which is a mark of when people have lost a temporary haven; and glad also to be rid of that whole bunch of depressives and trendies who mistake the fact of their lostness for the attraction of the outsiders' confusion.

As I walked down the darkened streets and inspected the curtained windows of the houses, I found that I had discovered something. I had found, in that sweet-tempered solitude of the streets, a huge and wonderfully small room in the sky that is composed of ten thousand taxi-cabs and pasted over with a quarter of a million pounds that belonged to a Nigerian. And in this discovery I dreamed of several silk-yards of myths and realities and enchantments with which to remake the cracked music of all wretched people.

I dreamed. I had discovered, for example, that there had been a mistake. Everyone had been fooled: I had perpetrated a hoax. Nobody knows it but: I WAS THE TAXI-CAB DRIVER. What a shock it was, coming to myself. Tramping down the grey streets, inspecting the houses, I followed myself, haunted by the desires in that hoax. This is how it happened, not too long ago. I was a taxi-cab driver, cruising along. This man in a brown suit flagged me. He had a briefcase. The first thought that crossed my mind was that he was a Nigerian. Rich Nigerian. I had picked up several of them before. I stopped and he climbed in. I looked at him in the mirror. He looked respectable and had an air of dismissive dignity and charismatic indifference. Politician or businessman. He told me where to drop him and before we got there he decided to stop off at Marks & Spencers. He stayed there a long time. He was probably buying up the entire establishment. I had picked up a few of them and had been pretty shocked at the number of stereos, videos, and boxes of cereal that they took back home. I waited for the man. Let it be known that I waited. Then I took one look at the briefcase and drove away angrily. When I discovered the quarter of a million pounds in it, the first thing I did was to dump the cab. I caught a plane to America, bummed around for a while, came back, and changed my colour. It seemed to me a simple matter. People have been hanged and guillotined for much less than leaving a quarter of a million pounds in a starving man's cab. People, in fact, should be hanged for carrying that kind of money around. What more could I do to help the starving, the miserable, the drought-ridden bastards of this world than to drive off with such money? That, however, is as far as my solutions got. When I came back, and changed my colour, and saw all those stupid television news stories of the anguished and disgraced Nigerian and the reward he was offering, I simply laughed my head off. I lugged the briefcase with me wherever I went. Somehow I trapped myself into one of those moods when you think the whole ineluctable mystery of life is caught in the iridescence of the river's reflections. I saw this white boy thrashing in the water flowing beneath the bridge. There was a group of people on the shore; they were shouting. Perfect fool that I was – I allowed a feeling of chivalry to come over me: I jumped into the river. When I splashed into the water I suddenly realized that the briefcase had gone. The boy was nowhere in sight. I swam around and soon saw a body floating, its head beneath the water. I swam after it and after several confused thrashings and water surging into my mouth I brought him ashore. The boy was dead and already bloated. The people who were clamouring on the shore, I discovered, had nothing whatever to do with the body. Then I remembered the briefcase. Hungry, wet, haunted by the faces of the anguished Nigerian, I shouted: 'There is a quarter of a million pounds floating on the river.'

Before I could dive back in, to rescue the briefcase, the inevitable happened. The Thames soon swarmed with a quarter of a million pirates, rogues, hassled people who had long had enough, madmen and what-have-you. They bobbed and kicked, a riot on the waters, for a leather briefcase that would open up a feverish haven of dreams and close up, for ever, the embattled roomful of desires. The police got into it and I slipped away angry and frustrated and cheated of myself. I hope that they never recovered the money. Foul thoughts.

That was a dream that drowned.

What a shock it was, coming to myself; when plane trees grow from cement and when the seasons of the streets yielded a dream of wonder. I found a house. I had always wanted to own a house. I inspected the place. Bats flew out of the windows. I went up the creaking stairs and peeked around the eerie rooms. There was excreta all over the place. But that was of no serious consequence. I lit a match and found one of the rooms more tolerable than the others. I sat down and took in the musty smells of rubble and suicides and the decaying of human structures and sheer rubbish. I looked outside the window and soon found that it was morning.

Coming to myself now, I know what season it is: it is the season of the sky. In this palace I can treasure discoveries. In the room up there, with an ENCHANTED BIRD for a companion, and the old man's weeping for music, there are indeed many things I could do with a razor.

PATRICIA CONNOLLY

Dead Flower

The metal bird screamed to him from the roof, a metal cutter on
the quiet of the late night.

He crab-walked up over the tiles approaching it in the silence
he used for everything. At the top he balanced himself
carefully, avoiding its bright-yellow eyes. But the bird was
watching an owl in a poplar watching a mole, listening to a
beetle frozen still under a dry dead flower, and it paid no
attention.

He tried to wring its neck, working in silence, looking past it
into the poplars, wondering what it had hidden there. He hoped
for a nest, woven tightly and packed with clay and spittle, a
waterproof vessel made by birds and full of their eggs. He
wanted to carry off worlds within a world and have the feeling
of it in his hands to take away with him, so this time he would
know what he had done.

But the pattern of the trees against the sky made no sense to
him, and he knew unless it was understood such a nest could
never be approached. He wondered why he only heard owls but
never saw more than their shadows passing. He wanted to hold
one and see whether it was plump under the feathers, or bony
and hard, whether each had a face you could know it by, or
whether the feathers were a mask to keep owls private. He
needed to know the inside world of owls, so he could turn away
from them full of what owls are and what owls are not. Then
they would not be able to stare at him unseen, gathering pieces
of who he was, who he was not, following his movements
through the walls of his house, the bones of his head.

His hands grew tired. The head spun back and he cut the nerves of his fingers on its sharp twisting feathers, splitting and curling with rust. As he bent tight over the pain, the bird shook itself, and left a neat semi-circle of blood to mark its territory. It thought the bowing over the hands was the first formal salutation of a dance, and so it loosened its wings a little, ready for a watching-the-owl dance. But he crabbed away down the roof, his pain clenched in his fists, and seeing that he was not for dancing that night, the bird let its feathers settle flat again.

Later, he stared in his mirror and saw no face, only the mid-morning sky, grey and empty. He drew the curtains to close out the sky, but the owls, though sleeping, still dreamed through them into his eyes storing up the images for future use. When night came he knew they would fly off with what they had learned, bring their fragments together in that same sky where he couldn't find himself, rebuild him the way they understood him to be, making the very image he couldn't catch in his mirror.

He photographed himself in front of a map marked with flags which showed all the market-places of war where he had dealt in metals and blood. They were the only places where he'd ever caught the sound of his life singing clearly. The print showed a mask and a robe of dried blood. The mask had no decorations, just ragged holes for the eyes and the nose. In the background was the mid-morning sky again, grey.

He had no use for a mouth, but he painted enough of a face on the mask around the openings to make himself feel dressed. Working blind, for the mirror showed him nothing, he drew lines to suggest holes were eyes, lines to suggest a hole was a nose.

He searched in garbage cans, digging through wet paper bags stuffed with bird bones. Their eyes watched him rip through the orange peels and fish skins, winking in the way birds have, without explaining themselves. But the eyes told him clearly that owls were behind it all.

He heard the metal bird inside a foundry singing to itself of what mirrors could show if they chose, and what they could not.

He stopped, thinking to ask the bird if it could help him with owls, but the bird and its metal hen were dancing a mirror dance which showed how birds can never lose themselves in mirrors. While he watched them, he fed his hands into a machine thinking to change its tune. He knew the owls had hidden his image in a moment of such a change, the winking told him so, the singing, the dancing. But the machine sang on, took his hands, told him nothing.

He hid in a hand-knitted building made of raw wool, which swayed in the wind on its frame and smelled of the spinner's kitchen. And there, across the street from the foundry, the metal bird discovered him, sitting inside waiting for his hands to grow again. It followed him into the stairwell, saw him try to hide himself under the swaying stairs. The bird was curious, thought it would sing to him about the owl that lived on the roof of a hand-knitted building, enjoying the logic of poplar trees. It thought they might try the owl-that-watches-down-through-the-weave-dance.

Through the pattern of the third step, he caught the bird's eye. It loosened its wings a little; a dead flower was in its beak.

Burn me, he said, when he saw the flower, coming out into the hall, the blood mask splitting into a mouth. Burn me. Put me out of my misery. Don't let me rot.

The bird dropped the flower. The light dry voice had spoiled its appetite for petals and dancing, for songs about owls, and it went back to the foundry where the hen sat by the machine, which, happy with discovery, now sang only of hands.

G.P. DAVIS

African Story

She left with the circus when it came to town. He owned a smallholding, away from the main road, a disorganized cluster of sagging buildings, huts and outhouses. Home – 'I like it like this!' he shouted after his wife's disappearing form. He knew where everything was, and could sit on the verandah and go through in his mind an inventory of his possessions in the dilapidated constructions, most of which he had built himself. The circus had come to town the previous month, and pitched its gaudy insomniac tents only a mile from the farm. The noise of their erection had drawn the couple to the perimeter fence, where they could see the billowing shapes going up against the setting sun, one lurid transience against another. They didn't hold hands. His name was Mylon, hers Fee. For Fiona.

Mylon had lived in this part of southern Africa for over a decade. He had lived in London and Paris, but had never intended to stay long. Africa appealed to a yearning for space and solitude, although once settled he slowly forgot his original motivations and became merely lonely, passing time fabricating gadgets to use on the farm. Life passed on, carefully noted in his diary, which was also a kind of log, recording daily events trivial or otherwise. He wrote – 'Sad day, wife left (1 p.m.). Cornmeal ran out again (4.30 p.m.) . . .' and so on.

They had been married only a year. She was the daughter of a local farmer who had fallen on hard times when the new nationalist government liberated his best land. Their better interest at stake. So Fiona, finding Mylon, their reclusive neighbour, attractive and a man of the world – he had after all lived in Europe – agreed to his request to be his wife after a few, mostly silent, dates. He asked with a strange entrapping look in his eyes – 'Be my fire wife.'

He had employed two black servants for many years, one to look after the main house and one to tend the crops, such as they were, and had grown accustomed to their ways. Their family and relatives moved around the farm freely, from the enclosure by the riverside where they all lived in a concrete breeze-block hut roofed in corrugated iron. A cock strutted possessively around the clearing. Children, black and sandy from digging the dry soil, searched out termite nests banked against trees and overflowing with life.

Inside the workshop, Mylon tested his latest invention, a mad scrabble of wires and wood, springs and cloth that clenched when a tiny lever was pulled. Fiona had left the main part of it in the aftermath of one of her rare visits. A mechanical hand from a magician's sideshow, with a grip at once sedulous and lazy, rotting now from age and misuse.

When Mylon had lived in London he had been described by an acquaintance as a 'remorseless extrovert'. That had been a long time ago, he reflected as he sat on the verandah, rocking slowly on the back legs of his chair and gazing at the children playing by the riverside. They had caught a small slow snake in the sluggish water and were beating it to death with sticks.

So Fee had run away to the circus. Or rather, it had engulfed her and carried her away like a stick in a strong current. She had gone one evening with her younger sister, a scrawny and impassive thirteen-year-old. They visited a stall featuring the 'Ugliest Man in All Africa', a genuine case of gushing volcanic facial horror. The sisters were deeply shocked by what they saw, despite their belief that the creature was a fraud. The stallholder was a dwarf with curiously unmemorable features, not the typical screwed-down midget face. Even when looking directly at his face, his features seemed to change, melting and reforming around hard interrogative eyes. Seeing the sisters' distress he rubbed his pudgy hands together and, as they passed through the exit, murmured: 'Do not be upset, these are merely forms of no meaning, he is blind and does not know.' Fee was surprised by his concern. Later she saw the dwarf, who was known as Mr Moreau, walking at the edge of the lights and stalls with his 'Ugliest Man'. He was, when erect, very tall, but in the dark contrast of the bush it was difficult to make out details. She left her sister at a stall watching puppets and made her way over to them. As she approached, she gasped and froze – the Ugliest Man appeared to have lost his head. He was wearing a three-piece suit, grey pinstripe, a white shirt and a blue and silver paisley-patterned tie – but the neck of the shirt was buttoned up at the top of his head, with his jacket shoulders padded up to the same level. This was how he hid his face from the world. Mr Moreau moved with him always, touching his thigh as they navigated obstacles. He had a captivating stare. Fee moved closer, horror turning to acceptance. On any terms. When she returned to her sister, who now knew the puppet show by heart (an Africanization of Punch and Judy, black faces, tribal dialect, an army captain instead of the policeman), she had been absorbed into the life of the circus. She was to become Mr Moreau's apprentice. A speciality act breathing fire, using her vagina as the bellows. She had assiduously developed this trick while living on the lonely and unstable smallholding.

Mylon continued working on his latest invention. An aunt in England sent, dependably but irregularly, food parcels containing delicacies – Marmite, jellied eels, Eccles cakes. These never lasted long. He had sat on the verandah and mused on the problem of their manufacture or multiplication. He hit on the solution while watching birds swoop down from the spindly trees to the river's surface to catch fish. As they flew a reflection travelled with them, sometimes doubling a struggling fish. So now, in the workshop, a new type of furniture was evolving – a table around which was clustered an array of mirrors focusing on to a central area where he would sit eating. The mirrored panoply could be tilted or revolved by a system of levers attached to foot pedals transplanted from an old organ. Gradually the magnifier took shape, resembling a shiny space satellite that had dropped on to a writing desk. The Africans were intrigued, but they had seen many unusual objects assembled recently in the workshop. Something to talk about by the riverside.

A constantly changing diet causes constipation. Mylon had tried all the commercial cures but to no relief, and was growing increasingly irritable and choleric, even when rocking on the verandah. Iridescent beetles had eaten all the flowers by the drive, chewing at dawn, dew forming on the vivid lawn at the front of the house. He had been up at three that morning exploring the flowerbeds, shining a torch on the voracious bugs as they gobbled the closed buds. He had seen an enormous land spider – as big as an egg – pulling an equally large stunned moth, wings wet and wrapped around its body, into its dark sandy burrow. Mylon thought immediately of childbirth, of Fee's stillborn baby girl. He shuddered and walked back to the house to watch the sun rise over the river, bringing the Africans out of their concrete shelter. As he breakfasted on the verandah, a shiny red and blue humming bird shot from one flower to another against the railings. The same bird kept him company at breakfast every day. He realized that what was lying within, his malodorous waste compacted in dark tubes, needed some help to effect its removal. He remembered the mechanical hand that Fee had contemptuously deposited in the gate-box with a note – 'Use your filthy hands. You need this now. Goodbye for ever, filth.' She had placed this in the box after her last visit, a particularly stressful affair. He wanted her back, didn't want her showing her tricks in a circus. 'Have you no respect, how do you think I feel?' he complained, forcing a show of bitterness for the occasion. He just wanted to make love to her again, to feel the tiny bristles of her pubescence. Hair soon burnt away. She sneeringly dissembled – 'We smoke cigars and swap stories, what do you do all day? The flowers are all dead, can't you invent something to get rid of the bugs, something useful?'

The mechanical hand was soon in place in the bowl of a portable chemical toilet. Mylon had just collected a food parcel from the post office containing his favourite whisky marmalade, eels and whelks, and laid out a glorious spread on the mirrored table. He would consume and radiate and then have a trial run on the extractor toilet. Like an apple corer, he thought as he feasted, watching his mouth in the mirrors, reflecting repetitions into the shimmering depths of the device. As Mylon opened, a thousand times, a jar of jellied eels, he had a sudden urge to defecate. He moved the extractor toilet in to replace his chair and sat on it as he tucked into the eels, a delicacy he loved to spread with whisky marmalade on toast. He pressed the button that started the prestidigitations of the synchromeshed hand, now wearing a pink rubber glove, under his bare buttocks. As the eels slithered easily down his throat, he felt a withdrawal from his interior, but not an accompanying feeling of relief. It felt as though his entire visceral mass was turning inside out and being pulled into the orange chemical toilet. Mylon knew this was impossible. Alarmed, he looked into the mirrors, and saw his teeth and mouth moving away from the rest of his face, now fixed in a frightened stare, and merge with their most distant reflections, pulling the rest of his face with them. He felt a tightening under his chest, and a feeling of rapid movement as his solar plexus turned into a thin sinew connecting the two inventions. Mylon was surprised.

A blue and red hummingbird settled on the string between the bright-orange bucket and the attractive glinting table. It began to clean its beak against the trembling thread. Far away the fire wife breathed out, always fearing involuntary internal contractions. Mr Moreau fiddled with the long wispy ends of his moustache and decided that it needed a trim.

T. WALSH

My Other Grandmother

That there are some things which flesh and blood cannot endure was an oft-repeated maxim of my grandmother. Her own life was at once the proof and the disproof of this principle. I am not now writing about my fictitious grandmother who regrettably remains very much alive and who while never having achieved a full-length story continues to feature in many anecdotes. The most recent depicts her as wife to a man who has devoted, indeed shortened, his life in restless investigation into the nature of truth. Now he is dying. (I hope you share my personal preference for biography which doesn't waste words on that meaningless interlude between the subject's birth and his dying.) My grandmother, with a liberal interpretation of a death-bed vigil, is in the kitchen making marmalade. Calm claims the dying one's hitherto trembling body. A smile breaks over his fleshless face.

'I have it! I have it!' he calls out from the parched depths of his dried-out lungs. 'All statements are true to the extent that the contrary to what they assert is equally true.' Exhausted and triumphant, he collapses into his pillows. With a wooden spoon my grandmother removes a little scum from the simmering marmalade.

'But if that is to have universal application,' she calls through to the sick chamber, 'then it must apply to and invalidate itself.' My grandfather crosses to the great beyond a broken man; my grandmother enters into one more chagrined widowhood. And it wasn't as though she hadn't attempted to make his passing more notable, having the previous evening, reading the signs, slipped under his pillow an *Anthology of Famous Last Sayings.* Grandmother's own problem was not What to Say when the Time Came. She worried that through stroke or other mis-adventure her speech might fail her in that vital last moment. She had often considered compiling her own *Anthology of Famous Last Words Lost to Us*, giving thought principally to safeguarding herself against being a future contributor. By some mechanism which none of the family fully understood and which was activated by the tradition-hallowed death-throes' last plucking at the eiderdown threads, she had arranged that, words failing her, a great banner would unfurl itself over the head of her bed with the text reading, 'Was that It?' Replaced in later years, reflecting perhaps incipient tranquillity, with, 'The Rest is Commentary.'

Apparently, my fictitious grandmother is my grandmother on my mother's side but the sole anecdote that makes mention of this, unspecified, daughter of my grandmother only obscures the line of descent. As the story goes, my grandmother had two daughters of husband-worthy years. One of them was assisting my grandmother who was up a ladder carving that evening's fodder from the hayrick when the all-observing eyes of my grandmother noticed that the sweet child was in the first stages of pregnancy. Screaming blue murder, the ladder swaying under her from the force of her transmitted outrage, my grandmother swore if only the girl could be sure who the culprit was, which perhaps fortunately she couldn't be, that on what *he* couldn't put correction *she* quickly would, with the hay-knife.

To calm herself, my grandmother retired indoors and to her room and a volume of short stories. Nothing heavy. Among them, *The Bedchamber Mystery* by C.S. Forester of Hornblow-er fame, which tells the tale of three sisters, one of whom commits an indiscretion, but which one is never known since all three act out the role of the transgressor so that the baffled speculator must needs give the benefit of the doubt and his full admiration to all three. My grandmother, on finishing this story, closed the book, rose up and, having checked that she had not in her earlier lost quiescence left the hay-knife where it would endanger life, called her two daughters to her and commanded that both of them go about visibly pregnant.

The whole mountainside, not being able to tell which was the daughter who had fallen from grace and which the one so noble in character as to sacrifice her reputation that she might shield her erring sister, could but take both girls to its heart. But on this occasion my grandmother had overreached herself. The daughter of my grandmother who is my mother went on to give birth to twins. Bloodied but unbowed, my fictitious grandmother moved on to the next anecdote.

However, it is not of my anecdotal but my other grandmother that I now wish to write. My other grandmother really lived and is now dead: the price of having lived. She was a fervent believer in life after death. I shared so fully in her expectation of this, as in all things, that I feel the betrayal that, ironically, her being dead protects her from experiencing and write to assuage a sense of injustice. Not her but, as I am aware, my sense of injustice.

The first years of life with my other grandmother were as a time spent in Eden. It was a world of play, of flowers, of food, of singing, of snugness, of safety, of warmth. A delayed awareness of hostility, cold, injustice, isolation, when they did break in upon me served only to heighten the power of my grandmother. Not only was she the source of all good; as vital, she was the one refuge from all evil. In her presence lay safety; beyond it lay darkness, an inhabited darkness, inhabited by fearful monstrous beings. She was the point of all departures, the alighting place of all returns. Joy was when she was happy; anguish when she, her person, her happiness, was threatened.

The energy of my grandmother made her the object of an unceasing interest: working indoors, cooking, sewing, cleaning; in her backyard wrestling, as with a great serpent, with long wreathing blankets over the washtub; in her garden, weeding, digging, clipping. Even during this period of endless activity there were mysterious visits to the doctor. Was she seriously ill? About to die and leave me alone in a forbidding country? Not that she ever complained of suffering except to sigh at morning time as she rested on the bedside before putting her skirt over her head and jested that she was tired before she was tackled. There was the night when I awoke to see her standing naked to the waist before the wardrobe mirror dressing a large sore on her breast. There were too her attacks of palpitation. Frightened and unwittingly transmitting her fear to me she grasped my hands, squeezing them, so that I could not without greater pain straighten my fingers after they had been set free.

A different kind of threat to the happiness of my grandmother, and in consequence my happiness, was posed by her unmarried daughter. Jane went dancing every Sunday night, travelling on her bicycle to halls as much as seven miles away. To make free, dance, with men whose people you knew nothing about horrified my grandmother but did not leave her speechless. She lectured incessantly on the dangers to health and morals of late-night dancing. Only the wanton were abroad after midnight; knowingly to enter into the occasion of sin was itself, as her catechism told her, a grave offence to purity; pride came before a fall; she would mark her words, when it was too late; play enough with fire and you always ended up burned; as long as the jug went to the water it was bound to get broken; you needn't tell her what men were, they were all the same, wanting what they wanted; if after all her warning she still got into trouble she would not lift her little finger to help her.

This last threat at least usually served to bring the argument to a head, causing Jane to go to her room, bang the door and put on the gramophone at its loudest. A long period of laden silence between the two ensued, on occasion lasting for days and leaving me frequently wondering if it were not better to have them openly in conflict which had the merit of revealing to me their worst intentions. That I might know what was happening and to happen, every step, every shift of head, every movement of eyes, every twitch of muscle, had to be observed and deciphered.

'Why are you doing that?' I asked my grandmother, seeing her tear an old garment into inch-wide, foot-long strips.

Her reply, slow in coming, was delivered with grim emphasis:

'I am going to hang myself.' The rest of the day I lived through bereft of all feeling. The end of everything had come. It did not occur to me to reason or plead with my grandmother. Did I question nightfall? The end of summer? In fact she used the strips to set Jane's hair in ringlets, the act being performed with no exchange of words though in time there was the usual reconciliation. That night my grandmother did hang herself, in my dreams.

My grandmother had good reason to fear the ruination of her daughter, there being, it seemed, a tide in such matters, and the tide a high one. Prevalence increased rather than moderated disgrace, a disgrace which embraced the girl's whole family: even long-dead members being dug up and their misdeeds recounted. It was, none the less, considered impolite to make open reference to the girl's condition to any member of the family, so long as all showed due outward awareness of their disgrace, but usually the mother found it necessary to unburden herself to a sympathetic listener, where she could find one.

Because my grandmother abhorred all scandal-mongering and was of the oft-expressed opinion that any exchange with any of the other village women that went beyond 'Good morning' or 'Good night' brought something double-meaning from them – an expression and an achievement that filled me with wonder, as I considered it amazing enough that people were able with words to express one meaning – because of this side of her character, I must now suppose, she was the recipient of several such unburdenings. Always across the wall between her front garden and the road, this being a line she allowed few people ever to breach.

Where previously the attitude had been that the girl involved was bold and shameless, now she became a child, a little child, too innocent for the ways of the world and the wiles of men, deserted, left to bear her Cross for the rest of her life, her Cross, to be borne with the patience that God had borne His Cross; it was His way of testing us, our opportunity to unite with Him in His suffering. This shifting of responsibility, the invoking of the Divine, united the two women and raised them above all who lacked the charity to see the terrible terrible business for the trial that it was.

This social backcloth I did not feel any need to invoke as justification for my grandmother's acrimony. All justice, order and right derived from her. (When, one Christmas, my grandmother sent me back to Moore's store to have the meat they had given me changed for a better cut and Mr Moore, referring to my grandmother by her full maiden name, said she was all her life a contrary woman I staggered out and down the street, indignantly and repeatedly telling myself, 'What does that man know about my grandmother?') To desire that she on occasion speak and act differently was to desire alteration in the nature of right, and cause the sky to fall in, the fields to flood and sweep away everything that gave ordinance and security. My one prayer was her unchanging perpetuation, a continuing place in her presence. Fortunately Jane took a job at the nearby house, living in, her weekly visits thereafter anticipated and looked back on with pleasure.

But my grandmother's days were now marred by frequent attacks of violent pains. She blamed the gardening and ceased to work out of doors. Her only outings for years had been to the chapel, the dispensary, and a Sunday-afternoon walk as far as Gorman's pump. Now the walks were shortened and the dispensary visits stepped up. It was at nighttime that the pain was most severe. She sat upright in bed moaning. I sat upright at the other end of the bed keeping vigil until finally overcome by sleep. In the morning when I awoke she was there, still upright, and in time she was the one who remained on in bed while I got up and lit the fire as she used to do and boiled the kettle and made the tea to her instructions and took her a cup together with a slice of blackened toast before setting off for school.

The doctor now called to the house. I had no knowledge of what my grandmother was suffering from though I heard talk of rheumatic pains, weak heart, high blood pressure. I provided him on each of his visits with a basin of water I had poured from the kettle and a clean towel. He wrote out prescriptions on spotlessly white paper which he folded and placed in an envelope on which he wrote the name of the chemist in Callen, Mr Kenrick. Even when she became worse he went on doing the same, taking out his fountain pen, slowly removing its cap, shaking the pen over the fireplace, writing rapidly on his spotlessly white paper, of which he seemed to have an inexhaustible supply, and placing the folded sheet in an envelope: except that now he wrote on the envelope the name of the chemist in Carrick, Mr McNamara, some difference having arisen between him and Mr Kenrick.

There no longer was a meal waiting when I got home from school; my grandmother got up in the late evening and then only for a few hours. Sometimes she remained for three or four days in a row in bed and finally, being unable without help to stand on her feet, did not get up at all. Now that she was totally incapacitated our lives were as one, I sharing her pain, being her hands, feet, and eyes, aiding her in her bodily functions, acting it seemed only to her instructions.

At the end of the Emergency my grandmother's husband, an occasional visitor in previous years, was among the first to be demobbed – they couldn't get rid of him quickly enough, my grandmother said – and returned to stay, bringing with him a sum of money, gratuity from a grateful government, and an ugly bar and ribbon. My grandmother bought herself a new bed – it was all, she said, she would ever need in this world – but her further desire to have a wireless was vetoed by her husband on the grounds that he was not having English smut coming into the house. By law, my grandmother's husband was entitled to his pre-Emergency civilian job as delivery man for Moore's store but he declined the option on the grounds that his wife needed him at home.

The neighbours, as he frequently reported back to my grandmother, sympathized with him in his having an invalid wife demanding all his care and attention but my grandmother complained that she had been better cared for when he was away in the army having a gentleman's life and vowed that she would expose him, could she get up from her bed, to the whole world for what he was: a street angel and a house devil. Her contention that his army years had been days of leisure, pubs, cinemas, and card schools was one of the main issues they disputed. In proof, my grandmother quoted her husband's own incautious words back to him and cited the fact that in all the years he had been away he had never sent her a penny of his pay, her allowance having been sent to her by the government, which was a good thing because if she had been depending on him she would have starved to death long since.

And what had he to show for all that money he had been getting all those years? Nothing. Not a damn thing. He had come back in the same suit he had gone away in. Where then was all the money? Gone. Spent. On cards and on pictures. She had seen a lot of pictures breaking her back in the garden which was what had made her the way she was, crippled. Not that she was surprised, not for a minute; he had always been the same, selfish; always was, always would be: the leopard never changed its spots. He could go to the clubhouse and hear anything he wanted to hear on the wireless but where could she go? Could she get out of her bed? The army had not changed him; it had only made him worse.

Waves of sickness rose up in me with each daily repetition of this diatribe. If at the time I were in her bed, which I continued to share, I nudged her; if up, I found reason to stand by her silently imploring her silence. Why did she distress herself arguing with this outsider and intruder? His smoking and his getting up in the dark hours of the morning, making lots of noise and doing nothing, the only hours when she could snatch some sleep, his pretending to be sleeping when called at night, his reluctance, even when he was up, to put down his Western and take her in a cup of tea caused my grandmother to revert to me for all her needs and their arguing became the only link between my grandmother and her husband. The one thing of his she found useful, to defecate on to, was his tin, harp-engraved, army dinner-plate. And that, she said, he brought home because it was the army's and not out of his own pocket.

She now suffered little pain but much discomfort. Any

attempt to lift or alter the position of her body or her legs caused her agony. Her head was at all times supported on three pillows, her back supported on one pillow; her legs were arched and they interlocked at the knees which had an ointment-rubbed cloth inserted between them and were supported by a fourth pillow; the soles of her feet pressed against further pillows wedged between them and the endboard of the bed; the toes distorted under the weight of bed clothing and in spite of an elaborately structured crib. She found a rubber cushion intolerable and inevitably urine overflowed on to the rubber sheet protecting the mattress, soaking into her nightdress which, slit down the back, she wore day and night, and pasting the crumbs to her back.

There were plenty of crumbs, as she had a splendid appetite and could eat half a loaf breakfast and teatime; in between, a dinner that always included three or four potatoes. Her eating and tea-drinking meant that she sat on her army pan almost all day. My only concern, and not for myself but for my grandmother, was when she was constipated, even after several liberal dosages of castor oil, and I had with my fingers to remove the head of the blockage. It would be difficult to say which one of us strained the more or, with success and the emergence of laden platter, heaved the greater sigh of relief.

The nightly business of restoring some order and comfort to a degree that did not prohibit all prospect of rest developed into an hour-long ritual of urine-mopping, crumb-chasing, nightdress-changing, blanket-shaking, pillow-beating, washing, ointment-rubbing, massaging, powdering. She still found it impossible to go through a whole night without some rearranging of pillows or of the cloths binding her feet. I grew to being able to attend to her without waking from sleep, not hearing or not remembering hearing her calling me. But frequently I did hear her calling me in school hours, her voice startling me from whatever group or individual task I was engaged in.

My grandmother's husband came, also ritualistically, to her room each night to ask how she was, to make comment on those subjects which he was permitted to refer to, and then to sit in silence in the semi-darkness – for my grandmother's eyes could endure only the Sacred Heart lamp – incapable it seemed of speaking his good wishes for her night's rest, which would have allowed him to depart. There was no arguing, only silence now. My grandmother had told me how, when Jane was a baby, they had quarrelled until she had run from the house with the child in her arms into the rain and he had followed her and struck her when she had refused to return with him. Every night, waiting in that silence for him to get up and go, I felt the blow he had struck her.

What my grandmother termed a new trick of his did rouse her to words. When she spoke of having been unable to sleep, he too had had a sleepless night. When she spoke of being in pain, he too had his ailments to recount. In his youth he had received a gun wound in his left leg: the one Irishman that got himself shot fighting for the British and didn't get himself a pension, according to my grandmother. Now he developed a limp, most noticeably on entering and leaving her room. To raise himself from his chair when finally he had said his 'Good night' was an agonizing operation. He felt about him blindly for some means of support and on occasion when almost upright collapsed back, his face lined with suffering, to be charged by my grandmother with flying in the face of God: a young man still and pretending not to have the full use of himself.

O Jesus, Mary, and Joseph, wouldn't she thank God on bended knees to the end of her days to be able to walk as far as the door and there was him denying God's mercy.

A new dimension was added to our world with the return of a married Jane, and husband. After a honeymoon enjoyed by all parties old battlefields were newly bloodied. Jane's husband was excluded, except by Jane. He was not a single man any more; she did not mind his leaving her to go footballing every Sunday of the year, she did not expect her feelings to be considered, but as a married man now he had certain responsibilities; if he got hurt and could not work and was out of a job and there was no money coming in, would the football club pay his bills; she was only asking, because someone had to do the asking.

Her husband made no reply. He scarcely ever spoke and nothing angered him. Without his co-operation, the emotional peaks on which Jane might have found repose remained always out of reach. To my surprise I found myself wanting to leave this world. I felt myself uncoiling beyond its confines, hungering to be out and off. I would return and rescue my grandmother and take her away with me to where she would again wear shoes, once again grow prize vegetable marrows. Jane's presence made my departure possible. My grandmother herself made all the arrangements. I felt guilty about my excitement, trying not to let it show. My grandmother displayed no undue emotion on the morning of my leaving, checking that Jane had made enough sandwiches for the journey, that I had taken an apple, and in the last moments sprinkling me with holy water, and half of the leaves of the sprig of fresh privet she used as sprinkler. I said an impatient 'Cheerio' and dashed from the room and out of the house but not quickly enough to miss hearing her heartbroken sobbing.

Though my grandmother lived for another twenty years, narrowly outliving her husband, I never did take her away. She never walked again and she remained for all of those twenty years, cared for increasingly selflessly by Jane, on her back, her knees interlocked and, to the end, ruling her house: luring Jane's errant offspring to her bedside and then laying into them with a hastily produced stick.

Throughout those twenty years, and to a lesser degree in the years since, my estimation of my grandmother has undergone violent swings; linked to, even reflecting, my different re-evaluations of her husband. Who could ever not always love someone who introduced love into our lives? Not sometimes hate someone who taught us how to hate, even one not overly attractive person? One last point. Necessarily last, because it is, as it always was, the most vital in our relationship. My other grandmother was my mother.

MEIRA CHAND

The Gift of Sunday

Sometimes on a Sunday, at his wife's insistence, Mahabirlal Goga drove his family out of Bombay to Juhu, and the beach hotel there. On these occasions Mrs Goga dressed herself and the children in appropriate clothes, her sari exchanged for various stretchable, westernized items, in confirmation of a holiday mood. Mr Goga knotted, as always, a broad tie in a careful shade against his shirt. On the beach he trod warily, careful not to sandlog his crocodile shoes, his only concession to the day a snappy pair of green sunglasses. The children rode mangy camels on the dirty sand with oblivious enjoyment. A supercilious nip once from one of the beasts had permanently dissuaded Mrs Goga, to her husband's relief, from hoisting both herself and him aboard. They waited instead at the sugar-cane stall, for the return of the camels and their children.

Mahabirlal watched an old iron press squeeze sweet juice from tough sugar-cane stems; the shifty-eyed child who manned the stall drained it from them into tall, thick glasses. Then, sipping his drink meditatively, deep in depression as always on Sundays, Mahabirlal squinted at the bright dots of colour lurching precariously in the distance, on the backs of the irritable, lethargic camels. Mrs Goga had quickly finished her sugar-cane juice and moved already to the ice-cream stall. The two yellow-clad cheeks of her ample hips pushed purposefully through the crowd. Mahabirlal turned his back upon her, and sought strength to endure the day in the limitless calm of the sea. That Sunday, as usual, after the camels Mrs Goga decided on eating lunch at the beach hotel and the children ran screaming ahead. The air-conditioning in the hotel lobby momentarily froze the sweat on their backs before they passed out to the garden pool, and a whole world of bronzed nubility.

Mahabirlal Goga often dreamed secretly of the sights enclosed in this golden world, but dreaded an entrance with his wife. Mrs Goga always marched ahead of him through the lobby doors into the sunlight and laughter, the clink of iced glasses and splashings from the pool. She could if she wished have walked to the right and come quickly upon the lawn and tables with umbrellas where they usually sat. Instead she turned to the left, in a long circle about the pool. This was not an inspection by Mrs Goga of the latest trends in bodies and beachwear. It was a test of strength brought to bear upon Mahabirlal Goga on each of their visits to the beach hotel.

As she walked ahead, Mrs Goga glanced to her right and left, like a general reviewing a disreputable army. On the pretext of following some interesting sight, she looked frequently back at her husband to judge his fortitude before a wanton world. For this promenade around the pool, Mrs Goga affected a particular swing to her hips. This gait was unknown, except at parties, when she manoeuvred herself through a roomful of men. Hidden then within the depths of a sari, she achieved a certain success absent now from her rotund form, in its Sunday wear of slacks and red tank-top. Blinkered and meek, Mahabirlal trotted behind her, not daring to look to either side, concentrating his steps in time with the yellow pendulum before him. He hoped the toes of his shoes would not involve themselves with his heels, to bring him down shamefully among the half-naked bodies, deck chairs and laughter. Everywhere about him fleshy spheres dazzled, distracting him long enough, from the corner of an eye, to pick out the symmetry of a polished golden kneecap and other anatomical items. The pure beauty of these liberated forms took his breath away, and made him wish to examine them further, even to give a friendly pat here or there. Hastily he recovered himself, focused his eyes again in front, and followed where he was led.

At the table on the lawn he was beached as usual with his

back to the pool, his gaze up against a hedge. He accepted this blind seat with resignation. His wife always reached the table before him, the children automatically sat each side of her, and even if the table differed, he was left with the same chair and the hedge. Today Mrs Goga appeared in a good mood. What she saw pleased her, and what he refused to see pleased her even more. She ordered snacks for them all, then turned to the children.

'Now go and play over there. No swimming today with those sore throats. And no fighting, Sanju! Don't cry, Ritu, don't speak to him. Horrid boy. I said no kicking, Sanju.' Mrs Goga's voice rose loudly in agitation. She lunged forward at Sanju, pushing her chair over in the process. Mahabirlal picked it up and set it back in place. She sat down heavily upon it again.

'That son of yours is just like you. Never listens, never does anything anyone tells him.' Mahabirlal did not interrupt, he followed the progress of a caterpillar upon the dry and dusty hedge.

'Don't try and take his side,' Mrs Goga admonished, but as Mahabirlal continued to stare in silence at the hedge, Mrs Goga gave up. She returned her attention to the pool, a popular place with the Bombay film world, and frequented by actors and actresses of unchanging notoriety, whom Mrs Goga never tired of watching.

'A lot of the film crowd here today,' she announced with satisfaction, looking straight over her husband's shoulder. He knew better than to crane his neck at her observations. 'They don't look all that good off the screen,' Mrs Goga continued. 'And just look at the way they behave in that pool. Quite shameless. And why even bother to wear that much, when they're already showing *everything*.' Except in her imagination, Mrs Goga had never worn a swimsuit, never entered a swimming pool; she was modest and traditional. Apprehensively, Mahabirlal watched her absorb the shameful sights of the pool. By the flicker in her eyes it was clear that a far worse sight than naked men was naked women. Naked men could be looked at and disposed of, but naked women must be torn apart. Mahabirlal gazed down at his hands and waited for the blessing of departure.

When snacks and surveying were finished, they left as they had come, in a circular route about the pool. Mrs Goga reached the door of the hotel lobby first, Mahabirlal lagged behind, absorbed in adjusting his sunglasses, while simultaneously keeping down a tuft of hair the afternoon breeze played with. He did not see the young woman, chased by several boisterous men, dashing for the door he reached to open. The collision that occurred was to affect Mahabirlal's future severely, but all he immediately felt was the touch of warm wet flesh, and a tang of suntan oil and cologne. Unable to disentangle his toes from his heels, Mahabirlal and the girl came down together in an untidy arrangement of torsos and limbs. He found himself clutching, all at once, several of the anatomical items he had appreciated earlier in the day. His head ached where it hit the concrete path, and his vision blurred the moment his glasses were pitched from his nose. Looking up at the yellow mass looming ominously above him, he failed, in his shock, to recognize his wife. He smiled foolishly instead at the girl wrapped about him, loath to release the gifts she had thrust so suddenly into his hands. Then he heard his wife's voice; the girl giggled and withdrew unhurt; he pulled himself up and replaced his glasses. His wife's faced focused again before him, dark as the sea before a storm.

There was little conversation within Mr and Mrs Goga's small car as they drove back towards the town. The children were tired and subdued, and neither the rigid ring of the steering wheel, still ablaze with stored heat from its wait in the sun, nor his wife's contemptuous silence, could erase from Mahabirlal's fingertips the secrets he had so recently touched. He heaved a heavy double sigh, once for the gift of that afternoon, and once in relief that the weekend was over.

The following Saturday morning Mahabirlal had to reach for his glasses before he could thread his shoelaces. He said a number of things under his breath, as the metal-ringed eyelets defied him. Mrs Goga sat before her mirror, in a short sari blouse and long petticoat, her midriff a bare fleshy tyre between. She watched Mahabirlal critically in the mirror as he cleaned his spectacles. Aware of her scrutiny, he turned his attention quickly again to his shoes. But that second bending to his laces was a momentous event. A series of revelations flooded his mind, heavy enough to curve his spine for the rest of his life. After thirty-four years of life, he realized at last, he had no gift for weekends. He could barely support his own Sunday; to sustain the leisure of others was abhorrent.

Mahabirlal regarded himself as a thinking man: he pondered often on the inevitable acceptances of life, love, marriage and the future of his children. The thinking usually came in sudden flashes, as he put away account books at the end of the day, or shooed a beggar from his car window at traffic lights. He looked forward to these illuminations as proof of God's conscientious-ness working in him. This Saturday morning was no exception. He looked up at his wife as he fumbled with his shoelaces, as if seeing her for the first time.

Mrs Goga strained forward, mouth open, near her mirror to lipstick her lips, and afterwards drew carefully a customary *tikka*, a matching red dot in the middle of her forehead. It sat like a setting sun upon her brow, squat and smug. Its proportions had grown over the years in accordance with Mrs Goga. When she first married the *tikka* was long and slim, and Mrs Goga had resembled it. With the thickening of years both Mrs Goga and the red mark came to look as if they had borne two, and miscarried several children; they expanded in maturity.

As Mahabirlal watched, his wife took a sari from a hanger and started to wrap it about herself. While she tucked and pleated, she reminded her husband of their weekend itinerary: a cocktail that night and on Sunday, lunch with her parents, and a film and snacks with them too in the evening at the club.

Still involved with his shoelaces, only the hem of his wife's ankle-length petticoat was in Mahabirlal's line of vision. Its symmetry was broken by the odd hanging thread, and her bare feet beneath it showed determination, in round blunt toes and thick ankles. It was those very feet that had enabled Mahabirlal to marry her, for his wife was of a different community, and from both sides their parents had opposed the match. During months of slow courtship there had been few meetings between Mahabirlal and his future wife. From the first time he saw her until his wedding, they communicated from the balconies of their adjacent buildings. He had fallen in love the morning he saw her plaiting her long thick hair at an open window in the early sun. She had smiled coyly once, then giggled and turned her back upon him. From that moment he pledged himself, with romantic vision, to all manner of gruesome fates unless the match took place. On both sides the parents anxiously approached each other and conferred. Mrs Goga's hands and horoscope were examined by religious men, without success. But, at last, in the lines of her feet, the necessary luck was found, making the acquirement of her stars an asset to Mahabirlal. It was solely on account of her feet that his parents had relented about the marriage. But his mother soon found solace, and even a certain pleasure, watching the shocked expression of friends when she announced he was marrying a girl from another community. 'What can we do? Times are changing. We must be progressive. It is a love match. It is God's will.'

In the beginning, after they married, Mahabirlal had been proud of his wife. The diamond jewellery she brought as part of her dowry proclaimed him a man of substance to society. His children, when born, were neither too dark nor too thin. Mrs Goga made every effort to create a comfortable home; vases of dried ferns stood in corners and competed with hanging baskets of plastic flowers, a plaster bust of the god Shiva crowned a showcase of foreign dolls and chinaware. She did not put up with slovenliness from the servants and, in spite of afternoon card parties, was always home when he returned from the factory at seven. But looking now at her feet on the carpet before him, it was difficult to remember that, balcony to balcony, he once loved her to distraction.

Now, as he tied neat bows on his laces, he realized at last that

Sunday was too great a weight to drown beneath. He straightened up with decision. 'From tomorrow I shall have to go to the factory on Sundays. There is too much work with those weekend shifts. You go to your mother's with the children. I don't want to spoil *your* Sunday. I'll join you at the club in the evening,' Mahabirlal said firmly, taking care not to meet his wife's eyes.

'Work, work, work. You businessmen are all the same. I should have married that Ranjit Mehra; his parents also made an offer for me. Now he's president of the club, besides the Rotary, and the life and soul of any party. Go if you must then, if that's how it is. We can enjoy ourselves as well without you.' Mrs Goga shrugged and shouted loudly at the sweeper boy, a child of twelve, whose broom of loose twigs made an appearance at their half-open door. He scuttled away in fear, never rising from his haunches, like a great brown breed of spider. She slammed the door upon him and turned back to scowl at her husband. But Mahabirlal was already reaching for the door she had closed, mumbling about an appointment.

'Breakfast. . .?' admonished Mrs Goga. Mahabirlal shook his head.

The following morning Mahabirlal Goga found what he was looking for at the back of his cupboard, and set off in the direction of his factory. When the road reached Juhu, he turned sharply off towards the beach hotel. After parking his car he adjusted his green sunglasses before walking jauntily through the lobby and the garden doors beyond. Before the pool outside, he turned to the left as his wife would have done, but in deviation to Mrs Goga's patrol, he stopped at the changing-rooms and disappeared behind a blue door. There, amid smells of wet elastic and chlorine, he pulled on a pair of swimming trunks. He jumped about before a small mirror high on a wall, trying to see if, after years of disuse, his piece of beachwear sagged or clung too blatantly about him. Looking down vertically was no help: his view was blocked by a ledge of paunch. At last, hoping for the best, he opened the door and walked gingerly in unaccustomed nakedness towards the world of bronzed nubility that now constantly filled his dreams. Smiling down hesitantly at his deck-chair compatriots, he observed at last, in lingering and uninterrupted detail, the smooth limbs and orbs of gold that gleamed dazzlingly around him. He smiled and sighed, and smiled and sighed, at the sheer beauty of release.

Under a palm tree some distance from the pool he found a vacant deck chair, a small white table beside it. He stretched his legs out and relaxed, letting the sun stroke his bare skin, while he savoured the voluptuous waterfalls of flesh about him. He studied with equal care and precision each small perfect fragment or exposed drape. He turned his head slowly from right to left, large sunglassed green eyes on a long thin neck, like a lonely, inquiring mantis. Soon he detected what he was searching for among the sensuous inventory of the garden. Beyond the thunderings of life and the clink of chilled beer bottles, he saw again at last the girl who had catapulted his life on to these new planes. His heart gave an uncomfortable lurch; he gripped the frame of his chair and stared concentratedly at the golden nodules of her backbone, as she sat on the grass with a circle of friends. Eventually, as he knew she would, she turned her face to him and smiled in recognition. Just as he had dreamed, he waved brightly to her, pointing to the beer bottle beside him as he beckoned. Smiling and nodding, she returned his wave. She stood up and began to walk towards him, her smooth body held lightly together by two black straps. Mahabirlal swallowed hard and licked his lips in apprehension. Soon she stood before him.

Regarded from the lowly position of the deck chair, she was all and more than Mahabirlal had expected. Her mouth when it smiled was a mouth that had smiled at many men, and so knew in what way to arrange itself. Mahabirlal was quick to notice that several male eyes had followed her oscillating route towards him. He felt at once unquestionably established, in the garden and in his chair.

'Hi.' The girl smiled down at him. 'Come every Sunday? I'm sorry to have rushed at you like that last week, but those guys chasing me were crazy.' Her voice held a phoney Americanized twang; she nodded toward the group she had left. She sat down casually upon the grass beside Mahabirlal's chair, her nearness and her nakedness making even the prospect of conversation with her overwhelming. Mahabirlal found his voice had dried suddenly, like exposed glue. He tried silently to unstick it.

'Where are the family today?' the girl asked, raising her eyebrows and widening her eyes. She shook long damp hair from her shoulders and gave him a deep and intimate look, as if this was not their first acquaintance. Mahabirlal quickly mumbled something about contagious diseases. He could not say the girl was pretty; there was a coarseness about her features. But something he could not name emanated from her as she chatted and giggled, it seemed to swim around then bury itself firmly within him and begin to expand warmly. It was obvious she liked him. He smiled, and began to feel that he might really be an attractive man, attractive to women; he never felt like this when he was with his wife.

'Are they all your friends?' he asked, growing suddenly more confident, looking in the direction of the group of young men she had sat with.

'Those guys? Sort of. But they're all boys, I prefer *men*.' Mahabirlal was meaningfully impaled by her eyes. 'Tell me what you do? I bet you're rich and important, aren't you?' Her words fitted exactly Mahabirlal's expanding vision of himself; his self-importance swelled at such instant recognition. It was not so difficult after all; he would soon be as suave as those other men he observed, steering strange women about dance floors.

'I'm not *that* important. I just own some factories near here.' Mahabirlal laughed nonchalantly, exaggerating his inheritance by the plural term. He began to feel a new man was emerging in a beautiful astral body of confidence. He saw it glow and settle upon him, looking with disgust at the old Mahabirlal.

'There, you see, I did guess right. You are rich and important. I could tell the kind of man you were, at once,' said the girl, smiling with her bright monkey eyes.

Mahabirlal was pleased.

'And you know, you look definitely better like this, without that tie and things, you look more . . . powerful.' She drew back to assess Mahabirlal's nakedness the better. Immediately, he wished he had more hair on his chest.

'What about the beer you promised?' the girl pouted suddenly.

Mahabirlal could see her friends beginning to gesture impatiently. To prolong her departure he ordered beer for them as well.

'Aren't you sweet,' she said, reaching across his bare legs to pour their beer into glasses. He smelt her tangy odour again, as her arm brushed his knees. The muscles of his thighs tightened to such a degree he feared his toes might curl with the contraction. He looked down at them anxiously, as the girl handed him a glass.

Between sips of beer he learned she was an air hostess, flying the dull local routes. Mahabirlal watched a beery foam collect upon her upper lip. The hair fell softly back from her face as she lifted the glass to her mouth. Her neck was long and soft, like a bird's, thought Mahabirlal.

'Leave those friends,' he coaxed, speaking suddenly and urgently. 'Have lunch with me. Afterwards we will drive to Marve. We have a small house right on the beach there. We don't use it much, my wife doesn't like it. She says it's too cut off, she prefers this hotel and all these people.' He could not believe he was suggesting what he was.

The girl moved nearer, placed a finger on his arm and ran it down to circle the large ruby ring on his hand. 'Marve. That's great.' She drew her nail lightly round his ring.

'Then you'll come?' Mahabirlal questioned in disbelief.

She nodded. 'I'll tell the boys and then change. Won't be long.' She threw back her beer in a single gulp and then stood up. With a smile she walked away in the direction she had come. He followed with his eyes the slim bronze undulation of her. He seemed to have entered a kind of trance. She reached her friends, and he saw them take her hands, to pull her down among them, but she resisted, talking and laughing. Suddenly, several of the boys turned to stare incredulously in the direction of Mahabirlal Goga. He did not mind. He leaned back in his deck chair for a moment, before going himself to change. Through a bamboo fence on his left, he could just see the camels far away along the beach, the bright specks of terrified children clinging to their backs. To his right the tables were mostly empty and forlorn.

Mahabirlal was dressed and waiting when she returned. He guided her quickly to the air-conditioned restaurant, before she could change her mind.

'They have a band in here. Do you like lobster? Or they have a good prawn curry,' Mahabirlal advised as they settled at the table, unable still to believe the words and actions tumbling from him with such ease.

The girl wore jeans seamed tightly about her buttocks, and a low-necked sweater. Accustomed only to the heavy yellow pendulum of his wife, Mahabirlal had all but forgotten the exact effect a pair of well-proportioned and -defined buttocks should have upon a man. Her hair was tied carelessly with red ribbons into two bunches, which fell forward over each shoulder. Sitting across the table from him, eating not only lobster but, it seemed to Mahabirlal, almost everything else on the menu as well, she looked like a wanton schoolgirl. In his present mood this slight tendency to fantasy did not displease him. As they ate, the beer flowed between them, and Mahabirlal felt his head grow heavy; he was not used to so much drink. The girl seemed to feel no effect. Her lips were printed in a scalloped pattern around the rim of her glass, her fingertips were oily from the chicken she held and bit at with sharp tears, like a hungry dog. Mahabirlal could summon little appetite; food seemed irrelevant; he nibbled half-heartedly at some shrimps, preferring to watch the girl. Now and then she paused between mouthfuls as if remembering him, and gave a wide, greasy smile. Conversation was rendered useless by the noise of the band. At last she sat back with a sigh of contentment, laughing and patting her stomach, a shred of chicken caught between her teeth.

125

Mahabirlal looked at his watch and suggested they should go. Outside, he started the car with a nervous jerk. His heart began to beat. He wondered how he should proceed once he arrived at Marve. What did the suave men do? Maybe there were rules of etiquette in circumstances such as these that were yet unknown to him. He did not want to put a foot wrong, he was a late starter in the art of deceit; there were wasted years he must catch up on. He eased the car out on to the road, keeping his eyes with an effort on the road ahead. It was a long drive to Marve, and the girl and the road seemed to demand a feat of schizophrenic concentration. In companionable understanding the girl put her arm through Mahabirlal's as he drove, and laid her head gently on his shoulder. She said little, giving only an occasional caress to his knee or thigh. Mahabirlal relaxed and began to enjoy the anticipation that seemed around each bend.

Eventually they got there. Mahabirlal drew up before the little house and had to admit, looking at it critically, that a new door and a coat of paint were needed. Still, to a newcomer, the tree in the yard overshadowed most faults, and the beach spread out before them in all its blue and magnificent daring. The girl jumped out of the car in excitement.

'You really have got a place, then?' She laughed, as if she had not believed him. Mahabirlal looked at her, surprised. She ran up to him and took his arm. He liked the feel of her weight clinging to him in unsolicited intimacy. Her spontaneity saved him much groping embarrassment, she broke down the barriers he would otherwise have had to break. He was grateful and determined to learn from her the rules and artifices of his brave new world.

With a smile and a wink, he disengaged himself and turned back to the car. He pulled down the flap of the glove compartment and felt for the key to the house that they always kept there. After a moment he withdrew his hand, empty. An unthinkable thought had entered his mind. The elation of conquest and beer sank slowly and coldly within him. He saw a picture of himself taking out the key, along with other items, the week before when the car had gone for servicing. He had given the key to Mrs Goga, to include temporarily on an immense bunch she carried about with her, hooked on to the waist of her sari. He had not yet retrieved it from her.

The girl's smile faded slowly as he explained. 'I thought as much,' she said. 'You men will try any trick.' She pouted disagreeably.

'No, really. It's just the key. We'll come next Sunday,' Mahabirlal hastened to assure her. She made him feel suddenly foolish, as if while he told the sad truth, he was lying. He felt the old Goga rise again above the new, with a devilish, knowing grin. He turned roughly and kicked the front door of the house a few times, but nothing moved. He tried the windows, and with his nose pressed against the dusty glass, glimpsed half a sofa, and the back of a bed. He gave up and stared dejectedly at his toes. The girl tapped him on the shoulder, she was smiling again.

'It doesn't matter. As you say, we'll come again. Let's try the beach today,' she invited. Mahabirlal's hopes rose slightly.

They sat down beneath a shady palm, with cool dry sand around the roots. As soon as he leaned back against the trunk, the girl pressed close to him, running her hand under his shirt, pulling at the buttons.

'No,' said Mahabirlal in alarm. 'Not here, someone might see us.' He looked nervously along the empty beach, thinking of the aged Parsi couple who sometimes stayed in the next-door house. The events of the day, culminating in the loss of the key to the house and the vulnerability of his desire and position on this open beach, struck him suddenly, like an illness. He felt a slight nausea, and his head began to ache. He wished he had not drunk so much beer. Perhaps it was enough, he thought, for the first day, for an introduction to this new world. He would keep its treats for the next time.

'All right. If you don't want to, don't.' The girl seemed uninterested again. Then, immediately, in a more persuasive voice, she said, 'Have a little rest. You look very tired. Come, put your head here, it'll be more comfortable.' She patted her denim thigh. Mahabirlal nodded gratefully, appreciating her understanding. He gladly lowered his aching head to its inviting resting place. But settling his neck upon her thigh, he was unprepared for the flood of sensations that speared his dorsal nerves and spread berserk to his remotest of reflexes. Only the thump of his head outweighed it all. Through half-closed eyes he could see she had blackheads under her chin, and lipstick flecked her teeth. It did not matter; he lay upon his pillow and smiled, his eyelids began to droop. Here he lay, a man among men at last, while in a cinema his wife and children chewed popcorn, fixated no doubt by the wanton simulation of the very life he led at this moment. Who, he wondered sleepily, would have thought that Sunday had such milk and honeyed gifts to bestow, gifts so easily taken and got away with. It was a revelation like no other in his life. Under his neck the sensations of the soft denim pillow fought with the beer. The battle was short; the beer won. Mahabirlal closed his eyes and slept.

The sun was low when he awoke. Under his head the sand was cold, some trickled uncomfortably down one ear. The girl was gone and also, he soon discovered, three hundred rupees from his pocket, and the ruby ring from his hand. She left him, however, a small exchange, for which he was not entirely ungrateful. Tied in a neat bow, on a large safety pin, one of her red ribbons was pinned to the zip of his trouser fly.

As he drove back to town his head was still muzzy, and Bombay came oppressively down upon him, with its dirt-streaked buildings and the droves of beggars who flooded forward to his car at each traffic light. Eventually, he parked the car before the open, colonnaded front of the club, and walked through to where he saw his family, settled in basket chairs about a table on the lawn. They seemed little interested in him, nobody questioned his day. Mrs Goga was discussing, with his mother, the subject of film censorship, and the sad deterioration in public morals that could make so popular the film they had seen that afternoon, about an apparently respectable man, who led in reality a raucous double life.

'But he came to a bad end, just as he should. That much I will say,' Mrs Goga decided with firm satisfaction, staring meaning-fully at her husband. Mahabirlal coughed nervously and looked away. Only his father-in-law, by way of greeting, gave him half his attention from a plate of cheese toast.

'If you have to work shifts on Sunday, things can't be that good. You should have taken my advice, and not have jumped into a lot of expansion before you were sure.' Mahabirlal's father-in-law burped gloomily above his plate, and prepared to take another bite of toast.

'It's nothing like that. It's these power cuts. We can't afford to fall behind schedule. It's hit all the industries. Many people are beginning to work Sunday shifts,' Mahabirlal explained brightly. The gaps between the buttons on his father-in-law's shirt widened as he breathed; a few wiry hairs poked through.

'We all suffer. By two o'clock it's gone. No power, and not a gas cylinder available anywhere. How do they expect us to eat lunch? Do they cut it off in Delhi? Does Mrs Gandhi eat cold pre-cooked *chappattis?*' Mrs Goga's mother grumbled. Finishing the last chip on her plate, she wet her finger and wiped up the crispy remains. A large diamond pierced the end of her wide, flat nose.

'Will you please call your children off. They're kicking my little girls,' a woman at the next table shouted angrily across at them.

'Sanju. Come here. How many times have I told you, no kicking little girls. Don't answer me back like your father. Shut up, I said. Shall I show you what shut up means?' Mrs Goga lunged towards Sanju, pushing over her chair in the process. Mahabirlal picked it up and set it back in its place. Mrs Goga sat heavily down upon it again.

On the dark evening lawns of the club, floodlights encircled family groups about white metal tables. Mahabirlal was grateful for the patch of shadow about his chair. He was not in a mood to be scrutinized, for he knew his face must lack the familiar mould that habitually held it together. His features felt sharper, and a smile broke sometimes, inadvertently, on his face. But the family was too busy to notice, involved in gossip and a fresh

129

round of snacks that a waiter delivered with a bottle of tomato sauce. Mahabirlal smiled at them with tender magnanimity. He leaned back in his chair and looked at the sky.

Above the floodlights that engulfed the lawns, the sky was immense and dark. But in that blackness each small star was held carefully, and turned to an angle where its treasure could shine, by some all-knowing hand. Mahabirlal sighed and felt at one with God's clear plans, as he contemplated the gift of the Sunday behind him, and a lifetime of Sunday bonanzas to come.

ANTHONY EDKINS

What's Eating You?

Just as he was leaving, she said: 'Don't be late! Remember the Upanishads are coming to dinner.'

It's funny how one phrase rather than another plants a poisoned dart in the fuck-it part of the brain. Almost any other remark and he might have returned home – for dinner, toothbrush, copulation, sleep, mouthwash, breakfast, and off again.

But the Upanishads had come to represent everyone and -thing he no longer believed in. He remembered the first time they had met (and it had been exactly the same the last time, too): tedious talk about the artful dissemination of birth-control techniques, cricket in Kabul, and how your tribal warriors wouldn't put up with the Russkies for long.

But it wasn't *only* the Upanishads; it was the Upanishads *and* his wife (called by him not Ulla, or even Mrs Fastnet, but Fastnet Senior because she was a day older than he was), a combination that had come to prove debilitating for his morale, along with several others: Fastnet Senior and the Smythe-Bastuds; Fastnet Senior and the Hungerford-Bridges – a whole series of saga-long middlebrow novels! They were like great edifices built by dreams to dwarf him and keep him out. It was other people who brought out the worst in Fastnet Senior. She and he had occasional moments – usually sexual – when they – what? – esteemed, trusted, appreciated each other; no! – it was more probably a sort of reciprocal animal warmth, embellished by largely fanciful conceits about the past. And there were other moments, usually when she was curled up like a cat – that animal thing again – reading, but the trouble was her attention-span for reading wasn't much better than a cat's, and she'd yawn, stretch, and stalk off to phone the Upanishads (or the Hungerford-Bridges) for midnight croquet or nude scrabble.

The Upanishads didn't like him very much. As an aggressive defence mechanism, he was always bringing the conversation round to *Lives of a Bengal Lancer*, a film he'd enjoyed as a boy, with Franchot Tone having his nails tortured and Gary Cooper being brave. (He was half-American – so was Fastnet Senior, and this, he thought, was why they didn't really mesh: 'Meet my wrong half,' he'd once introduced her, a joke she hadn't appreciated, of course – anyway, that was why he rather admired Gary Cooper – always helping the French out in North Africa, the British on the North-West Frontier, and homesteaders in the Wild West.) But the Upanishads were both nationalists and snobs, and didn't really care for references to Clicky-Ba, a Khyber Pass character who used to turn up weekly in the *Wizard*. The last time the Upanishads had come to dinner had coincided with Russian tanks round Kandahar, and he'd gone into a routine about stiff upper lips wearing Old Leningradian ties and singing 'We all love the Screw Gun' to the tune of 'The Volga Boatman', while Garodny Coopervitch bled bravely to death holding aloft the Hammer and Sickle. Later that night, Fastnet Senior had lectured him about lack of taste and done a tasteless Lysistrata on him – another nail in the Upanishads' *turbeh*, had she but had the sense to sense!

He was working himself up into the nearest he could get to rage – mute whining. Not a pretty sight – and not a pretty sound either, he admitted ruefully, wondering whether the fact that self-pity was quizzical was a redeeming feature. His argument was: to stay with a woman just because you both like fucking is immoral, humiliating, and lazy.

What about the children? sneered the voice of conscience. He grinned with glee: we haven't got any children, he trumped. He had always despised conscience, not as a generality – *his* conscience, which he had inherited from his Irish grandmother.

What about better or worse, sickness and health, bread and circuses, sticks and carrots? He nodded, as though checking an inventory; gone through the lot, every clause in the contract – not our contract, by the way, one drawn up by persons unknown – crossed and dotted, used and exhausted. Time to change: the Upanishads can stay the same, tireless, unchanging – the Upanishads and Fastnet Senior.

Right, but why not explain before going, why slink away like a lover in late afternoon? He was indignant: I'm striding out in broad daylight. There's nothing to explain – only the possibility of pointless argument: equal disenchantment never happens at exactly the same time, always one of the two is left with a sense of grievance; there's always the deserter and the deserted, even if the former is sometimes less to blame. He flicked an old bus ticket into the gutter: everybody has got to leave home sometime, otherwise you sink into psychic death; no! – nothing so dramatic: merely deadness. . .

A little before dawn on the following morning, Fastnet walked to a mainline station and boarded a train heading south to the sun and the hour of waking alone.

Bloody tired, he felt, du-di-di-dur-du-di-di-dur, the grimy backs of slums and tenements, warehouses with broken windows and missing slates, junk dumps and yards of battered cars, du-di-di-dur-du-di-di-dur, suburban houses and gardens trimmed by Procrustes, du-di-di-dur-du-di-di-dur, the country at last with first light beginning to break the indistinct blackness of the sky.

His copy of the *Morning Sickness* slipped unfolded from his knees and, as the train thundered into a tunnel, he nodded off to sleep.

The sudden reduction of noise as the train emerged from the tunnel made his eyes flutter open. He tried to hang on to his dream – something about twins with weirdly disparate hats – but an awareness that night had now turned to day dawned, distracting him, and the dream floated away. He looked out of the window at the hurrying landscape, then for a confused moment thought he'd gone back to sleep and was dreaming again.

It wasn't that the landscape was different in degree: he found himself looking at a completely unknown terrain which bore no relation to what had gone before. He saw arid heights and pitted canyons, and, on the horizon, hard high mountains. The architecture of the sparse buildings was in a style he'd never noticed in fact or photo. The sheep were a strange shape and the infrequent humans, one or two mounted awkwardly on mules, all seemed to have blankets like bandoliers about their bodies and they were wearing bulbous rope sandals.

This prompted him to look around the carriage. There were differences: more wood, frillier curtains, small square pictures of costumed folk smiling and dancing in front of fussy castles, and, prominently displayed, a notice saying: *NOCHTA BIS-MIRCHEN.*

He hadn't paid much attention to the couple on the opposite side of the aisle when he'd entered the carriage but he was pretty sure they'd been a typical duo drawn from the international student fraternity, guy and girl both be-jeaned with large light-weight packs on the seats beside them – certainly not the squat stolid pair, dressed up like peasants on their way to a wedding in the city, now sitting there.

They were watching him out of the corner of their eyes, so he sighed, hunched himself up, and turned his face to the window, trying to give the impression he was composing himself for a return to sleep.

The train rushed through a station. He attempted to decipher the name – blue lettering on beige board – CERNYWYZKA-WA, it looked like.

But what consolidated unease and sobered consciousness was the realization that the wheels were no longer humming du-di-di-dur-du-di-di-dur; instead, they were striking a looser, more leisurely note: dik-dik-dik-dik-dik-dik, they went, and he had a vivid vision of a gloomy smalltown *pension,* soundless except for a grandfather clock.

He sat upright, said aloud, 'Christ! we've been hijacked,' and realized that the couple in the far corner were now whispering – obviously about him – but not a single recognizable syllable registered in his anxious ear.

'Where are we?' he almost shouted at them. The man nodded and smiled; the woman looked out of her window. For some reason, the purply-grey complexion of the Upanishads came to mind. 'Afbloodyghanistan, probably,' he snorted, answering his own question.

The man nodded again, encouragingly. '*Shuckska*', he said, making an obscure gesture with his hands, '*Shuckskásha!*'

His turn to nod but he couldn't be bothered. He looked out of the window and thought of Fastnet Senior, plump in bed probably and, simultaneously, tears came to his eyes and an erection to his cock. He lit a cigarette, nearly gagged on it, then noticed that the woman was pointing; he followed her finger and saw *NOCHTA BISMIRCHEN*.

'*Scusi*,' he said, stubbing out his fag and burning a thumb in the process.

SVEVEROLT, a tiny station, with an official in a comic-opera hat and a sardonic goat, flashed by; the official had been holding something that looked like a red wand.

The name of the next station was PHALLUS. Pity it didn't stop, he thought, might've been a resort! Perhaps it never stops: I'm dead and this is how it is in death's other kingdom – an unending stream of halts, with gibberesque names, where your train never stops.

The countryside was beginning to look lusher and more inhabited. Terraced hills replaced the earlier barren mounds, and trim new-looking white houses with very red roofs sprouted instead of shacks and sheds; primitive pines had given way to orchards.

He tried to think what to do but the thing was he'd always been very bad at thinking; he lacked concentration and tended to believe that thinking, like learning languages, was a skill some people possessed and others didn't. He was essentially a

135

tangential person, and thought always shunted him off into the sidings of daydream and fantasy.

They were speeding through OPS at the time and, instead of pulling the emergency lever – a fleeting impulse triggered by 'thought' – he found himself imagining their coming to a majestic terminus in a baroque station – FASTNET, perhaps – and his being ceremoniously greeted by a rather gigantic young woman in an embroidered blouse with a little badge, representing the Union Jack or the Stars and Stripes, pinned like a brooch above her left breast. He rushes over and buries his face in her stakhanovite bosom.

She bends her head indulgently and says: 'I can't hear what you're asking.'

'Doesn't matter – you have. You do!'

'Do what, darling?'

'Speak English. Where am I? You're wonderful! – What's your name?'

'You're here in my arms,' she says tenderly, gently levering him to her left and grabbing his bag with her other hand, 'and I'm called Migale.'

'Migale! A marvellous name. Suits you – it's somehow statuesque. Where are we going?'

'To bed, of course, but first we must eat.'

His stomach was grumbling and the pair in the corner were now regarding him with apprehension. He tried to smile: 'Restaurant car? Buffet?' He arched his eyebrows and pointed to his midriff. The woman shrieked and hastily moved off down the aisle, followed, a little sheepishly, by her man.

'Shit!' he said, as they went: he had wanted to explore but now he felt inhibited, in case they thought he was following them.

A minute later, the man was back, apologetic and hesitant: '*Upanishad?*' He seemed to be asking a question. Then he beckoned.

Might as well follow him. As they entered the next

compartment, the peasant stood aside and pointed. It was a dining-car, empty except for one table, where four men wearing loose tunics and baggy trousers were eating. He sat down one table away from them in the opposite side of the aisle.

Almost immediately, a waiter appeared with a bowl of soup: it was muddy brown and tasted vaguely of vegetables. Course followed course: a fish he couldn't identify; then a minute bird on a small piece of toasted black bread. This was followed by a very dark stew with dollops of white curd on top; then a salad consisting entirely of something like radish and very bitter little purple round things with an orange stone in the middle. The four men were laughing uproariously and seemed to be drinking a series of rapid toasts out of thimble-sized glasses. The waiter next brought him an extremely strong and smelly cheese – produce of strangely-shaped sheep or sardonic goat, he decided – and, as though they went together, a second plate of an abrasively sour rhubarbish fruit, cut into symmetrical logs. He burped. The waiter smiled and hurried back with the blackest coffee he'd ever experienced; also a finger bowl and one of those thimble-sized glasses with a colourless liquor, its schnappish taste quickly obliterated by fire.

The bill, as incomprehensible as a prescription, came to 297–270 plus 10%. He drew out his chequebook and looked at the waiter, who leant over and scribbed £5.50 on the bill. He wrote down that amount in words and figures on his next blank cheque, then dated and signed it, the waiter watching him as though he were a small boy learning to write.

Usless to try approximating: 'And the payee?' he queried, pointing.

The waiter understood at once: '*Upanishad. U-pan-i-shad.*'

This endorsement almost made him retch but he managed to downgrade his disgust to an inner belch, and, muttering '*Merci,*' he rushed back to the safety of his corner seat in the neighbouring carriage. His travelling companions had disappeared.

He groaned and looked out of the window. The landscape had changed again (the restaurant car had had frosted windows) and a desolate plain stretched to infinity. Hamlets were practically non-existent but he thought they sped through one called SOLEREIN before gluttony's torpor sent him to sleep.

When he awoke, they were emerging from a cutting. Du-di-di-dur-du-di-di-dur went the wheels, and he was suddenly wide awake and singing at the top of his voice: '*Non! Rien de rien. Non! Je ne regrette rien.*' The sun was shining on a countryside blooming with understatement but the students who were swarming about the carriage were staring at him and laughing.

'Drunken old sod,' one of them said with disgust.

'I'm not drunk. I'm happy! Off to Migale, you know. First holiday I've had in years. Maybe mouth my memoirs, do some snorkelling – that sort of thing.'

'Where's Migale?' asked a girl the colour of Mexican honey.

'Migale's a woman, love. I've got to find her.'

But when they pulled into the Channel port the only people on the platform were the Upanishads, dressed in heavy motoring coats and carrying goggles and gauntlets. As soon as they saw him, they waved exaggeratedly, hallooed, and marched towards him, their purple-grey faces suffused with pleasure, their white teeth shining. They looked hungry.

DEBORAH SINGMASTER

Stella Artois

The room was clean: that was her only reaction as she lowered the sleeping infant into the cot which the hotel management had provided; he had finally dropped off after crying continuously throughout the Channel crossing.

Lacking the energy to undress completely, she slid, half-clothed, between the stiff, cool sheets on the double bed. The room seemed to be rocking with the motion of the boat but her insides, exhausted from the upheaval of sea-sickness, had relaxed now that she was back on land, and within minutes she sank into a deep dreamless sleep.

Her awakening was violent: she started up from the pillow, the top half of her body lurching forwards into the darkness, her heart thundering. The room was airless, stifling; there was a faint smell of cigarette smoke. Her head ached from want of oxygen and also the pressure of the hard bolster-shaped pillow. She got out of bed, went to the window and wrenched it open; as the damp air enveloped her, she gulped it down gratefully. Behind her the infant let out a wail, summoning her. She fumbled with the catches that held up the collapsible side of the cot. He wailed again, more loudly this time, enraged by her slowness, his clenched fists pummelling her descending hands.

She took him back to bed with her and switched on the bedside lamp to see what time it was. The dim disc of orange light shone down on to an ashtray advertising Stella Artois beer; in the ashtray lay a cigarette butt from which a thin wisp of smoke curled upwards and vanished under the tasselled fringe of the lampshade.

The girl recoiled: someone must have entered the room while she was sleeping; that was probably what had woken her so abruptly – the sound of the intruder leaving; she must have forgotten to lock the door. The infant, conscious that he had lost her attention, twisted his head sideways, his mouth juddered open and his face puckered, then his cries came like the muted rattle of a machine-gun.

'There, there!' she tried putting him to the breast but he would not take it, he squirmed and his back arched away from her arms. She got up again and paced the room, rocking the damp wriggling bundle against her. Grey light was filtering through the half-opened window before she got him back to sleep. In the distance a pneumatic drill started up, together with the whirr of a crane. Closer, outside the window, she heard a *camion* go past.

It was raining. She carried the infant in a baby-sling and held the sides of her opened coat around him. A building site occupied the square in front of the Hotel Celtique. Foundations were being laid several feet below ground level and palisades of rusted reinforcing rods stuck up above the surrounding mud like the teeth of monstrous mangled combs. The crane was swinging piles of concrete slabs from one group of helmeted workmen to another, shifting its load forwards and backwards on a squealing pulley far up in the air; from his control cabin the crane driver would be able to see over the rooftops to the harbour and across the Channel to the horizon. The girl could not walk more than a block beyond the site – either the rain, or the infant's cries, or her own state of suspense, drove her scurrying back to the hotel as if she had just remembered something vital.

'*Rien, Madame*,' the proprietor of the Hotel Celtique, thin as the angle-poise lamp clamped to the reception desk, answered her query. No phone call, no telegram, nothing.

The room they had given her was on the top floor; she asked

if she could be moved: it was tiring having to carry the infant up so many flights of stairs. The proprietor sympathized but regretted that he could do nothing, all the rooms on the first floor were taken – perhaps the following day. . . She said she might not be staying, it would depend. He bowed, courteous but unconcerned. His wife, rotund and chatty, ignoring her husband like a carefree bird scavenging around the foot of a scarecrow, viewed the infant with a critical eye; a mother of three, she knew all there was to know about infants and if she was not mistaken this one looked '*mal nourri*', to her trained eye. Was she nursing? Yes? Madame shook her fair frizzy head, she believed in the bottle, '*toujours le biberon*'. The girl said bottles were less convenient for travelling.

All evening she sat in the room. Doors opened and closed on the floor below. The hotel plumbing hissed and shuddered and flushed and gurgled. No one came up to the top floor. At midnight she woke the infant to feed him; he hated her for it. Eventually, after a lot of coaxing, he took from one breast but resented being moved to the other. She changed him and put him down again. It was half-past one when she got into bed, frantic for sleep. She leant over to turn off the lamp and her eye fell on the ashtray; it was clean and empty. Her hand remained over the switch as she hesitated, suddenly nervous of launching herself into the dark. This time she knew she had remembered to lock the door.

The infant's cries woke her at four. He fed well, pressing his fingers into her breast as he suckled. Later he fell asleep in her arms and she kept him in bed with her, comforted by his contact.

When she next woke – this time of her own accord – it was still dark. For some seconds she could remember nothing, not even the infant; she knew only that she was terrified: a few inches from her face an incandescent dot glowed and winked – the burning head of a half-smoked cigarette. She leaped out of the bed and ran to the door expecting to find it had been broken open; it was still locked. She opened it and looked up and down the corridor; there was no one there, nor any sound of footsteps on the stairs. She drew back into the room, locking the door, checking it. The flimsy curtains were billowing inwards from the half-opened window; she ran across the room, pulled them apart and looked out. The street below was deserted; on the wall a few feet away from the window, the neon sign of the Hotel Celtique flickered and hummed.

She searched the room, looking under the bed and opening the superfluous clothes cupboard with its mass of jangling coat hangers. Nothing. She sat down on the edge of the bed and stared at the small cluster of ash pellets beneath the tip of the cigarette, neatly positioned in one of the grooves on the rim of the ashtray and still glowing and winking as wisp after wisp of white smoke spiralled upwards into the cone of the lampshade. Suddenly, as if she was possessed, the girl grabbed the cigarette, put it between her lips and inhaled. The smoke bellied inside her, she could feel her lungs bulging against her rib cage, her head swam and the room tilted; she lunged towards the wash-hand basin and vomited.

It was clear that the proprietor thought she was mad – or up to something. His manner, still formally polite, betrayed underlying hostility and suspicion. Madame's peremptory salutation was unsoftened by subsequent pleasantries; if the infant was dying of malnutrition it was no concern of hers – all this conveyed in a single 'bonjour, Madame'.

Again the girl pressed for a different room, knowing it was useless; she had wrecked her chances of enlisting their co-operation by suggesting that all was not well with the Hotel Celtique, that people passed through locked doors during the night. The language problem did not make things any easier. The proprietor cut short their discussion with a reminder that the room would have to be vacated by midday if she decided she did not wish to stay for another night.

Outside, a fierce, salty wind battered against the hoarding around the building site, muffling the noise of the drills and bulldozers. She tried to find another room in a cheap hotel nearby, but it was Friday, they were all booked up, or said they were when they saw and heard the infant. She bought a roll of bread, some cheese and a bottle of mineral water, and took them back to her room. The infant had been awake all morning and she let him cry in his cot while she ate. Afterwards she tried to compensate for her neglect, hugging him to her, kissing his cold mottled little fists and screwed-up face. It was not what he wanted, he wanted more milk and this she could not give him.

She wanted to sleep now, before it grew dark so that she would be able to stay awake during the night. In the morning she would leave. If she had heard nothing by then it would be pointless to wait longer. The infant slept only fitfully, waking every half-hour or so, rousing her sometimes from a state of semi-consciousness in which daydreams dovetailed into actual dreams; at other times jerking her brutally out of oblivion from which she emerged nauseous, her limbs trembling, chilled from the sluggishness of her blood's reluctant circulation. She gave up trying to feed him and shoved her crooked little finger into his mouth instead. He was, she thought, beginning to feel lighter in her arms. She gnawed on the heel of cheese left over from her lunch and forced herself to drink glass after glass of mineral water in the hope of increasing her milk.

Later that evening she went out. The wind had softened and become almost balmy. The building site lay silent and the pavements were chequered with parallelograms of light spilling from the open doorways of cafés and bars. She ventured into one of the bars and ordered a black coffee. There were no other women present. The men standing by the counter glanced briefly at the solitary girl, their curiosity turning to indifference as soon as they identified the bundle slung across her chest. She looked for somewhere to sit. An old man with a single brown tooth got up from his perch on the end of a bench by a crowded table and ushered her towards it. The men at the table, wreathed in a cloud of cigarette smoke, were shouting at one another like sailors in a blizzard. They paid little attention to the girl until she started to cough and the infant let out a small and, for him, well-mannered whimper, whereupon they all stopped talking and laughed kindly. They spoke to her but she could not understand them; the smoke was beginning to make her feel sick and dizzy. She swallowed her scalding black coffee and left.

The room repelled her: at first merely bare and comfortless, it had now acquired an almost animate awfulness – the wallpaper writhing under a ghastly blown-up paisley pattern whose red and green coils twisted and slithered like trapped snakes. She locked the door and laid the infant on the bed. Ignoring his screams, she dragged the cot from the far side of the room and wedged it against the door – no one could now force an entrance into the room without her hearing.

'Coming, coming, coming.' She picked him up and tried to soothe him. When she opened her blouse he shot his face against her nipple, held it between his gums for a second, then lost it again, too desperate to co-ordinate his most basic functions.

'There, there!' She spoke to him through his screams. Gradually he relaxed and began to suck; despaired-of peace came like the blessing of a tooth removed from an abscess. She leant back against the headboard and closed her eyes. A sharp rap on the door startled her and she jumped, dislodging the infant, who instantly resumed screaming.

'*Qui est là?*'

It was the proprietor. Was all well? He had heard some noises. . .

'*Oui, merci.*'

He knocked again, not hearing. She shouted, yes, yes, everything was fine – had been, that is, until he came knocking. It took another eternity of patting and crooning to persuade the infant to continue nursing. And with the silence that grew as he fed and dozed came paralysing terror of the hours stretching ahead. She focused on the ashtray, clean again, gleaming under the lamp: if she could concentrate on it, never take her eyes off it until morning, nothing would happen, of that she was certain.

Fewer cars passed beneath the window. The occupants of the rooms on the floor below, if there were any, gave no indication of their presence; the plumbing system was silent. She placed the sleeping infant on the bed, her arms quivering under his small weight as she did so: the lack of food and sleep was beginning to tell. Afraid of dropping asleep if she were at all comfortable, she knelt by the bedside, her aching eyes still trained on the ashtray. Stella Artois. Stella, star. S.

She forced her mind to keep turning but it moved in ever smaller circles, like a spinning top losing momentum: s for sugar, s for slipper, s for sleep. Artois: a for apple, a for answer, a for agony, a for. . .

She woke to find herself lying curled on the floor in a pool of sunshine. For the first time in months she was aware of feeling happy, as if some miracle had occurred in the night. She lay still, basking in unfamiliar sensations of warmth and well-being. Then she heard voices outside the door and the first blow of the axe splintered the wood. A hand stretched through and undid the lock; the cot was shoved back into the room, one of its legs caught in a crack in the linoleum and it toppled over, landing close to where she lay.

They pulled her roughly on to her feet and held her upright. They said things to her which she scarcely heard, as if her head were underwater or swathed in invisible bandages. Only the ambulance siren sounded clearly through her confusion, and at first she thought it must be the infant crying for her; it was time she fed him. She looked round for him, her eyes searching the rumpled empty bed. Her scream took them by surprise and they were not quick enough to restrain her from floundering across the room to the open window and looking down at the small bundle, covered with a white table cloth, on the pavement below. If they had not dragged her back she would probably have flung herself out on top of it. They had to half-carry her out of the room sobbing and raving in an incomprehensible mixture of French and English of which they could make no sense – apart from catching her endless repetition of the name of the beer: Stella Artois.

Madame stayed behind to clean up the room; the first thing she did was to empty the contents of the ashtray into the waste-paper basket.

ANDY SOUTTER

S F

Dear D,

Thanks for your communication.

I guess the best way I can be of help is to give you a little run-down on the more recent evidence of SF and the cult attached.

Mainly because SF is so long dead, all that remains are fairly scattered and indistinct shreds of information from addicts, admirers, detractors and exploiters; and though it has been clear for a long time that whole individual and social theories, attitudes and structures were based on SF and once exercised a powerful influence on the world – yet today the Thing Itself remains elusive.

The famous Fleisch silent film is only one example of the unreliability of SF evidence: we don't know whether the people we are watching are real people or just actors. (Much of the material – though by no means all of it – is clouded by this same doubt as to its authenticity.) The movie sheds a jerky light on the affair; it's very short, and the action is spliced with screen-size caption boards with arabesque borders, carrying an elaborate script:

'THE SPIRIT IS WILLING'

THE HANDSOME YOUNG ARISTOCRAT VON FLEISCH – DYING OF CANCER IN HIS BATH

Fleisch is seen, Marat-like in his bath in a darkened room

where shafts of sunlight creep through the heavy drapes and play over the scene

A HOPELESS DRUG ADDICT

Close-up of his terribly sore-infested body

HE FINDS SOLACE IN POETRY

Fleisch takes a book and his lips move in recitation:
'ALL IN THE GOLDEN AFTERNOON
FULL LEISURELY WE GLIDE
FOR BOTH OUR OARS WITH LITTLE SKILL
WITH LITTLE HANDS ARE PLIED
WHILE LITTLE HANDS MAKE VAIN PRETENCE
OUR WANDERINGS TO GUIDE'

Fleisch pauses and his face shows ironic relish before continuing:

'A CHILDISH STORY TAKE
AND WITH A GENTLE HAND
LAY IT WHERE CHILDHOOD'S DREAMS ARE TWINED
IN MEMORY'S MYSTIC BAND
LIKE PILGRIMS' WITHERED WREATH OF FLOWERS
PLUCKED IN A FAR-OFF LAND'

SF appears wearing a surgical apron over his suit

HIS STUDENT FRIEND SF

SF empties a jug of steaming water into the bath
Fleisch recites:

'SHE STILL HAUNTS ME, PHANTOM-WISE
ALICE, MOVING UNDER SKIES'

SF prepares a narcotic injection

'. . .NEVER SEEN BY WAKING EYES'

Fleisch offers a vein and is injected;
he lies back and recites:

'EVER DRIFTING DOWN THE STREAM
LINGERING IN THE GOLDEN GLEAM
LIFE, WHAT IS IT BUT A DREAM?'

Fleisch falls into a swoon;
SF sits at a table behind him, puts head in hands.
Close-up on SF's sad young face.
Cut to Fleisch suddenly coming round, shouting and
threshing,

'THEY'VE COME DOWN FROM THE CADUCEUS!
THEY'VE COME TO GET ME!'

Fleisch subsides and speaks to SF:

'THERE'S NO WAY OUT SF OLD CHAP
HOLD ME UNDER EVEN IF I STRUGGLE –
IT WILL ONLY BE THE CRUDEST INSTINCT THAT YOU SUPPRESS'

Fleisch slides below the water till his head has disappeared.
SF watches.
Fleisch re-emerges, speaks:

'I IMPLORE YOU'

Fleisch submerges himself again and SF holds him under for
some time.
Close-up on the agonies passing over SF's features.
Finally SF relents and Fleisch emerges spluttering.
SF speaks:

'A CURE MAY COME TOMORROW'

Fleisch looks up at him and replies:

'I'M HIDEOUS AS A MONGREL'

SF replies:

'NONSENSE. YOUR BREEDING IS IMPECCABLE'

Fleisch swoons again.
SF returns to the table and injects himself with the narcotic;
then he encloses a smidgeon of the drug in an envelope
addressed to an unmarried woman; he replaces the envelope
in his pocket.
He gets up and stands over Fleisch.
Close-up on Fleisch's almost peaceful figure.
SF picks up one of Fleisch's books and reads:

'AUTUMN. OUR BOAT LIFTED UP, THROUGH THE MOTIONLESS
MISTS AND TURNED TOWARD THE PORT OF POVERTY'

SF shakes his head and continues:

'THE ENORMOUS CITY WITH ITS SKY STAINED BY FIRE AND
MUD. AH, THE PUTRID RAGS, THE RAIN-DRENCHED BREAD,
THE THOUSAND LOVES THAT HAVE CRUCIFIED ME! WILL SHE
NOT STOP, THIS GHOUL-QUEEN OF MILLIONS OF SOULS WHICH
WILL BE JUDGED? I SEE MYSELF AGAIN, MY SKIN PITTED BY
MUD AND PESTILENCE, MY HAIR AND ARMPITS FULL OF
WORMS, AND EVEN BIGGER WORMS IN MY HEART'

SF ponders:

'MOTIONLESS MISTS'

He checks the book:

150

SF replaces the book.

Close-up on SF's arm retrieving a dripping copy of *Alice in Wonderland* from the bath-water between Fleisch's knees. SF lays the book down, looks at his watch, speaks to himself:

'I MUST HURRY TO MY LECTURE'

He adjusts his appearance and hurries off.

THE END

A PSI FI PRESENTATION

One thing is certain – that SF was alive and well and living in Paris at the time when Jane Avril used to perform her dances, which she called Vexations, to the waltzes of a Scottish pianist named Satie. A contemporary newsreel shows Avril (a tall, graceful blonde dressed in a full skirt with a mass of petticoats) beginning her performance with smooth and expansive gestures before gradually and with almost imperceptible progress causing her body to stiffen to a paralysis – starting with the eyes, spreading to the rest of the face, then down through the neck, arms and torso until finally not even her toes move and her rigid figure jerks awhile upright before falling to the floor and lying still as the music ends. But what is interesting is that as the camera holds on Avril's body it also shows, sitting at a table on the opposite side of the cabaret stage, what is clearly the figure of SF joining in the applause.

This evidence lends credibility to the rumours that SF was much influenced by a guru named Charcot (the man knew Avril), to whom the following tract has been attributed:

Our plane trees are coming into leaf. The city is fresh and

sharp today. The smell of light disinfectant used to wash down restaurant terraces. A brief, light shower of rain. Blackbirds on the garden lawn. Bright laburnums. Blossom-scented air. Two slender young people in white cotton clothes standing between café tables on the boulevard. A fluttering sound that repeats from time to time, sometimes close to, sometimes far off. Hot sun on the face. The smell of malt from a brewery. A celebrity in genial mood standing at the counter of a patisserie and joking with the shopgirl. A young man buying a bunch of irises. A nursemaid pushing a pram with two giggling twins in lace bonnets. The strong smell of ink from a newspaper. A fluttering sound. A waiter laying fresh table-linen. A crowd watching a balloon drift upwards; a blue sky, a few clouds here and there in white puffs. Silk scarves blustering. Steam escaping from a window. A light carriage pulled at a trot by dapple greys. Fresh vegetables. People walking briskly out of buildings. The smell of coffee. A shout from the crowd. A handkerchief dropped from the balloon. An old man in a baggy suit carrying an easel. Short dogs on long leads. Drifts of pink blossom at the foot of walls and in gutters. A window cleaner's red ladder. The squeak of chamois on damp glass. A fluttering sound, close to. Pigeons taking off. Children ringing doorbells and then running away.

Charcot is said to have spoken these words to magical effect whilst preparing and dissecting corpses. Apparently for this task he wore wellington boots, a large rubber apron, and a black top hat. He would remove the complete brain, intact (they were said to be those of virgins who had died of despair) and present it to a follower (such as SF is rumoured to have been), who, mesmerized by the speech, would hold the brain close and whisper gentle and loving words to it. The brain was then replaced in its body. It hasn't been established whether the bodies were reanimated by this process or whether it was a burial rite; there are conflicting views held about this. But it is generally recognized that SF did not ever make a detailed physiological study of any of the brains that came into his hands, but nevertheless constructed an increasingly elaborate model of their operations.

Some time after this it became the fashion to pay to relate dreams to another person. From this we might figure that listening to dreams is hard work. But it looks like SF tried it at least once: the evidence comes in the manuscript of a certain Hesse of Frankfurt, a leading artist. Her handwritten auto-biography was discovered quite by chance in a baker's shop at Archangel. This is how Hesse discovered SF:

. . .I hoped SF would give me the flushing I so earnestly desired and had been used to receiving from B. I told him I would pay to have him act as B., but at this point he became very indignant and said that his act was no one's but his own. I questioned him further and discovered that it was in fact B.'s act, but I did not pursue the matter because he seemed rather highly strung (he excused himself – I nearly said exposed himself which is correct in a sense of course – twice before we began) and anyway, it didn't really matter to me. Boys will be boys, I remember thinking; and I settled down to talk. I gave him my string of pearls, my latest dream; beginning with a labyrinthine flight along endless corridors pursued by an unnamable horror, followed by mingling in a large crowd of women taking pictures of themselves, then the large electric sign over the arcade – AMUSEMENTS with the letters S-E-M-E-N flashing on and off, then a café with the sign VALPOLICELLA with the letters P-O-L-I-C-E flashing out. At this point I turned round to discover SF asleep in his chair behind me. Obviously he was quite incompetent, and I woke him up and told him so. I refused to pay him and left. It was the last I had of that kind of business. It all happened shortly before my woollen chains exhibition.

It is probably after this period that SF became then a literary phenomenon; but although he produced hundreds of adventure stories, none survives – they have all been lost or burnt. What has survived is a single charred page of what is claimed to be a housewife's diary from September 19— (year indistinct):

or not. Was putting usual toothpaste on SF's brush when he came in and dropped ash on it. In awful mood because he'd sold an adventure. Then he told an awful joke and did usual rebellious act with trowha. Said some awful thing about Communism meaning misery and chaos. What was awful was that he wouldn't come out in time, again. No more baby joy's, please! Before I went to sleep I said hello to Clitorina. It is nearly

The page is owned by someone claiming to be a descendant of SF; but the uncertainty about its validity is on the same scale as the Turin-shroud controversy.

Another chance find, a telephone monitor retrieved from an ancient tip by a historian's young daughter, supplies a further piece to the puzzle. The tape is understandably in a dreadful condition, but nevertheless the vestiges of three conversations have been transcribed from it. Only one side of the conversation is heard, and experts say that the voice is that of SF.

VOICE: Yes. (*a painful cry*) No, I didn't mean that. Isn't it obvious? . . . burned myself. No, not on the tile stove because we have no fuel for the tile stove. (*pause*) With a match, yes . . . to light my . . . Take it or leave it. No I won't . . . you. . . We've gone . . . and again . . . I'm sorry, you . . . sir (*click*) . . . (*a number of beeps and hisses*) . . . Hallo . . . Well, times are . . . are hard to find and even harder to . . . plagiarizes . . . least . . . killed himself most honourably . . . scandal. . . The British . . . dachshunds. . . me. . . Yes . . . food parcels and . . . tennis balls . . . shot himself you say? And hung himself at the same time? How aggressive. . . Yes, my books . . . never examine them except through the patient's clothes . . . Oh, that reminds . . . whom you distinguished a while with your friendship, er. . . I was trying to be discreet. Yes. . . Yes. . . Yes. . . So you think successful suicide is a proof of health? Mmm. . . could be right there. . . Wednesday. (*tape ends*)

The gaps in the transcript correspond to the sections of tape too damaged to decipher.

It appears that SF's constant drug abuse eventually produced hospitalization. Our only solid reference to this is from a small entry in a collection called *Hospitals of the Suicide Age*, where this account of a patient invalid (name unknown) is given:

I came round from my operation still groggy from the anaesthetic. I was not able to speak but I could observe all that went on in the tiny ward. Opposite me and next to the bed where SF was sleeping, a dwarf sat resplendent in a gold-braided dressing-gown, eating grapes; one of which slipped from his grasp and rolled beneath SF's bed. At this the tiny man leaped down from his mattress and crawled under the bed in pursuit. He was clearly a little excited and began to shout things like 'Where are you?', 'Come to the Almighty', 'I saw you go under', 'You can't escape me', and such exclamations, at which SF began to wake. SF, who clearly had not realized that a frantic fruit-pursuing midget was beneath his bed, began to believe he was in the presence of his Maker. 'I am dead then, yet still in pain,' he murmured, 'there is some rewriting to do.' Then to the dwarf: 'Who are you exactly?' From under the bed the dwarf explained that he was the owner of a spectacularly large circus that had taken six days to erect before the main supports had given way and the whole project collapsed. I saw SF reach for his urine bottle upon hearing this. The dwarf then appeared with the recovered grape, introduced himself as Almighty Alberto, and pointed to his head injury which he said he had sustained as a result of two kicks from a pair of fleeing zebra. No sooner had he said this than there

155

came a violent clumping from outside the ward, and seconds later a moustachioed stranger lurched through the doors on a pair of crutches and came to a halt. 'I arrived by bicycle,' he announced to the astonished SF in a broad Spanish accent, 'and I sawed the front part of the seat off in your honour.' This appeared to make SF extremely anxious and he asked the stranger who he was; whereupon the man claimed to be El Salvador, and promptly produced a manuscript of an adventure he had written and wanted SF to read. He explained that the adventure was about the following subjects, as I recall them: (1) Ten-metre-long *churros* sodomizing great vats of hot thick chocolate and announcing their presence in clouds of greasy steam that float along hot morning streets and land in the outstretched palms of squatting beggars; (2) Jets of flame spurting mysteriously from the heads of babies lying in shop windows; (3) Gypsies forcing carnations into all his orifices and offering limp medallions of generalissimos while shouting '*DIOS*', '*FUEROS*', '*PATRIA*', '*REY!*' and '*VIVA TEJERO!*'; (4) Six helicopters in ascension, each carrying a dead bull on a rope, on their way to dive-bomb the graves of Breton and Eluard. After this claim SF still appeared most unsettled and the stranger noticed this and said he would take his leave in order not to tire SF. He rose from where he had been crouching over the bed and announced that even though SF was finding it difficult to speak, nevertheless homage was due to his mouth, which he saw as the fount of great wisdom. The man then spoke effusively and reverently of a procession coming forth from SF's mouth led by the Egyptian baboon-god of wisdom, followed by scores of madonnas, then a black bull charging forth followed by an accountant, domestic servants, a submarine, a taxi, a patisserie, a park, and a group of industrialists and publishers; themselves followed in turn by the heroes of Antiquity: Christ, Moses, Oedipus and Leonardo in procession, with a string of popes bringing up the rear. 'El Salvador' spoke of SF's tongue as a river of gold in which were dissolved the most expensive tinctures of bronze, amber and cocaine, and upon this river there floated libraries, concert halls, theatres, royal yachts, royal miles and royal males, beautiful women, handsome men, and the great 'keys to our kingdom' which the stranger said had already placed him in a state of 'permanent intellectual erection'. At this he bade SF adieu, flung away his crutches, turned with a flourish and walked elegantly from the ward. Meanwhile the object of his admiration had dozed off again. It was then that I realized that blood was trickling from SF's mouth, and I could only watch as this became a torrent. Luckily the dwarf noticed at this point, and ran to fetch a nurse, so the haemorrhage was soon stopped.

I've already mentioned that no original work of SF survives. The only substantial reference to it is a microfilm of a short magazine item, in possession of the university library at Kabul. The article, entitled 'Is Hitler an SF fan?', is from *Eye* (New York), April 1935 issue. (It has been suggested that *Eye* is an example of an SF fanzine):

Is Hitler an SF fan?

It could yet be that Nazism is just another Jewish conspiracy – because close scrutiny of recent speeches by the Führer seems to suggest that he has been reading a lot of SF lately. Take this latest delivery from Deutschland's demagogue, given at a torchlight rally in Nuremberg last week: 'It is only through obeying individual leaders that the masses can do the work and make the sacrifices upon which civilization depends. It is innate in man to be a leader or follower, and at all times an élite must give direction to the dependent masses. The bonds that unite group members depend on their common bond with the leader. Our task is doubly important today because uncultivated races and backward strata of the population are already multiplying more rapidly than highly cultivated ones. . .'
This little lesson is lifted almost word-for-word from the

latest SF book; and further on in his wanderlogue the Vituperative Viennese also made unacknowledged references to SF's theories about women. Nothing is as it seems, it seems, and 'civilization' is producing some bizarre bedfellows. Is AH a Jewish agent? Is Zionism subtly persecuting itself in order to gain world sympathy? More next week.

There is no trace of next week's or any other edition of *Eye*, and the above remains the nearest thing we have to an actual quote from SF's writing; although there are ample clues to suggest that in those days SF was an enormous influence in the US. Nor does any record exist of the birth of SF; but there is however a taped interview with the doctor who assisted SF's death. Most of the interview deals with the doctor's own life and times, but this is a transcript of the relevant part:

INTERVIEWER: I believe you were present at the death of SF, Doctor Sure.

SURE: Yes. It was a misty September morning in 1939, I believe. I remember walking from Swiss Cottage underground station along a sidewalk carpeted with plane-tree leaves, and stopping to buy a newspaper from the seller at the corner of Eton Avenue and College Crescent. A few hundred yards further lay the house of SF, which was recently built in the Georgian style, but was already half covered in ivy. I was always amused that SF had put down in the middle of a neighbourhood resplendent in gloomy Gothic mansions, miniature castles, and mysterious convents; it seemed that something in SF's soul had clearly sought out those tall oaks and hidden gardens, and chosen this haunting venue as a last resting place.

INTERVIEWER: How did you find SF that morning?

SURE: He was sitting on the edge of his bed, which had been covered with mosquito netting to keep the flies off. A bowl of dog food was at his feet and he was trying to persuade his little dog to come and eat. The dog stood some distance away and clearly had mixed emotions, given the smell of his meal coupled with the unpleasant odour that SF's cancer was producing. The dog finally fled the room, and I remember then SF turning to me slowly, and saying, 'And so much for Pavlov, eh Fleisch?' I had to remind him that I was not Fleisch.

INTERVIEWER: So he was in good humour?

SURE: It prevailed for a little while. I remember asking him – somewhat histrionically – what he thought had been his greatest achievement, to which he replied that spelling the name of the hero with an uncapitalized p had convinced the world that it was a real phenomenon rather than an invented one. He reminded me that he never began a sentence with the word. But it was hard for SF to sustain his joviality and finally I was informed that the pain was too great, that the indifference to the world was overwhelming, and that he would be obliged if I would take his life with my needle, with 'the wife' as he called the opiate.

INTERVIEWER: Was his real wife present?

SURE: He wished that only his daughter should know, and then only after the event. Several times his wife and daughter came to fuss and in their presence I had to delay the injections, where were clearly overwhelming doses. After I had administered to SF, his wife came into the room again and I told her that he was asleep. She sat down to talk to him nevertheless, saying that he could always hear her better when he slept; I went to tell the daughter.

INTERVIEWER: A strong experience.

SURE: Most certainly. For a while I felt that it would be the correct thing to take my own life also. I remember leaving the house, sniffing the damp, fertile air, and hearing an air-raid siren starting up nearby. . .

And that is all the recent stuff I can find. I guess it's all just a withered wreath really, but I hope it's of some use to you. It is not my period of course.

By the way, did I tell you my grandmother died back in the spring? And that there was nothing at all wrong with her? We will all miss her. She always attributed her perfect health to the Victoria plums from her garden. She raised a brood of hard-working republicans like herself. She was a day short of her hundredth birthday; now of course suicide never existed in her day either, but it is interesting that Grandmother always said she could not bear the thought of receiving the King's telegram.

keep it up
— F.S.

RONALD HAYMAN

Urchins

'Mummy, I do wish those boys would go away,' Emma complained. 'They're so irritating, and they've got no right to be here.'

Chattering in loud Greek, the three brown-skinned boys were splashing about in the shallow water under the ornamental bridge. The German, French and Italian guests at the beach hotel were vastly outnumbered by the British: along the curving, rocky beach, it was mostly Anglo-Saxon bodies that were sunning themselves or relaxing in the shade under the brightly-coloured straw umbrellas which were planted irregularly along the sand and on flat areas of concrete between the rocks. To Jake the day seemed windless, but in the bay the blue, red, orange and mauve sails of the windsurfers were kept briskly in motion. Apart from the vigorous splashing of a fat man who was swimming on his back and the scraping of a canoeist's oar as it touched the rocky bottom of the shallow, man-made inlet, the only sound was the shouting of the boys.

Running across to the shower, they turned on the taps, sending out jets of water in all four directions and, laughing, the three of them chased each other round in a circle, in and out of the water. Yesterday, when twelve of them had invaded the swimming pool, the Greek barman had beckoned them out of the water and sent them away with a smiling reprimand, but generally nothing was done – nothing could be done – to stop them from coming ashore after swimming past the fence which divided the private beach from the thickly crowded public beach.

Hanna yawned and then stretched out voluptuously on her sun-bed. Already the soft skin on her lean body was tanning beautifully. The first time Emma had complained about the boys, Hanna had told her that they had more right to be there than the tourists. Which made Jake wonder whether it had been a mistake to bring them to such an expensive hotel. Hanna had canvassed for the Labour Party before the last election, and twice she used the word 'colonialist' in arguments about whether it was unfair that the hotel should own so much of the coastline while native sunbathers had either to spread their rush mats on uncomfortable stretches of rock or join the huddle of horizontal and crouching bodies on the small public beach. 'It's like the field hospital in *Gone with the Wind*,' she had said when she first saw it. Now, when they passed it on their way to the town, he would make uneasy jokes about Florence Nightingale and Vivien Leigh.

'Hanna,' he said, 'do you feel like going into the water again?' He noticed, just too late, that she was rubbing suntan lotion into her legs.

'Not just yet,' she said. 'Thanks.'

'Shall I do your back for you?'

'It's all right, thanks. There's no need.'

Of course there was no need: if she was lying on her back, why would she want oil on it? For the hundredth time he warned himself against being too solicitous. Just let the relationship evolve.

'Bored?' he asked Emma.

'I wish there were more children here.'

'There's lots of children here.'

'Yes, but either they're too posh or they're boys.' She watched a boy of her own age digging a moat around the elaborate sandcastle he'd built.

It was the first time since her divorce that Hanna had involved Emma in a summer holiday with a man: all he needed to do was behave naturally, trying to think less about her awareness of his awareness of the play on him of her awareness. He must give the same tips, for instance, as he would if she were not there: if he gave more than usual, or less, it would look as though he were trying to seem more generous than he was, or more socialistic.

'Oops, sorry,' Emma said to an ant she had just squashed.

Should he offer to take her in for a swim? He should do what he wanted to do. After forty-nine weeks of hard work in the office, he should stop asking himself questions that started with 'should'. He closed his eyes to cut off the incessant feeling that he must do something for Hanna. The crickets were keeping up their pointless, dry, mechanical shrieks, insisting pointlessly on their territorial rights, while in the harbour the crane creaked persistently. The heat pressed down on him. 'Let's recharge our batteries.' The phrase floated into his mind from the distant past – his father, when the family sunbathed at Torquay. With his fingers Jake rubbed at the mosquito bite above his left elbow, simultaneously rubbing with his toes at the bite on his right ankle. On his chest and thighs there were also areas of skin which the sun had made pleasantly irritable. Mediterranean holidays made him feel that his skin enjoyed an independent life, but this year Hanna's presence was more sunlike than the sun's. Without opening his eyes or hearing any sound from her, he knew exactly where she was.

'Why don't you take your tee shirt off?' she asked.

'I can't,' answered Emma. 'I'm embarrassed.'

'Everyone else is topless. Why shouldn't you be?'

The child's ankle brushed against the sole of his foot as she moved closer to her mother. 'It's those boys,' she whispered. 'One of them keeps looking at me.'

He wondered what it felt like to have breasts which twelve months earlier had not been there. When he opened his eyes, a dragonfly was hovering like a miniature helicopter. It swooped away towards the cactus plants on the edge of the garden. The buildings around the harbour looked like an arrangement of cardboard cut-outs, with a toy car starting its climb up the steep road that led inland. Near the crane something unidentifiable was sending out a bright glint.

Penguin-like, two Italians were walking over the sand,

holding hands, their flippers flapping noisily. On the first day, he had bought flippers for Emma, but she had used them only once. After glancing at the Italian girl's breasts, his eyes met Hanna's. No woman had ever given him such a strong feeling that there was no need to be careful about how he looked at other girls.

Clutching her fishing net, Emma was stepping gingerly over the rocks towards the sea. One of the windsurfers kept falling into the water as if the main pleasure were clambering back on to the board. Jake was beginning to enjoy idleness: there was nothing to do except be there. On the two uninhabited islands, the striations on the mountains were more clearly visible than yesterday. Leaning back, the water-skier sent out a feather of white spray. Under the nearest umbrella a girl was lovingly rubbing oil into the plump bronzed back of a man. Earlier they had been talking with Midlands accents. Suddenly he felt hungry to have Hanna's fingers massaging oil into his back. It would be nice if she offered, but he didn't ask.

'Look what I've caught.' Emma was coming towards them with something black in her net. It was a sea-urchin, the black spines gleaming like the bristles of a wet hedgehog. 'They can hurt people,' she explained.

'Only if people step on them,' Jake retorted. 'They can scarcely move.'

The child looked crestfallen. 'Do you think I should throw it back?'

The question was addressed to both of them, but Hanna's eyes were closed.

'What would you like to do?' he asked.

'Keep it.'

'Then keep it. It's no worse than eating a fish.'

She shook the net. The animal tumbled out on the hot sand, its black spines moving unhappily. Emma seated herself cautiously next to it.

'Will it take a long time to die?'

'Not very long, I expect.' He sat up on the sun-bed.

'Is it feeling much pain?'

How much sensation was there underneath the distressed movement of the spines? 'I don't know.' He didn't even know how its body was shaped under the bristles. What would be left if they were plucked away? Something soft and mouselike?

'How do they breed?' she asked. 'Are there males and females?'

Each time he had to say 'I don't know,' he felt more uneasy.

'They're disgusting,' Emma said.

'No,' he said. 'They aren't pretty or endearing, like a bird or a butterfly, but they're no worse than any other animal.'

What was Hanna thinking under her closed eyelids?

'But they're sick,' said Emma. 'Horrible.'

He watched the helpless movement of the spines. 'They're not,' he said. 'The bristles are a defence against fish that could otherwise eat them. It's just that. . .' He hesitated. 'It's hard for us to feel sympathy with something that looks alien.'

'What does alien mean?'

'Other. Dissimilar.' He was thinking of racialism, but didn't want to lecture her about it with Hanna as part of the audience. 'Something with no eyes and no visible mouth is bound to look sinister.'

'It's not dead yet,' she said.

The spines were still moving, more slowly, and when the wind blew a white thistledown seed against the ball of black needles, the thistledown looked more alive. Caught only momentarily, it escaped happily as the wind blew it on.

'I think I should throw him back into the sea,' Emma said. 'I never thought he'd take so long to die.'

'It is taking rather a long time.'

'Do you want me to throw him back?'

Probably it was too late to save the creature's life, but not too late to cultivate the right attitude in her. 'If I'd caught it,' he said, 'I'd throw it back.'

She touched it with her net. 'The prickles are still moving. How can I get it back into the net?'

Levering himself off the sun-bed, he found a stick for her.

'Pooh,' she said. 'It stinks.'

Meaning that in the hot sun, the flesh was already rotting. But he let her go on pushing gently till it was back in the net.

'He's still alive,' she announced when she came back. 'He went on moving after I threw him back into the water.'

'Good,' he said, unconvinced.

Hanna's eyes opened. 'Is it nearly lunchtime?' she asked.

Further up the beach, camped around a yellow umbrella, was one of the better-spoken English families. Twenty years ago the hotel must have been a reserve for the upper and upper middle classes; today you heard a range of British accents. Wearing a wide-brimmed straw hat with a scarf over it, sunglassses and a green bathing costume, the mother of the family was sketching, alternately looking out at the bay and down at her big sketch-pad, while the daughter, a pretty short-haired girl of about nineteen, worked with a brush and a small black metal paint-box, not unlike the one Jake remembered from childhood. She was facing away from her mother and several times when she looked up from her painting, her eyes met Jake's. After exchanging a smile with her, he grinned at Hanna.

'Why did you smile at Mummy like that?' Emma demanded.

'Like what?'

Mimicking the smile, the child produced a startling impression of smarmy condescension.

From where she was sitting, Hanna could not have had a good view of the simulated smile, and Jake wasn't even sure whether she'd been watching her daughter. In any case, she said nothing.

'Let's have a swim,' Emma pleaded.

'I don't feel like it,' said Hanna, nestling against the orange sun-bed like a woman who doesn't have to get up for another five minutes. 'Do you want to take her in?'

'OK,' said Jake, getting up slowly.

It was windier than yesterday, and the windsurfers were moving faster. Unable to soak in the sun as he had yesterday, Jake had been sitting on his sun-bed, watching the pedaloes, the canoes, the water-skiers and the boats in the harbour. On the islands the mountains were less clearly visible than yesterday. In the water which had been so clear, bits of rubbish had accumulated by the pier and along the edge of the rocks. Floating next to a cigarette packet was a dead sea-urchin.

Emma had been in the water only for a few minutes when she screamed.

'What is it?'

'I've been stung by some seaweed or something.'

It was only then that he noticed nobody else was bathing. On the little pier, four Greek boys were chattering excitedly, pointing at something in the water and shouting to him. Emma was closer than he was to the ladder. Already she was scrambling out of the water. The boys were beckoning him to come back. Emma was clutching her arm. As he swam hastily towards the ladder, he felt a sharp pain, like an electric shock, on his right leg.

'Shall I help you?' called the tallest of the Greek boys. Jake was surprised he could speak English, but there was no need for help. The pain in his leg was like that left by a whiplash, but he had no trouble in pulling himself up the ladder.

'There are three of them,' said the boy, pointing. 'Very dangerous. The current brings them. Little red octopus.'

Jake peered into the water, but he could see nothing. Emma had run to her mother, who was gently rubbing ointment into her arm.

'Is it much pain?' asked a bespectacled blond German man of about fifty. Jake had often seen him wearing his glasses in the sea.

'Not much.'

'Cortisone would be the best, I believe.' He gazed at the red weal on Jake's leg with ill-disguised pleasure.

Reappearing with Emma's net in his hand, the smallest of the Greek boys made a sudden, accurate dive from the pier into the water. Almost immediately he was climbing up the ladder with a jellyfish in the net. He handed it to Jake, who took it over to Hanna and Emma.

'Not dangerous at all,' he announced. 'Just a jellyfish.

167

The pain won't last long.'

'She's being very brave about it,' said Hanna.

'It's nothing much,' Emma declared.

He tipped the jellyfish out of the net. It lay on the sand like a giant's sperm, bulbous, obscene, transparent, faintly iridescent. The tallest Greek boy had wandered over to them. 'You can touch it there,' he said, prodding the back of the jellyfish with his finger, 'but it is dangerous to touch there.' He pointed to the almost amorphous underside.

'As if I'd want to touch it,' said Emma, when the boy had wandered off.

'Let me rub some ointment into your leg,' offered Hanna.

The cool cream on the pain was soothing; the touch of her fingers was affectionate.

'Has yours stopped hurting?' he asked Emma.

'Not quite. They're disgusting things. What are they for?'

'They aren't for anything,' answered Hanna.

'They used to be called sea-nettles,' added Jake.

'But they're alive,' objected Emma.

Barking excitedly, a mastiff was chasing a mongrel all over the beach. The mastiff resembled a jowly ex-colonel who had recently asked Jake for a job. Yesterday's sandcastle lay in ruins, and in the harbour the crane squeaked persistently. Alongside the quay, the flat cargo-boat was almost colourless, a greyish-brown silhouette. Emma was crouching on the pier, reaching down into the water with her fishing net. The nineteen-year-old English girl was in the same position, painting again, but this time, when their eyes met, she did not return his smile. She went on looking up at him, though, as she painted. He felt mildly irritated at being a figure in her landscape, with no control over what she made of him, no right even to see it.

'There,' said Emma. Out of her net she tipped another jellyfish on to the sand. It was larger than the first one. The bulbous body sagged in the middle like a huge glob of sputum. 'I'm going to see if I can catch some more,' she announced as she trotted off.

PAT REVILL

Book Review

It is one of the tenets of literary criticism that good literature feeds on literature. It is also true that literature feeds on the science of the age, hence the mechanistic novels, with their strict chronological and causal structures, that abounded in the nineteenth century and, indeed, still survive anachronistically into the twentieth. Hence too the about-face of many of this century's novelists away from concrete, external reality and towards internal, subjective uncertainty as relativity and quantum theory ushered in the new physics.

The writer, like the scientist, is no longer the detached chronicler of a solid, immutable and predictable universe. The distinction between external and internal has been shown to have been a spurious one: the observer is now also a participant, creating and re-creating an essentially insubstantial universe through his or her subjective observation of it.

Only in the twentieth century has it become truly possible for the novelist to respond to Sterne's complaint that we 'forever make novels as apothecaries make new mixtures, by pouring only out of one vessel into another . . . forever twisting and untwisting the same rope'.

Many writers, and readers, have ignored the challenge posed by the new *Weltanschauung*, as the best-seller lists reveal only too well. Others have responded to this apparently vertiginous perspective with a fragmented and shifting vision of reality, hostile to the individual and dehumanizing. Others again have given us the 'psychological' novel, with the self's tortured emotions and fragile relationships as the only true knowable.

Some, notably Doris Lessing in her 'Canopus in Argus' series, have embraced the challenge and explored the new freedom.

The latest contender is Pat Revill, whose first novel, *Book Review*, deals with a book of short stories called *Book Review* by Pat Revill, and with its writer.

The novel begins familiarly enough with a woman of thirty-four taking stock of her life and finding it lacking. An English teacher working in Sweden, she knows she is both successful and contented but at the same time she fears that, by always keeping her options open, she has failed to achieve anything at all (like puberty, midlife crises are happening earlier these days).

Her contemporaries are all mothers, career-women, artists, writers, even skilled and talented amateurs but only, she has always believed, by having compromised their integrity and ideals, forced themselves into a narrow specialization and bowed to social pressure. She, by contrast, has emerged with her integrity intact, but empty-handed. Suddenly the wider knowledge and experience she has gained and valued so highly seem insignificant and she longs to be able to hold up something praiseworthy to the society whose standards and censure she thought she had learned to ignore.

She attempts a literary solution when she recalls the words 'Everyone is the author of his life.' She has always tried to regard the events of her own life in terms of the consequences of her own decisions and non-decisions. Now she begins to write *Book Review* and goes one step further.

She relates how a thirty-four-year-old woman regrets that she has, in the eyes of society, apparently failed to achieve anything praiseworthy and so decides that, as each of us is the author of his or her own life, she can easily repair the damage by writing herself a past. But why stop at one? She notes some of the things she would like to have become and done and then systematically works through the list.

In 'Family Ties' she creates a tender and loving yet humorous and headstrong mater familias. 'Words Apart' is about a successful writer; 'Images' about a television personality;

'Ebony Towers' about a university lecturer; 'Contract Bridge' about an advertising executive; 'Platform' about a politician and 'Strip Me' about a cartoonist.

The stories themselves are meticulously detailed, yet delicately and economically written; and they do not appear anywhere in the book. In the title story they form part of the catalogue of the works of the now highly successful writer. In each of the subsequent stories, which take their titles from the fictitious stories, a story is reviewed and the background to its writing is given, meticulously detailed, yet delicately and economically written.

The author of the novel quotes Jorge Luis Borges in reviewing the book of short stories: 'Why take five hundred pages,' he asks, 'to develop an idea whose oral demonstration fits into a few minutes?'

The novelist continues, through one of the personae in the short stories: 'Furthermore, which of us hasn't at some time created lesser or even greater fictions about our own past, and never been called upon to "prove" their veracity? What form could this proof take anyway? What difference is there in the present between a real past event and a fictitious one? Aren't they both effectively fictitious, existing only in the subjective mind?'

In other words, these bits of fictionalized reality are also realized fictions. The writer of the short stories becomes, through the act of creating them, each of the characters she creates, indeed has always been them. Thus she presents not one version of her own life but eight, if we include the writer herself, and so manages both to keep her options open, and apparently, to close them.

But is this an acceptable solution? The writer of the novel thinks not, and goes on to demonstrate that the seemingly finite collection of short stories is no more than an incomplete fragment.

In the rather less successful second half of the novel in which 'the writer' is clearly intended to stand for the human individual, she tries to show how the stories that do not appear in the collection are nevertheless an essential part of it. These include stories that were actually written (or more accurately not written) but not incorporated into the book, those that were only ideas that the writer rejected, and those that did not even manifest themselves as ideas but remained buried in the writer's unconscious as unrealized ideas.

The writer/individual is totally free to move at will in time and space, creating a potentially infinite number of characters/identities. Therefore, so long as she remains passive, she contains within herself the possibility of immortality. The act of creation immediately makes concrete that possibility and so negates it unless, the novelist insists, the creation is never completed. Each creative act must contain within itself the implicit statement of its own imperfection, as the boy Liang in the traditional Chinese tale 'The Magic Paintbrush' must leave his painted birds incomplete or else they fly away.

This is, of course, merely an extension of what great artists have always known. Which painter could ever claim that a painting was 'finished'? Which composer would make the same claim for a piece of music? How many writers would want to explain every action, every symbol in their work? The good work of literature, as of all art, must be ambiguous (Borges again).

Therefore, the novelist would no doubt argue, it is essential that the novel raises at least as many doubts and questions as it tries to answer. Is the second, philosophizing half of the novel really less successful than the first and, if so, is this deliberate (in which case is it really successful)? Can the book even be called a novel? Is the analogy between writer/novel and individual/life a valid one? To what extent can we change or influence the past or our experience of the past? What restrictions do the laws of probability place on our freedom of choice? Or to put the last question another way – as it is essential to the author's argument – can the uncompleted chain of creation continue indefinitely?

For the novelist it apparently can. She has created of the present writer a reviewer of the novel *Book Review* and no reviewer, however immodest, can ever claim to have written the definitive analysis of a book. The review has in its turn created its own readers whose opinions and judgements must be – with all due respect – similarly and inevitably incomplete.

Thus the immortality of the writer would seem to be assured not, as conventionally, through any merit in her work but as a scientific probability.

And yet, and yet, we object: we know that eventually we will die. But the novelist has anticipated us.

The new physics, she reminds us, is revealing a universe that is finite but unbounded. While we live, the options open to us are unlimited. Even when doors slam and keys turn, past and often tragic experience has shown that the human will can and does go on choosing and inventing. And when we die, the author believes, we will merge once again with the unified whole whose component parts are constantly shifting and changing, yet are always and inescapably there. The chain of creation is infinite.

> we are the earth and stars
> we always were
> and will be
>
> we are the past and future
> we are now
> and always

This, claims one of the novel's characters, is the message of the new physics and of the literature it is spawning.

At times disconcertingly ingenuous, at others irritatingly over-ingenious, *Book Review* is nevertheless a brave first novel and provides a further, hopeful antidote to what the author somewhat clumsily calls 'the holocaustics that would try to corrode the human spirit'.

D. J. TAYLOR

Dreams of Leaving

The walls of the studio had been whitewashed a fortnight ago
and the raw scent of ammonia still hung in the air. Fuchs
unscrewed the cap of the zoom lens and snapped a fresh reel of
film into place. Mr Van Oss said: 'OK. So give us the fuckin'
works, whydoncha.'

Someone switched on the arc lamp, drenched the room in
pale-white light. 'Fuck those asshole bulbs,' said Mr Van Oss.
Somewhere in the background a fan began to rasp. The two
girls, one black, one white, who had spent the last five minutes
shivering behind the canvas screen, removed their robes and
began listlessly to belabour each other's rumps with dull, heavy
slaps. The smoke from Mr Van Oss's cigarette wreathed their
breasts, hung in dense clouds over the camera. Fuchs tried to
shoo it away with his hand.

Fuchs had seen it all. Guys and girls. Guys and guys. Girls
and dogs. Brawny dykes romping in thigh-high bracken.
Banana shots. Fladge. He had graduated from taking twenty-
dollars-a-reel pictures for the kind of magazines Mr Van Oss
thought 'there ought to be a fuckin' law against' to a staff job on
a Brooklyn glossy called *Cocksure* and thence to Mr Van Oss.
'And you can cut out that back-street crap,' Mr Van Oss had
told him, when he had suggested a few variations on the usual
display of Technicolor pudibunda. 'Jeez, do you think I'm some
kind of fuckin' pervert? That stuff with cripples, it's depraved,
it's for sickos. What sells this magazine is *class*.'

Fuchs snapped a few pictures. The white girl, having finished
chastising her partner, allowed her breasts to be fondled while

174

emitting gusty sighs. The bodies clinched, broke apart, came together again. 'OK, OK,' said Mr Van Oss impatiently. 'OK. So you had the hors d'oeuvre. So make with the fuckin' main course.'

Fuchs sometimes wondered why he took this sort of picture for this sort of magazine. For Mr Van Oss was not classy. The studios up at Staten Island or on the Bronx were classy, where the models arrived in Bentleys, had stockbroker boyfriends and cooled you out if you made a pass at them. Moreover, Fuchs found the sight of so much female flesh, so freely available, strangely unnerving. Fuchs had tried telling this to Ellen. Ellen had dismissed this as 'just what a porno photographer would say.'

Fuchs tried to stifle the yawn of boredom that rose in his throat. Before him the two girls began to lick each other's goose-pimples. 'Yeah, OK,' said Mr Van Oss. The white girl, spreadeagled like a starfish, writhed in simulated ecstasy. Her nipples, Fuchs reflected, looked like coathooks. He remembered the conversation he had had the previous night with Ellen, at the end of which Ellen had announced her intention of leaving 'this whole motherfucking east-coast asylum' and by implication Fuchs as well. This conversation had been calculated to impress Fuchs with a sense of his own insignificance. Oddly, it had left him almost jubilant. He had felt so good, he remembered, he could have reached out and pummelled the sky.

The girls were by now amusing themselves with a curved, ebony dildo. Fuchs trained his camera on the black girl's hand as it caressed, without interest, her partner's mottled thigh. 'Fuck it,' said Mr Van Oss. 'Cut.' The girls disengaged, looked at him sheepishly. 'Waste my fuckin' time, whydoncha,' said Mr Van Oss bitterly. He looked suddenly woebegone. 'OK. Same time tomorrow.' There were, Fuchs reflected, good days and bad days. This had been a bad day.

Sometimes Fuchs thought (thinking it now as he wandered back to his apartment on the fringes of Harlem, where giant spades surveyed you coolly from street corners) his problems were a result of his name. Check-out assistants sniggered when he handed them his credit cards. Postmen smirked as they delivered his mail. For a time he tried to get people to pronounce it 'Fookes' or even 'Futch', had even gone so far as to ask Mr Van Oss to call him Ralph, but Mr Van Oss had just said, 'Aw, fuckit Fuchs, whydoncha.' Fuchs gathered that the amusement Mr Van Oss derived from his name was one of the principal reasons for Fuchs' employment. He had tried explaining this to Ellen one night, after the third successive occasion on which he had failed to achieve an erection. 'Jesus, why are you so hung up?' Ellen had said and Fuchs had wanted to reply 'Because I'm thirty-one years old, because I'm going bald, because I take dirty pictures for a living. Because my name is Ralph Waldo Fuchs. Fair enough, wouldn't you say?' Instead he had not said anything. 'Maybe,' Ellen had suggested unkindly, as a reminder of past infidelities, 'maybe you should try making it with one of the broads at the studio.'

But Fuchs had long ago given up attempting to score with the models. You could never be sure of their predilections. Fuchs remembered how a casual invitation from a Swedish girl and her friend had led to some very unpleasant tripartite goings-on (no thank you). Half of them wanted you to beat them up, and the other half wanted you to let them beat you up. Fuchs remembered. He remembered them all, the one who had wanted him to dress up in feathers, the one who had produced a cache of wooden phalli. Fuchs couldn't take it any more. He remembered especially a girl called Rosa Russo, Mr Van Oss's 'Lay of the Month' in three successive issues who, it transpired, had never laid anyone in her life. 'So Jesus why didn't you tell me?' Fuchs had demanded. 'You never asked,' Rosa Russo had said after she had smacked him across the face. And Rosa Russo had been a speed-freak into the bargain. There were some girls, Fuchs thought, who were just not cut out for the modelling business.

'OK Fuchs,' said Mr Van Oss the next morning. 'So I want

three reels of fuckin' A-Grade kiss-my-butt film.' It was so cold in the studio that Pedro, the Rican who did the lighting, had brought in a twin-bar electric heater which he placed in the corner with an injunction to Fuchs to 'keep y'fuckin' hands off it turdass'. Fuchs' breath rose to the ceiling in mushroom clouds. They were filming a short sequence based on 'a mutha of an idea' that had come to Mr Van Oss the previous evening, to be called 'Women in Uniform'. Two brunettes dressed in GI battle fatigues prodded each other experimentally with dummy sten-guns, sat astride them, finally (having removed the battle fatigues) clasped the barrels between their breasts. Fuchs bobbed between them, sinking to his knees as the girls slipped into a prolonged horizontal clinch. 'Fuck me,' said Mr Van Oss, 'if this doesn't give Joe Public one hell of a horn.'

Fuchs found himself, as he found himself most mornings, mentally checking off the reasons why he hated Ellen. Because she wore vast maternity smocks while remaining adamantly unpregnant. Because she lay in the bath like a great white whale reading Gurdjieff. Because she had been abroad. Because she expressed dissatisfaction at the ideological shortcomings of Fuchs' job. Because Fuchs couldn't fuck her enough.

Fuchs slammed a new reel of film into the camera, wondered about using a filter (Mr Van Oss liked those crepuscular, fumbling in the shadows shots) and decided against it. Five shots into the second reel Mr Van Oss clapped his hands together with the suddenness of a cap-pistol. 'OK. Cut,' said Mr Van Oss wearily. 'Look, we have to rethink this thing.' The girls stood around, hands on hips, while he rifled through a back number of *Penthouse* for exact situational details (most of the major magazines found themselves being ripped off in this way sooner or later). Fuchs, unlit Marlboro scooped under his lower lip, asked Pedro if he had a match. 'Don't smoke, asshole,' said Pedro amiably. 'You forgot, huh?' Fuchs watched the back of Mr Van Oss's neck as he bent over the glistening pages. It reminded him of red tyre-rubber.

Fuchs collected travel brochures, some of the West Coast and the Rockies (Fuchs had never been further west than Cincinatti) but mostly of England. Misty, early-morning shots of the Cotswolds. The Norfolk Broads (Hell, Fuchs thought, what a title for a picture spread). His favourite brochure had on the cover a picture of St Paul's Cathedral looming up behind the words 'London in July'. Fuchs had a feeling that he wanted to see London. He had a vision of himself drinking beer in some quaint English pub, checking out (from a purely professional angle) Soho. Mr Van Oss was properly dismissive of English competition. 'Amateur crap,' he had been heard to say. 'Like some photographer gets his girlfriend to wave her fanny about and they call it "Vixens at Play" or something.' Fuchs had often wondered about the price of an air ticket. Fuchs had been wondering about the price of an air ticket since Watergate.

'OK Fuchs, let's hit it,' said Mr Van Oss. Pedro flicked a few switches, bathed the stage in lurid, blood-red light. ('Yeah,' said Mr Van Oss, 'tasteful.') The girls, naked except for peaked caps and buckle belts, began to march up and down. A dummy machine-gun was brought out and fingered. Fuchs monitored the arched backs, hovered anxiously as one of the girls straddled the barrel. 'Yeah, yeah,' said Mr Van Oss as if he were singing the chorus to a Beatles number. Outside the rain spattered on the window in translucent, coin-sized blobs. Fuchs bent his head over the tapering cylinder of the zoom lens.

Fuchs tended his collection of brochures and posters better than most people did their pets. His bedroom, in fact, was a sort of shrine to the places he had never been to. It was one of Ellen's favourite apophthegms that you couldn't see the wallpaper for pictures of exotic camouflage – gauchos busting steers, llamas teetering on Nepalese mountain passes. There was a line of squat, plastic-backed box-files, divided up by continent, running along the top shelf of one bookcase and a map of the world (a 'political' map borrowed from one of Ellen's friends so that the NATO alliance countries were shaded electric-blue and places like Ghana had per-capita income statistics printed alongside) bluetacked to the door. Fuchs spent a lot of time in there, slicing pictures out of the *National Geographic* with a

Stanley knife, reading illustrated travel books, bringing the box-file card index up to date. It was a good feeling, this having the world at your fingertips. Hell, Fuchs thought, it was like being a Pentagon hawk, the globe staked out in front of you, lacking only the ability to punch a few buttons and send that map on the wall shrieking up in flames.

Mr Van Oss, Fuchs realized, was losing his grip. For every reel of film shot by Fuchs that ended up on the page, underwritten with prurient captions, approximately five went into the garbage can. This fundamentally stemmed from Mr Van Oss's inability to handle temperamental models. There had been the time when the famous Cindy Lu Win, imported at great expense from a studio on the Bronx, had concluded one session by asking him who did he think he was, fuckin' Van Gogh or something? (Miss Lu Win had further disgraced herself by telling Fuchs 'that goes for you too, pervert'). This meant that the studio was having to rely on inferior models, high-school girls who thought that all you had to do was take your clothes off and pout. Hence Mr Van Oss's gloom, hence it was hinted falling sales – not, Fuchs thought, that the readership had any particular discrimination – hence, more importantly, a cut in Fuchs' salary. Hence too a series of late-night conversations between Fuchs and Mr Van Oss in various down-town bars. Mr Van Oss unquestionably needed a confidant. 'It's like this, Fuchs,' Mr Van Oss had said morosely, 'I get these ideas, you can't expect an ordinary model to handle them at first. That's why we're wasting so much film. Hell, that's art, I suppose. If we were one of those get-that-camera-halfway-up-her-ass studios I wouldn't mind.' Gradually the confidences became personal rather than professional and Fuchs had heard the tale of Mr Van Oss's first wife whom he had married fresh out of high school ('hell, we were just kids') and whose centrefold appearance in *Up Front* had made Mr Van Oss's reputation. Fuchs sympathized. In fact, Fuchs was prepared to sympathize almost indefinitely. He enjoyed Mr Van Oss's reminiscences of his picturesque past, the stationing in the South China Sea during 'Nam, the hitching across Europe. Fuchs had asked Mr Van Oss what he thought of England and Mr Van Oss had looked at him solemnly and said 'it is a Goddamned shit-hole, Fuchs' and Fuchs had nodded, inwardly disagreeing. The drinking sessions snowballed. Afterwards Fuchs went back to his apartment light-headed with alcohol, listened to Ellen extrapolating her horoscope, smoked dope, lay on his back trying to bite the head off the twisting darkness.

One day Mr Van Oss said, 'Hell, Fuchs, if the studio goes I'll see you're all right.' It was true that twenty minutes and another aborted photo session later Mr Van Oss had called him a 'Goddamned shit-stabbing motherfucker' but on the strength of this Fuchs went to his favourite travel agent's on 53rd and treated himself to an unusually lavish selection of brochures.

There remained the business of telling Ellen. 'So you want to go to England?' said Ellen incredulously, eyes darting like fish behind her aquarium spectacles and then, when she realized what Fuchs was getting at, 'So you want to go to England without me?' 'Sure,' said Fuchs, trying to sound reasonable, 'sure, I want to go to England without you.' 'Fine,' said Ellen, 'if that's the way you want it.' Fuchs gazed out of the window at the pale, early-evening light, suddenly hating America so much that he wanted to smother it. Three hours later he discovered Ellen lying in the bath, nervously contemplating the two-inch razor blade with which she had halfheartedly nicked herself. 'Oh Ralph,' she said mistily, 'oh Ralph, you shouldn't have said that. You just shouldn't have.' Fuchs called an ambulance, stood in the kitchen thinking of the early times with Ellen, concerts, Zappa and the Mothers at the Filmore East in the early seventies, the day Carter got the Democratic nomination and Ellen saying that she always preferred Kennedy and anyway where was he on women's rights. It all seemed a very long time ago.

In the studio the air was already a smoky blue, though it was barely eleven o'clock in the morning. Fuchs lounged by the electric heater. Pedro said in an amphetamine monotone: 'Yeah, I been to Cal. man, Frisco, but that whole West coast scene is dead.' Two kimono-clad strawberry blondes sat in the corner under the arc-light, one painting her nails, the other reading a paperback. Mr Van Oss said suddenly, 'Yeah I got it' to no one in particular. A light bulb fizzed and then went dead. Fuchs thought of Ellen staked out on the hospital bed in Central, surrounded by levees of friends, each of whom regarded Fuchs with thin contempt. 'Yeah,' said Pedro. 'The surf out there. Coming through the breakers, man . . . it's like fucking.'

Mr Van Oss clapped his hands. 'OK,' he said. 'I got it.' He began to run his fingers through his sandy, greaseball hair, capered crazily in the middle of the floor. 'Yeah, this centrefold, no make it a whole fuckin' series (Fuchs get off your ass and grab that camera).' The room lurched into activity. Fuchs wearily manhandled a tripod. Mr Van Oss went on: 'Right. We call it "Dreams of Leaving" see. This chick, her boyfriend's away and she's lonely.' He began to pace up and down, punched the empty air. 'So she looks at his photograph, right – first frame – then she starts packin' suitcases: close-ups. Oh Fuchs – I want that camera so near you can count the Goddamned sitches on her appendix scar!'

Fuchs felt himself sweating, yanked his tie so the knot hung low on his neck. Tonight he thought, tonight he would collect Ellen from the hospital, hell, maybe even fuck her for old time's sake. He felt good. He felt like superman. 'Shit,' said Mr Van Oss, suddenly deflated. 'Gonna take us a day to get the props. Hell though, we can wait. This one's gonna be a mutha.' But Fuchs, who had run his eye over the morning's mail, whistling shrewdly through his teeth over the two biggest bills, hoped that it wasn't going to be a mutha, hoped, in fact, that it was going to be absolute crap.

Fuchs went home that night to find Ellen, her left wrist still bandaged, hunched rheumy-eyed over a bottle of Bourbon. She appeared not to notice him. Fuchs tiptoed past, spun on his heel, snaked into the bedroom, stopped dead. The walls gleamed at him palely. Cascades of torn paper arched over his feet, undulated as he moved. A gawky pile of ransacked, split-open box-files lurched against the bed. Fuchs twitched the coverlet, discovered beneath it the greater part of the world, shredded and curling at the edges, Washington DC and Surinam lodged in uneasy juxtaposition. From the kitchen came the sound of keening. Fuchs dragged himself into the bed, fully clothed, and sobbed himself to sleep.

'Sheeit. Wow!' said Mr Van Oss the next morning. 'Ten minutes OK. Then we shoot.' Fuchs watched, resentfully, the assemblage of props, a chintz sofa, a framed photograph, a set of sleek leather suitcases and handgrips. Too many studios, Mr Van Oss explained, scrimped on the accessories budget. Fuchs, whose career had begun when the only accessory you needed was a bed, could believe it. Doors opened and slammed shut. Pedro ripped the plastic seal off a batch of 100-watt bulbs, plaited hanks of Rapunzel-hair fuse-wire. 'OK,' said Mr Van Oss. 'Hit it.' One of the strawberry blondes appeared on the stage dressed in a lacy if exiguous peignoir, clutched the framed photograph, after first holding it up to the camera for inspection, to her breast. Fuchs took a deep breath, the thoughts piling up in his head like windfall apples, took some pictures, obsessed by the memory of the previous night's reconciliation. 'Oh Ralph, lay it on me,' Ellen had sobbed and Fuchs had laid it on her strenuously yet with diffidence, as if he had been fucking an armadillo. The fan rasped. Pedro, unfurling a copy of the *NYT* said, 'Mandate my ass.' Mr Van Oss said, 'OK. Great.' On the stage the other strawberry blonde draped herself over an empty suitcase, arched a finger over the downy lining. Mr Van Oss said, 'Man, this is one way to pay the fuckin' bills whydoncha.' Fuchs remembered the puzzled look on Rosa Russo's face as he had backed away, thought of all the places he would never see, realized derisively how little he cared, and glared like a malignant sibyl down the aperture of the zoom lens, his eyes smouldering like dying suns.

ERIC SLAYTER

The Silver Fish

Visitors to the house of the celebrated poet and playwright, Sylvester Strangeways, were always puzzled at first by his strange obsession with moving water, both salt and fresh, and its various inmates. Particularly fish.

Their shining scales, flicking tails and jewel-like eyes formed the themes of innumerable poems of his. The shades of the sea, green and deeper green, the vast armies of its fantastic inhabitants with their gaping jaws and goggling eyes making a moving play of long-tailed shadows on the sandy bed of the ocean.

The tang of the sea, the smell of spray, the sound of heaving waters and waves slapping on rocks became such constant features in everything he wrote that many of his admirers began to fear for the balance of his mind. For it was becoming increasingly clear that all his waking hours and probably his sleeping ones as well were dominated by nothing else than thoughts of fish.

His house, with its sea-green carpets and sea-blue ceilings and wallpapers in which the waving tentacles of octopi mingled with the claws of crustaceans, also reflected his maritime tastes. Not surprisingly, the walls of his study were equipped at considerable expense with large port-holes through which he could look into the fish tanks on the other side as he sat writing.

There he would sit deep into the night, watching the silvery forms in the lighted water as they writhed their way through the waving weeds and bumped their heads on the glass to see who was watching *them*, and so they wove their way into his poems and fantasies.

In addition to the house and its known features, there was a mystery to guests and neighbours. In the extensive gardens at the rear of the house there had long been noticed a large water tank of opaque glass. That, by itself, was not remarkable. But the peculiar thing about it was that its size and shape kept on changing.

Some four feet high at first, it began to acquire new dimensions. The sides were extended. Then a new storey was added. Fresh sheets of glass, always opaque, were constantly arriving and workmen with ladders and rivets and all necessary tools of their trade were continually employed in making alterations.

This glass structure, tank or whatever it was, continued to grow until one day it was higher than the trees in the garden, and then it began to tower over the house itself. Fortunately the gardens were very extensive indeed, but even so the time was fast approaching when there would not be much more room left.

Naturally, as this huge structure rose higher and higher, people began to wonder what was inside it. The fact that they could not see inside made them wonder all the more, until their agony became unbearable.

Some of the guests who came to Sylvester's literary evenings and listened to his queer, sea-scented poetry with its sounds and colours of the deep, declared that they heard the distinct sound of movement from within the tank and others heard the noise of splashing. So in the end it was assumed that this monstrous building was nothing more than a huge aquarium in which Sylvester was busily breeding all the fishes his flights of fancy called into being. Or that he had gone into the fish business in a big way.

His daughter Magnolia, however, young though she was, not only shared her father's secret but understood the reasons for it, as events will show. For Sylvester had not always been interested in fish. At one time he had been captivated to the exclusion of everything else by exotic birds. At another time, it was tropical trees and flowering shrubs. In fact his daughter owed her name to that period in his career. But it was her chance visit to a pet shop which was to be the cause of his latest obsession.

One day Magnolia paused at the premises of Batsby's pet shop in the High Street, looked up at the advertisement in big letters underneath the name which read 'Why Not Take a Pet Home Today?', and saw the fish in the window. It was, or seemed to be, just an ordinary, solitary, silver fish in an ordinary glass bowl three parts filled with greenish, cloudy water.

The bowl also had a scattering of gravel at its bottom and a small, plastic archway, presumably to amuse the fish by allowing it to pass endlessly through it in its travels. A few strands of water weed which sprouted up from the gravel at the bottom of the bowl served the same purpose.

Magnolia stood and stared. She observed how the fish took a downward plunge, passed through the archway, made the water still more cloudy by stirring up the gravel with a flick of its tail and then rose again, gaping-mouthed and goggle-eyed, on the other side of the bowl.

Minutes passed unheeded as she watched its endless gyrations. Then she went into the shop, for one of her birthdays had recently passed and she still had some money left, and purchased the fish without hesitation. At the same time she enquired what it ate and was handed a small packet by the shopman bearing the name Magimeal, with the information that this was the finest and most nutritious fish food that any fish would wish for, and that there was always plenty in stock.

So, trembling with excitement, though careful not to spill the water, Magnolia brought the silver fish home and placed the bowl on a table in her father's study. Sylvester, who was busy writing a poem on Brazilian butterflies, his latest obsession, looked up and saw the bowl, its occupant and the rapt face of his daughter.

'Don't you think he's beautiful, Daddy,' whispered Magnolia. 'I'm going to call him Ferdinand. The man at the shop had just the right food for him and said he had plenty more there when we needed it.'

'I find him quite enchanting,' said Sylvester. 'The sheen of the scales and the tail movements. The effect of light through the water. There are three distinct shades of green, I see. Look at the flow of the water through his jaws as he approaches the side of the bowl. I must write a poem about him immediately.'

And he did so, sitting up late that night to complete it while Ferdinand blew bubbles and stared at him through the glass with rolling, greenish eyes as he worked.

The next day Magnolia was up at the crack of dawn and came down in her dressing-gown to make sure her treasure was safe and sound. Ferdinand was also wide awake, though whether fish slept or how they managed it, she was not at all sure, and he rose to the surface in response to a movement outside his bowl. Magnolia scattered in a few grains of Magimeal from her packet and the fish gulped them down greedily.

She threw in some more, enough, she thought, to make him a reasonable breakfast and watched him plunge this way and that, snapping at odd grains of food, weaving his silver length through the miniature archway and making his passage through the waving water weed.

All went well with the new addition to the family until one morning, after giving Ferdinand his regular feed of Magimeal with Sylvester busily writing at his desk, Magnolia noticed that the circular journeys of the fish were becoming less frequent. Ferdinand was also having trouble in passing through the plastic archway, after slipping through so effortlessly when she first bought him. He had also developed the habit of butting the glass with his head when passing, then looking up with an expression of pained surprise, as if wondering why she took no steps to remedy his uncomfortable situation.

'Daddy,' said Magnolia,' I do believe that Ferdinand is growing too large for his bowl.'

'Do you really think so', asked Sylvester, inspecting the bowl. 'Yes, I believe you're right, Magnolia. He's definitely not so supple. His body was a poem in itself when we first made his acquaintance. I suggest you go back to the pet shop and see if they have a larger bowl.'

Accordingly, Magnolia went back to the shop and explained the difficulty to Mr Batsby, the manager, who immediately showed great interest. He questioned her in detail about her method of feeding her pet, the fish's intake and output and a number of other interesting points while taking some notes in a book at the same time. He then supplied a larger bowl and another packet of Magimeal with full instructions.

Ferdinand was installed in his new home, continued his intake of Magimeal, and for a while all went happily. But before long it became apparent once more to Magnolia and her father that the fish was still steadily growing larger. Not only his size was changing, but his habits also.

Where he had once been content to swim placidly round his bowl, plunging gracefully through the archway and parting the water weed with a flick of his tail before rising to the surface, now he churned the water with an angry motion and butted his head on the glass as if impatient of obstacles. Even the bubbles he blew as he thrashed his way to the surface had an aggressive look about them and Magnolia noticed that they too were considerably larger.

'This is remarkable, I must say,' said Sylvester, dabbling a forefinger in the water to attract the fish. He succeeded and Ferdinand, thinking it was feeding time again, rose to the surface and made a vicious snap, causing the poet to withdraw his hand hurriedly.

'My dear,' he said, 'I'm afraid it will be necessary for you to make yet another trip to the pet shop and explain the situation. They will have to supply a larger container still, unless we can persuade them to take the fish back and I don't really feel inclined to part with him just when he's getting interesting.'

'Part with him,' echoed Magnolia. 'Oh, no. I couldn't dream of it for a moment.'

'Well, see what they can do for us, then,' said her father, nursing his forefinger. 'He's certainly going to jump out or push his way through the glass otherwise.'

With that he walked out of the room humming 'Scales, Tails, Whales' to himself, from which Magnolia judged he was going to write about a very large fish indeed.

At the pet shop, Mr Batsby showed even greater interest than before when she explained and went over his previous notes with care.

'This is a most unusual case,' he said solemnly. 'We seem to have sold you a very rare fish without knowing it. I might even be inclined to make you a very handsome offer if you would consider selling it back to us.'

'Oh, no. I really couldn't think of it,' said Magnolia with tears in her eyes. 'You see, he's a member of the family now and we have decided to call him Ferdinand. My father has just begun a new poem about him and needs to have him in the room while he is writing.'

'I see,' said Mr Batsby. 'Well, this is really a most amazing case. I simply don't know what to think. I'm afraid there are no larger glass bowls in the shop at present and the only thing I can suggest is a complete aquarium, which can be erected anywhere you wish.'

Magnolia said she was sure this was just the thing and would Mr Batsby be kind enough to have it sent round and set up in Mr Strangeway's study without delay. Mr Batsby promised to do this and sat thoughtfully in his chair after Magnolia had gone. Then he lifted the receiver of his telephone, dialled a number and asked for Mr Payne.

Mr Payne was the managing director of a thriving glass manufacturer's company on the other side of the town, trading under the name of the Brilliant Glass Company. 'Our Glass is Always Popular. The Reason is Clear,' said the slogan after the name. Although it was a little-known fact in town, Mr Payne was actually the brother-in-law of Mr Batsby and the two had been working closely together for many years, though neither of them saw any reason why this should become general knowledge.

'Cedric,' said Mr Batsby, 'A most extraordinary thing has happened. You know that last lot of fish food I got in from

Weedo Fertilizers? Well, I sold some of it to a crazy crank of a poet with fish on the brain and his daughter's been in twice to say the fish won't stop growing. They've already had my largest glass bowl and now they want a whole, utility-size aquarium for one fish.'

'Well, what's wrong with that, Dennis?' Mr Payne said with a chortle. 'Good for business, isn't it? Just what we want. Keeps up the demand for glass. May it never stop growing.'

'That's all very well, but I want to know what's going on,' said Mr Batsby. 'I've never known a fish grow as fast as that in all my life. That stuff you told me to add to the meal was only supposed to make it frisky, wasn't it?'

'That's right. So there wasn't much point in adding it in the case of a single fish, was there?'

'It was the only one of that kind I had at the moment. I was expecting a female in a few days and was going to encourage the customer to take a pair. I just thought I'd give it some advance treatment.'

'And you added the right quantity of derivative, as I told you?'

'Naturally. One tablespoon per packet, as you said.'

'One WHAT? A pinch, I said. Barely enough to cover the top of an old-fashioned sixpence.'

'Oh, my lord,' said Mr Batsby in an awe-stricken whisper.

'Dennis, we're trying to promote the sale of glass bowls by persuading more people to keep fish as pets, not creating marine monsters,' continued Mr Payne plaintively. 'Who do you think you are? Frankenstein, or somebody?'

'Good lord, Cedric, I could have sworn you said a table-spoon. What are we going to do about it now?

'I don't know, unless you advise the customer to take it to Loch Ness,' replied Mr Payne. 'I think I'd better get on to the lab and see if they can come up with anything.'

'Yes, do that and let me know,' said Mr Batsby in a quavering voice. 'I've got to ring off now, Cedric. There's someone banging on the counter.'

Mr Payne remained in deep thought after putting down his

receiver. Then he lifted it again, dialled a number from his private notebook and asked to speak to Professor Fullblower. The professor, who was a leading director in the well-known firm of Weedo Fertilizers, was also in fact Mr Payne's uncle, but this was normally kept quiet for reasons of trade and commerce. The firm's well-known trade slogan, 'Weedo is Wonderful for Weeds' was a somewhat unfortunate brainchild of the professor himself.

Professor Fullblower made no comment on the steady flow of Mr Payne's conversation except for an occasional 'Hmmmm' and at the end of it maintained a long silence, by which it was to be understood that his learned brain needed time to pronounce upon the problem.

'Hmmmm,' he said at last in a deep voice. 'Most extraordinary, Cedric, as you say. I shall have to look into this, you know.'

'Yes, but what do you suggest could have happened?' asked Mr Payne anxiously.

'On the face of it,' said the professor, 'I would suspect that a heavy intake of the chemical derivative $H2Q/4C$ compounded with the normal oxygen processes of the fish have had a severe inflationary effect upon the membranes of the lower bronchial tract.'

'Good lord. Do you mean the thing's going to blow up?'

'It's not as simple as that, Cedric. It never is, you know. There are bound to be other factors which will come to light in due course. Hmmmm. Yes. Well, it's obvious that we can't afford to be accused of manufacturing a chemical substance to increase the size of fish by distending them or by any other process, when our original purpose was merely to increase the fertility of fish in order that the pet shops could sell more which in turn would increase the demand for your glass bowls and our fish foods.'

'Sshh. Not so loud,' said Mr Payne.

'So having taken all the relevant factors into consideration,' the professor concluded weightily, 'I have decided to prepare an antidote, to be administered to fish who have already been given an overdose of H2Q. You'd better tell that idiot Dennis not to sell any more Magimeal until further notice. When the new product is ready I will let you know and you arrange for it to be supplied to the pet shop. I only hope the process has not gone too far to be arrested.'

With that the professor put his receiver down, made some very learned notes upon his pad and went off to his next board meeting to report the surprising effects of his firm's latest fungicide upon accidental contact with the local poultry population.

In the meantime, Mr Batsby and his assistant from the pet shop had arrived at the home of Sylvester Strangeways with the new aquarium, which they proceeded to erect in the study according to the poet's directions.

'You'd better put it over there by the window,' said Sylvester. 'The water will catch the early-morning sun obliquely in that position and give me the correct shade of ultramarine I need for my "Soliloquy on the Sea". It's largely a matter of harmonizing the shifting colours as they merge with the movements of the fish.'

'It will give you the effect of sunlight on the scales of the fish as it rises from the water. You remember how well that fitted into "Diaphanous Depths", Daddy,' said Magnolia.

'I do indeed. It was like being carried irresistibly into a voluptuous, whirling vortex of colour. The centre of a whirlpool where the head spins and the senses swim. Quite unforgettable.'

> See the Ocean Legions gleam,
> Scales of silver, eyes of flame,
> Tunny, turbot, plaice and bream,
> Out of Neptune's vast domain.

quoted Magnolia in reverent tones.

Mr Batsby and his assistant applied themselves to their task with vigour, bolting and riveting away until at last the large aquarium was ready and resting on its iron stand by the window

191

where it would catch all the poetic light Sylvester needed for his new composition. Then they connected the garden hose, filled the tank and added a large handful of fish tonic, another speciality of Weedo Fertilizers, and some fresh water weed.

'Bravo,' exclaimed Sylvester. 'Ferdinand is a fortunate fish. And now for the crucial moment.'

Mr Batsby took one side of the glass bowl containing Ferdinand and his watery world and his assistant took the other, and with infinite care they carried it to the new aquarium. It was a tricky operation, for the fish was suspicious of every movement, thrashing and swirling in the confined space of his bowl to the best of his ability.

They balanced the lip of the bowl on the edge of the tank, tilted it slowly and at last, with a resounding splash and a gleam of silver scales, Ferdinand half jumped and half fell into his latest home. He sank and rose again, flicked his tail, blew a long succession of bubbles and made a dive for the trailing green fronds of the weed, where he hid himself shyly.

'I really must congratulate you, Mr Batsby,' said Sylvester. 'That's just where I've always wanted him. He'll be both my companion and and constant source of inspiration.'

Ferdinand at this stage thrust his head through the forest of greenery surrounding him, gulped and regarded the poet with baleful eyes.

'Of course he really needs a mate,' said Mr Batsby. 'It's one of those things we normally look after but the snag in this case is to find the right kind and the right size. If it's the wrong kind it won't breed and if it's the wrong size it stands a good chance of being eaten.'

'That is something we wish to avoid,' said Sylvester. 'It would definitely spoil my metaphor. So we are prepared to leave both size and kind in your experienced hands.'

'He means if you can find the right female, we'll take it,' said Magnolia helpfully.

'But at the same time an arrest in the growth of the present specimen would be greatly appreciated,' continued Sylvester.

'I think we can be of help as far as that is concerned, sir,' Mr

Batsby said cautiously, recalling a very emphatic conversation he had had with Mr Payne before leaving to deliver the aquarium. 'We have reason to believe that the fish food we had been supplying was a trifle on the rich side, shall we say, and too much nutrient resulted in the fish putting on weight. However, after discussion with the makers, they have supplied me with a more balanced meal which I have brought with me today.'

'And about time too,' said Sylvester. 'We were beginning to think that the situation was getting out of hand. You'd better give Ferdinand his lunch, Magnolia. He looks as if he needs it to me.'

'I may say, sir, that your fish has aroused considerable interest in local circles and we were all frankly puzzled at first. However, we trust that Ferdinand's growth problems are now solved to everybody's satisfaction.'

With that, Mr Batsby and his assistant collected their tools and impedimenta and politely took their leave.

But Ferdinand, unfortunately, was not to live up to Professor Fullblower's hopes nor Mr Batsby's expectations. Magnolia, tripping lightly downstairs to breakfast one morning, suddenly noticed that far from shrinking as Mr Batsby had suggested he might, he was continuing to expand. The new aquarium literally rattled with the impact of the huge, silvery body bumping against the sides.

Ferdinand gaped hungrily as he thrust a blunt head through the curtain of weeds and goggled at her. A succession of greenish bubbles as large as small balloons rose to the surface.

'Daddy!' called Magnolia in alarm, 'He's still growing!'

Professor Fullblower was finally called in as an expert consultant on the subject of fish foods. He naturally looked very learned and used a vast number of inexplicable terms, but was of little real help. The language of science, like the language of poetry, is usually understood only by experts. In the end he had to fall back on his original thesis, that in Ferdinand's case there had been too heavy an overdose of $H_2Q/4C$ in the first place and therefore his growth could no longer be reversed but must take its natural course. He added, however, that the effect of light upon the water in the aquarium was greatly accelerating the growth of the fish.

'Well,' said Magnolia, 'he didn't ask to be supplied with H2Q/4C in the first place, did he? I couldn't agree to parting with him, whatever happens.'

'And I have just commenced a new series of extempore hexameters in which Ferdinand plays an important part,' said Sylvester. 'He certainly has to remain with us for that reason alone.'

So the professor said he knew, quite by accident, of course, of a very good glass manufacturer and what he suggested was the building of an expandable aquarium in the garden which could have new sections of specially prepared opaque glass added whenever necessary and be supplied with unlimited running water.

'This might at least have the effect of slowing down the growth of the fish until it finally dies of old age, or you eventually decide what to do with it,' he added.

And so, behind the strange, sea-haunted house of Sylvester Strangeways, there began to tower a monstrous, gleaming structure of glass and steel. Section by section, storey by storey it rose, dwarfing the house and looming largely upon the landscape. Within, still consuming vast quantities of Magimeal and blowing bubbles now as large as barrage balloons, lurks the problem that will not go away. Ferdinand the fish.

No one known how much larger he will grow or how many more storeys will have to be added to the giant structure, least of all Sylvester and Magnolia. But the local industries concerned continued to make a very handsome profit out of Ferdinand, as well as from the sales of all the other fish in the neighbourhood.

And although Sylvester's interests are now entirely concentrated on the tone structures of third-century Chinese ceramics, he still believes that if you want a good, live poem that bounds along like the running tide with the sound of the surf and the tang of the spray in its wake, you will never beat fish.

PENELOPE SHUTTLE

Ratón Ladrón

Their appointed meeting place was the field by the old burial ground. The boy arrived first, early, without weariness. He came through the dark cheerfully, a native of the place with no need of maps. But he was hungry. The town! Even at this late hour it might have been one entire kitchen. He could have bitten into the darkness and fed on it, so laden with the odours and zests of food. And it was not just from the restaurants, hotels and little cantinas, but from every house that the spiced and fiery flavours of food came, of this meat or that delicacy. . .

He left the town without encountering friend or stranger, skirting the main streets and sneaking through back-ways where he had played as a child.

The countryside began immediately, there was no zone where town and land mingled: the change was abrupt and exact; a threshold, from paved streets direct to a sandy track, going uphill through cultivated fields and rocky patches, groves and dry meadows of scrub. He walked easily into the dark. It felt soft as it moved against his limbs and face, smelling of fruit and flowers. It had its own range of scents: the clear and calm, almost learned orange trees, the fragrant flowers with their hints of happiness, the patches of herbs, all these odours pampered him. But there was a deeper smell; the raw almost rank odour of wild plants crushed by the wheels of carts and cars that had passed along the track during the day. The coarseness of it contrasted keenly with the serene, warm night he walked through.

The boy stood still, breathed in the vitality of the land. His mouth was slightly open, his eyes closed. Beneath his bare feet the dust was soft and cool, not as water is cool and gentle, but with a curious tingling texture, very like an electricity. He discovered for the first time since his childhood the intense softness and tameness of the earth. He dug his toes into the sandy dust and felt each grain as a separate anticipated entity. The earth, the dust. He scuffed at it, kicked it, and the grains blew up into the air, spun on the breeze. He felt the grains against his lips, on his tongue, and without warning experienced the accidental happiness those in his profession know on certain nights. Now for bravado he walked on with closed eyes, not stumbling, going forward like a blind man through the scented garden of his land, its capacious air. The insects whirred and whined, but their noise was placid in its way, had a gravity of manner; he relaxed to it without noticing.

In the long dry grass by the gate he squatted down, back against the stone wall, waiting. He hummed a tune. Yesterday, his elder brother, challenging the bull with a bright cloak, had almost stumbled, fallen as victim. The boy tasted the blood of fear for a moment before letting the thought, the memory go, making it go. His brother had sprung up, hadn't he, and made sense of the chaos of the fight, had done his job, used the wind cleverly, flicking his worn cape around, performed his task? Then he had faced the crowd, bowed to their chiding applause. As usual the men on horseback had dragged the carcase out on ropes, flies gathering on the caked blood of the bull's hide. There was the tell-tale groove in the sand. The people were yelling. Some of the old men grumbled. Then came the familiar unlikable grating sound of the ancient jeep dragging its rake over the dirtied sand, making the arena ready for the next corrida. And he could be as brave as his brother, couldn't he?

He laughed out loud. From his pocket he took out a paper parcel of food his sister had given him, though he had refused to tell her his plans. He gnawed at the bread, at the cold dry meat that tasted rougher, more stale than usual in his recognition of the night's perfume and possibilities. In disgust he spat out a lump of gristle, tossed the bread away.

196

His friend was late. He knelt up and squinted along the path, looking for any sign, but no one was coming, nothing moved, all was quiet up here on the outskirts of town. Lights were going out now down there, they began to sleep, well fed. He sat without thoughts, with fewer sensations than an animal, just waiting.

He looked up. When, as on a night like this, there is no moon, the night pours and spreads its dark so utterly that the everlasting existence of the dark cannot be questioned. Of course it will go on for ever. It is a strength that will not be broken, it holds everything together, the roots of men and animals.

But there was more than dark. The stars were there, their long broad wings glowing. Each constellation was a shining sculpture. They took his breath away. Aah . . . he gasped. There was the Constellation of the Bull charging and the Fighter dancing nimbly before him, and the starry blood from the wounded animal. The boy could almost reach out and touch it. There was the Constellation of the Unbroken Colt, forelegs rearing up, hooves flying. And the Constellation of Love's Arrows. A whole world of star-life to set against the dark, constellations that do not lament, but move confidently across the sea of the dark, all the stars in their shapes of men, beasts and ships, wiping out the drudgery of the dark.

The boy grunted, shook his head and blinked, sulkily shaking off the sleep that had taken him silently from behind.

'Hey,' he said softly as the man crouched down beside him. The man answered him, voice muffled by the scarf wound around his mouth. Both boy and man sat for another half hour, waiting. The silence was bigger now and somehow debased with the man's arrival, debased and abstract.

The boy pushed the long, damp, tangled hair back from his eyes, and signed. He felt the night penetrating him, searching for his weaknesses. He had enough cunning and courage for what lay ahead, but the waiting confused him.

'Is it time?' he asked, but the man reproved him, making an irritated gesture for silence. They went on waiting. The boy thought of the ugly old woman who had watched him all afternoon as he sat in the café; the man thought of the remoteness of cities. He loosened the scarlet and white scarf around his mouth and cursed quietly to get rid of the thick tender weight of dark and sleep and fear that threatened him.

The boy yawned.

'There was this gringo one year who came to our country,' said the man flatly. 'He came here and stayed in this town. One night he awoke and there in the moonlight, sitting upright on the floor, he saw a thing that frightened and angered him and in his harsh gringo voice he yelled, "*Ráton! Ráton!*" His cries "*Ráton! Ráton!*" created a panic. The household was roused, babies yelling, dogs barking, the men grabbing their wallets, the women shrieking with apprehension, the girls giggling; so much noise woke their neighbours who ran out of their house and down into the courtyard, shouting, "What's wrong, what's going on?" In seconds the entire household, even the old grannies, has rushed down into the yard and is gabbling the story to the neighbours, who are soon just as frantic . . . the next thing is, the officers from Guardia Civil are there and the people, seeing the officers, shout and yell again "*Ladrón, ladrón*, burglar, thief, help, *Ladrón!*" And meanwhile this poor gringo has been left alone in the house, in his room, the best room of course, with the mouse still sitting there upright outstaring him.' The man laughed and tapped the boy on the shoulder. 'You see? The foreigner's accent was so bad, his "*Ratón ráton*" sounded like "*Ladrón ladrón*" to everyone. . . Oh the confusion.'

The boy grinned. 'But what happened then, Miguel?' he asked.

'They all trooped back indoors, with the officers, to find it was only a mouse. But the landlord was so embarrassed. A mouse in the especially clean gringo's room! "Ah *señor*," he explained to his guest, "do not concern yourself, I see it is only"', the man began to laugh and nudged the boy, '"I see it is only a street mouse, not a house mouse, a street mouse, *ráton de calle!*"'

The boy flung himself back in the grass, repeating in a shrill stammer, '*Ratón de calle, ráton de calle!*' and twisting about with laughter. He laughed freely, the way he never did at home.

The man sat and watched the boy, smiling at his own story, but fastening his scarf around his face once more.

The boy rolled over suddenly and asked, 'Is it time, then?'

The man nodded. The boy scrambled up beside him and they both looked down at the dark town. The man gripped the boy by the shoulder for an instant, encouraging him, as they began their night's work.

In the garden of the big house they hid among the thick glossy immobile leaves of some overgrown shrubs, almost stifled by the foetid atmosphere of their bower, the yeasty peppery odour of the bushes mingling with the stench of cats. Far off a dog was barking, but without fierceness, a mocking deriding howl. They waited until the creature settled, and the silence was complete.

The man edged forward to the dark house with the boy gulping breath a few paces behind him. At the window he began forcing an entry. With a sharp click that the darkness would not hush, the fastening of the latch gave. The man caught his breath; the boy at his shoulder trembled and then stood motionless. They waited, listening with ears that ached with the dark. But no angry voice came, no cry of outrage; and neither man nor boy was a coward. So the man hopped lightly over the sill and slid quickly into the house. The boy followed more slowly, but not clumsily, turning his head to survey the grounds quickly before entering.

Inside the house they listened again, but the silence was unbroken. The room was lined with shelves of books that created another silence of their own in addition to the house's ordinary silence. Ignoring all these silent words, and with the sharpened senses of one who has often performed this task, the man made his way across the room to the door and gently, coaxingly tried it. It opened easily. Beyond the door lay the passage way and two other closed doors; also, the stairs.

A drizzle of light came from the uncurtained window on the stairs. From the stars, thought the boy suddenly, and felt pain.

The man moved silently towards the stairs, began to climb. The boy followed him, creeping up but blindly. He felt the sweat running under his arms, in the palms of his hands, but his mouth was dry, and hurt. *Ratón ladrón*, he thought, *ráton ladrón.*

Without hesitation the man made for the room at the far end of the landing. The door of this room was ajar. The boy stood still, sweat chilling him, while he watched the man disappear into the room.

He heard no sound but knew that was the room where their business had brought them, the old man's room. He was to wait here as instructed, while the other opened the safe and took out the money.

Waiting, watching. He trembled all over, as if he was already a prisoner. Time was an element that had stopped moving. It lay on him, a huge disabling burden he could not lay aside.

All at once the door he was standing by horrified him. He stared at it with fear and terror. He did not understand why he should reach out slowly and open it, did not know why he was entering the room, disobeying his instructions, leaving his station where he should be on watch. He closed the door behind him. His body felt light as an arrow.

The girl was standing by the window. She smiled at him and silently, finger to lips, beckoned to him.

He walked jerkily forward. He stood before her. She was about his own age, but taller. She was not ugly, she was not beautiful. It was the first time he had seen a naked woman. He felt proud. There was a candle lit and set in a little dish on the table. It shone youthfully for them. He looked down at his own bare feet then met her eyes again, felt his stiff lips trying to smile, but not succeeding. He mumbled something.

She took him by the hands pensively, casually. He felt both sleepy and violent, but did nothing, let her put his hands on her shoulders, her hips. They stood so for a time, he did not know how long, in silence. Then very quietly and seriously she said, 'Now you must go.'

Obediently, he went to the door. At the door he tried to

speak but she had turned her back. Her spine was a part of the room; her long thick hair plaited and lying over one shoulder was another part of the room; her strong bare legs a part of the room; she belonged to the room, to its four walls, its floor and ceiling, its patient bed, its old wardrobe.

He leaned back against the door, eyes closed, fingers gripped too tightly around the door handle. He heard her laugh, as if she had exposed his true character. Had she?

Her laughter unsaddled something in him, freeing him. Something new had come alive in him. He could have broken her back, could have ripped her apart like planks from a floor, his strength could have dismantled her. But he was too puzzled and happy to do that and quickly, before the spell could be undone, he slipped out of her room and resumed his watching, aware of her presence on the other side of the door as he was aware of the breath in his body or his own blood.

A moment passed, then another, and the man came rapidly, a shadow, out of the other room, the bag on his shoulder stuffed to the brim. Nodding to the boy, he led the way down the stairs, through the house, out of the window, through the garden and swiftly, unperceived, out of the narrow uneven streets of the town and back uphill to the field beside the disused graveyard.

They both flung themselves down on the ground, cornered, gasping, laughing, terrified, clouting shoulders, clowning about, free. Shakily the man unfastened the bag, counted out the boy's share, handed it to him with a brief word of praise. 'You did fine,' he said.

'Yes,' the boy said, 'I did fine, Miguel.'

The man grinned, scratched his beard, began to say something more but thought better of it and instead offered the boy a drink from his leather flask.

With his share of the money the boy planned to buy the girl in the room pretty clothes. He would go back to the house on Sunday morning and say, 'Will you walk by the river with me?' And she might say yes.

But next morning she had diminished to last night's dream, fading, a simulation, a deceit. He did not believe in her. He was older in the morning. He knew the money was real. Money had its own discipline, and he must obey it. It had decided that last night was over, finished, no sequel.

Next morning he lay in bed late, watching shadows drift and flush on the wall. The noise of the market down the street was loud, people were shouting, arguing, laughing. Later he would go out. He would find another girl. Plenty of girls about.

'*Ratón, ladrón*,' the boy murmured to himself, '*ráton, ladrón*.'

ALEX AUSWAKS

The Priest

Kagan had been in the camp so long that nobody knew any longer why he had been incarcerated there. Not even he knew any more. At the time he was arrested, people were being taken away all the time, but those who were left every time were sure they would not be touched. After all, they had done nothing wrong. And then one night there had been this frightful knocking on doors. It had begun at the next house and continued for a long time; then it moved to his.

'Don't go,' his mother had said.

'They've come to ask about the people next door,' he had answered, reaching for his boots sleepily. 'Well, I'll have to tell them they've been taken.'

'Don't go,' his mother persisted as the knocking went on. 'It's because there's no one next door they need to make up the numbers of arrested people. They have a quota to fulfil, just like factory workers!'

'None of us has done anything,' he answered. 'We're all right.'

But they hadn't come to ask about the people next door and he had not been all right.

'I haven't done anything,' he said to the three burly men who ordered him to come with them.

'We'll go into that later,' one of them answered. 'I'm fed up with all you innocent lot! Do you think an officer of the state security service has nothing better to do than argue in the street in the middle of the night?'

'I've done nothing,' he said when he was brought in.

'That's for us to decide, not you!' said the man in the prison. 'People with names like yours ought to be shot. For a start, no true citizen would have a name like yours!'

After a while Kagan gave in. The men who held him looked harassed and busy, as they must have been, if they were preserving the state from foreign intervention and internal subversion. They dazed him, physically, mentally, spiritually. It appeared that it was not enough for one's actions to be innocent of malicious intent. The state could still be undermined.

'You're lucky, pal. They've decided to be merciful. You're not going to be shot. Life, instead. Siberia.'

'I've done nothing,' he mumbled. 'I was so sure I'd done nothing. I'd swear I'd done nothing!'

'Look, pal,' said the warder. 'This is the new Russia. The prison system is like a crowded bus on a busy route. Some people are waiting to catch it, some have caught it, and one or two lucky ones are about to get off. Why complain? You're on the bus already. Stay alive, and one day you'll be able to get off it, too.' The warder laughed grimly. 'I suppose I am one of those waiting to catch it.'

Many years later he met the same warder, by then a prisoner like himself. He had identified himself to the warder.

'Don't tell anyone,' the man begged him. 'They'll tear me to shreds. They say ex-warders get torn to shreds by the inmates.'

'Don't worry,' Kagan had assured him. 'There's too many of you now. Your turn and the turn of many other warders came, too. But nobody gets off. They just keep on getting lots of new buses. It's called economic progress.'

In the beginning he had been too full of bitterness against the world that had betrayed him so. After a while, because bitterness was not second nature to him, he realized how many others there were, like himself, who were just as innocent.

'Don't be bitter,' said someone to him. 'You will take it out on someone else, or worse still, on yourself. They say that's how people get cancer. They eat themselves up.'

What about his family and friends? Why did they not plead his innocence? Why were they not petitioning the authorities?

Again, another prisoner said to him: 'If they dared, they would need the courage of gods, and not humans. Who dares tell our masters they made a mistake? Besides, our masters hear only what they wish to hear. If you want justice in a country, you have to have people who listen and hear and admit that mistakes can be made. In our country, to accuse someone of an error is treason.'

And so the time came when he accepted the fact that the perimeter of the barbed wire was to be the perimeter of his world for as long as he lived. There had been a priest among the prisoners who had said: 'When we are dead, we will have some five foot-odd length of earth to lie in. All these acres within the barbed wire are riches by comparison!'

Kagan lived.

Kagan lived a life of back-breaking toil, long hours, little food, constant supervision and anxiety. What little dignity he had as man, went. The guards left him and the others not the tiniest shred of self-respect.

They say that God misses nothing that happens on earth. It is just that He seldom speaks. And when God is silent, man cries louder than ever from his heart for God to hear. One day, the insulted, the injured, the incarcerated in body and soul, cried out. And when God did not answer they rioted.

Kagan was deputed to guard a warder who had been taken prisoner.

'Cut his throat if he moves,' he was told.

'Listen,' the warder said, 'this holiday won't last. The authorities can't afford it to get about what has happened. They'll raze the camp to the ground. The guards and us warders will be lucky not to be shot, as well, lest we ever let out the fact that a thing like this could happen. Take my advice, get the hell out of here!'

'It's all wasteland out there,' Kagan answered. 'There's nothing for hundreds of miles. I'd die!'

'That way you might make it. This way you have no chance,' was the answer.

Kagan waited till night fell, because it is at night that one escapes, and then he went into the tundra.

The snow was not very deep, but icy winds caught it up and swept it round and round, even as it fell to earth. Time and time again the same icy winds stabbed at his chest so that he could not draw breath. Time and time again they spun him round and round, so that he no longer knew in which direction he was going.

'This is the end of me,' he thought. 'I might as well have stayed behind. At least I might have lived a little longer.' And then he thought: 'It wasn't much of a life there, having my life constantly in the hands of others.'

He was so cold, he forgot he was hungry. He had hunks of bread inside his coat, but he dared not take his hands out of his gloves to reach in for one, lest they froze.

It had been a long time since passions and emotions had crossed his mind and his breast. Now he found himself torn apart by contradictory yearnings and regrets: to keep going, to have stayed behind; to live, to die. Peasants say that the man with the widest horizon plods the longest road towards it, and the man with the narrowest horizon plods the shortest road.

Thus Kagan may have wandered about, or been blown about longer than may have been necessary. Who knows? Finally, he fell down exhausted on the ground. The snow fell on him and the icy wind blew it off. He did not so much sleep as lose consciousness.

When he woke, he was huddled up against a stone wall. Its texture was only slightly rough to the fingers, as of a material likely to last, but there were no lines indicating brick or stone laid one against the other. Kagan recoiled from it. A wall was what people were placed against and shot. He recoiled and ran, but no sounds of pursuit followed him. He cast a quick look over his shoulder. Indeed, no pursuit. He kept on running, then looked back again.

'I must be going mad,' he said loudly. 'They say one sees mirages in the desert and that is all the prophets in the Bible saw. I suppose the tundra is a desert of sorts.'

He stopped. He pulled a glove off, reached inside his coat for a hunk of bread, bit off a piece and chewed on it.

The wind had abated and the snowflakes now fell gently to the ground. In the distance, through snowflakes, stood a building. It was carved out of one piece rather than put together from stone or brick. Blue cupolas shimmered atop it. No direct light fell on them and they seemed to be lit up from beneath. He looked again: could they be transparent? His curiosity aroused, he began to walk towards the edifice cautiously, still chewing on the bread like cud. No, the cupolas were not transparent.

'Could this be a witch's lair?' The thought crossed his mind, but was dismissed. 'Blue and . . .' Well, it wasn't quite white, but some shade of white. Nevertheless, whatever it was, these were not quite the colours of a witch.

'It's not a witch's lair,' he pronounced to the cold air.

He approached even nearer.

The doors were made of oak, beautifully carved. He looked at the carvings.

'It's a House of God,' he said, giving a vigorous nod with his head. 'I always knew they were wrong. There is God.'

He put his hand on the beautiful carved door and it swung open. The pews were arranged in a circle round the raised dais, which commanded his attention even as he entered. He went to the dais. An oak table stood on it and on the table a white damask cloth. There were candlesticks on the damask cloth.

'A tablecloth like that needs a feast to be set out on it,' he thought.

A natural instinct took him to the cellars. There was food and wine there. Because he was so hungry, his eyes were larger than his stomach. He took as much food as he could carry to the table on the dais. It occurred to him that he might soil the damask cloth and then they would know someone had been there. He looked for a newspaper to spread on it. There were plenty of books but no newspapers. Finally, he cleared the damask cloth from a corner of the table and began to eat from the polished oak. Even so, he felt uncomfortable. Finally, he retreated to a distant pew and picnicked there.

'I suppose one has to be a priest to feel at home up on that dais,' he thought.

He was still so much under the impression of how the edifice had looked through the falling snowflakes that it took him a while to notice how beautiful it was inside. There was a gallery on three sides, supported by pillars, and over the gallery, beautiful stained-glass windows. He could not remember seeing any stained-glass windows from outside, and, in fact, when he checked later, he discovered they were not visible from outside, though the light constantly changed and constantly refracted, changing the windows, alternating the stained glass, highlighting different parts of it.

'If only Litvinoff were here,' he said to himself. 'He'd really like this, the religious maniac!' And then he even shouted out: 'Hey, Litvinoff, where are you? I have a piece of beautiful glass to give you for a present, though God knows what what you would do with it.'

Litvinoff had been a fellow prisoner. His only possession was an old postcard of Jerusalem. A pilgrim from long before the revolution had brought it back from the Holy Land. It was frayed and tattered. Twice a day, morning and evening, Litvinoff went through the same ritual of finding the east, as if he had to discover it anew every time and affirm his discovery as correct. He would then put down the postcard and start praying, his lips moving virtually soundlessly. Some of the other prisoners would take turns to shout 'AMEN' very loudly in his ear. After a while, it dawned on everyone else that Litvinoff did not know how to pray. As a matter of fact he was slightly touched. He just moved his lips as if in prayer. The others had taken pity on him and had supported his charade. That is why they shouted 'AMEN' in such loud voices. It kept him happy.

Kagan slept.

When he woke it was evening. A sudden desire to pray overcame him. He did not know how. He remembered Litvinoff again. 'Well, I'm not Litvinoff! I'm not touched,' he said gruffly. 'I'm not going to stand here and move my lips and yell "AMEN" at myself.'

He realized he had not replaced the damask cloth. He now did so, and felt a little better.

'Perhaps I could make myself useful here,' he thought, 'dusting and cleaning and keeping things tidy.' But what was he to do about his personal plight?

'I'll be all right here till the Sabbath,' he thought. 'That's when they'll all start piling in and they'll have KGB agents amongst them to see who comes to pray here. I'll have to keep out of the way then.'

On the Sabbath he went out and hid himself, but nobody came all day.

'Some House of God,' he said to himself, and went back to eat and drink.

He padded round inside for a while and then stood on the dais. The House of God was still. He knew it was dark outside, but the stained-glass windows showed up as if lit from outside.

'I wish I knew what all these pictures meant,' he said to himself. He tried to read them, but however hard he tried, he lost track of the story.

'There must be a book somewhere,' he said to himself. 'Oh, yes, of course! It's been so long ago, I'd forgotten.'

He found the book easily enough. It had beautiful prints in it, many not unlike the pictures in the windows, and large clear type. He read deep into the night. He was enthralled. Though he gravitated to other books, he always came back to this one. When he came across the part where the escapees were fed by manna from heaven he thought of how he, too, was fed.

'I always knew there is God,' he said again. 'I always knew they were wrong, when they said He didn't exist. He existed then and He exists now.'

He never knew when the idea first came to him, but by the time he was aware of it, it had taken root so firmly, it was unlikely to be easily dislodged.

It began when, from time to time, either while he was cleaning and dusting, or reading and meditating, he would think, 'If only there were a priest here to conduct a service.' It crossed his mind at first occasionally, and then more and more often, with increasing insistence. And it was inevitable that this thought should turn into: 'Why don't I become the priest?'

He began by trying to say the prayers. This took him some time, but in the end he worked out which prayers had to be said when. He did not know how to read the music, so he chanted as best he could. With time he acquired confidence and even began to enjoy hearing his voice resound in the vast empty space. The mastery of the ritual and the constant reading of the Book gave him a depth and dimension he had been unaware of, and he began to probe deeper into the mysteries of religion and into moral questions. Unable to perform any but routine priestly duties, he plunged himself more than ever into these, as a kind of compensation for the lack of opportunity to do anything else. The frustration of carrying out any but ritual duties exhausted him. The books he read puzzled him. How could people be tormented by doubt, when to him all was crystal-clear? How could anyone doubt the existence of God Who had a house such as this which He had given to a creature so humble and undeserving as he was!

The fast days, which had never been a problem (Heaven knows he had been quite used to being hungry), became a positive joy. He lifted his voice up to fill the house. He knew that God heard.

The blow fell from a completely unexpected source. He knew that there was always the possibility of discovery. A stray hunter, an expedition, a chance aeroplane flying overhead to deliver supplies to a remote settlement. Even a helicopter. After a while he had ceased to be afraid. 'What else can life take away or offer me?' he thought. 'I have said prayers in God's house. Now I can die or go back to that living death without regret.' And when these thoughts crossed his mind, he would say very quietly to himself: 'Blessed be the Lord God Who has given me to live to this day.'

And so, when the blow fell, it was doubly felt, because it came from inside the House.

The Sabbath had just ended. He always lost a little of his inner peace when that happened. It was as if the real world was back and the peace of God had receded just a little. That particular Sabbath some nagging doubt about the performance of some ritual had come to him. Should he have done it this way or that? Yet another part of his mind reminded him that one of the prophets had denounced excessive zeal in the observance of ritual. His mind grew restless, then anxious, then strained. He went back to the books to check on what had bothered him. He found something else.

He must have seen the regulation set out dozens of times and yet it had not permeated his brain. Perhaps he had not really wanted to know the regulation! Now it struck him with absolute, with blinding, binding clarity. All the physical symptoms of depression brought on by loss of hope returned to him, overwhelmed him. You became a priest, said the books, when another priest placed his hands on you and invested you with some of his own dignity of priesthood.

He was no priest! He had taken upon himself a rôle he was not entitled to, that of conducting a service. He had raised his voice and hands to carry out parts of the service he was not entitled to conduct. Why, he had thought thoughts and wished for powers only a priest could have! In the small hours of the morning, when the night is chillest and the body at its weakest, tormented by doubts, undermined by uncertainty, assailed by misgivings, he turned his face to the wall against which he lay. He no longer rejoiced in conducting a service, or was enlightened by reading and meditating. He felt like an intruder. The day came when he could no longer even pray, much less conduct a service.

'Where God guides, He provides,' he said. 'If that is Your will, I shall go. I shall leave tomorrow, at daybreak, before sensible, rational thoughts prevent me.'

That night he had a dream. In his dream he walked a dreadful road. State security agents and dogs attacked him and dragged him to the camp where he had been incarcerated. Time and time again they said: 'Want a priest, do you? We've got a lot of priests here! Nicely behind barbed wire like you should be!

Take your pick of any religion, any denomination!'

He woke before the dawn broke. He prayed from the last rows of the pews. Somewhere he had read that on entering a House of God one must not push oneself forward, but sit in the last row, unless, of course, invited by those present to come forward. He prayed long and earnestly. He never raised his eyes, never deviated from the order of service laid down. There was nothing to say to God, although there was so much he wanted to ask.

He put on his greatcoat and tied a thick rope round his waist. He sliced off a few hunks of bread and put them inside his coat. He cut himself a staff and leaned on it to test its strength.

Then he went.

He went and he went and he went.

MANNY DRAYCOTT

Splices

It is a long journey from the suburbs to the city. The tube starts among lush, scented, flowering gardens and travels next to the mainline expresses that zip past, towards the major stations. Then it descends, suddenly, without warning, down – into the ground.

Mr Patel was jostled down the steps at Finsbury Park. He was in a hurry.

'Do you know the way to Moorgate, please?' said a voice at his side.

'I am in a dreadful hurry,' said Mr Patel, without looking to see who it was.

'I am from Bombay,' the voice explained, 'and I do not know the way.' The tone was anxious. 'And this place here, do you know, it is so vast, I cannot find a thing. Not a thing. I cannot find the place to go.'

'Bombay?' said Mr Patel.

'I want to get to Moorgate, please.'

'Bombay?' repeated Mr Patel.

'I arrived here on Monday.'

'My father came from Bombay,' Mr Patel's words came tumbling out.

'My father came from Hyderabad. I come from Bombay!' the stranger stated.

Mr Patel laughed. He explained how he had been born in Bombay, but then his family had gone to South Africa when he was very young. He had come here. Here he was.

An old newspaper rolled down the station as the train left.

'My train has gone.' Mr Patel shrugged, his arms stretched wide to emphasize the hopelessness of the situation. Then both men laughed and broke into Gujarati.

Mr Patel last saw his friend as he waved him goodbye – an isolated figure on a dimly-lit platform. Then the train hit the darkness of the tunnel.

Mr Patel arrived for his interview half an hour late. The tall plate-glassed building loomed before him and a uniformed commissionaire ushered him through the heavy doors.

'Mr Patel?' said a smart receptionist.

'That is who I am,' said Mr Patel.

'I'm afraid you're very late.'

'I am sorry, very sorry, actually.'

'However, Mr Pommerance will see you.' It was a concession.

The office was high up and from the wide windows you could scan the city. Mr Patel could see tall buildings and small ones; little squares and oblongs of varying shapes and colour. Square thirties office blocks, patterned Victorian buildings, and far down below, the Greek quarter which had yet to be demolished. Flags of multi-coloured washing bobbed and ballooned in the wind.

Mr Pommerance rose from behind his desk and thrust his hand towards Mr Patel.

'I am very sorry I am late. Really. I am truly sorry,' Mr Patel excused himself.

'Quite,' said Mr Pommerance.

Mr Pommerance sat down. 'I expect you came a long way,' he said condescendingly.

Mr Patel sat down.

'This job is a simple one,' Mr Pommerance opened. He leant across his desk, both hands clasped in front of him.

'Yes,' said Mr Patel.

'However, I see you are well qualified.'

'That is right,' said Mr Patel.

'You don't think you might be bored?'

'I am never bored,' said Mr Patel optimistically.

'There are a lot of applicants.'

'Yes?' queried Mr Patel.

'You will be required to collect and sort the mail, to stack it on to trolleys and deliver it from room to room.'

'There are a great many rooms here.'

'No more than usual, I think you'll find, Mr Patel.'

Mr Patel had not intended the remark sarcastically, and he continued with enthusiasm. 'This is a wonderful building, actually. Really wonderful. Remarkable, really. It is so large. And wide. And you can see so far.'

Mr Pommerance's desk did not face the window: the Asian had the view. Mr Patel could see the clouds sifting through the sky, and he noticed how the subtle, changing light altered the bulk and contour of the buildings.

'When did you come here?' asked Mr Pommerance.

'In 1963. I arrived here, in this country in 1963.'

'That is what it says here.' Mr Pommerance was checking. 'And why did you come?'

'I wanted to run.'

'Run?'

'Yes. That is it. That is it, actually.' And Mr Patel laughed, remembering.

Mr Pommerance raised his face sharply from the papers on his desk and studied the man in front of him. He had heard that kind of laughter before. He had seen that expression on the faces of the servants' children in the yard. His past sliced suddenly through his concentration and he caught the figure of an Indian stripped naked to the waist, washing. His father's chauffeur, that was who it was. What was his name? The name? Mr Pommerance could not recall the name. He had worn a white starched uniform and a white peaked cap. Before each meal he would remove his jacket, and gleaming dark and white in the sunlight, splash himself with water. The drops spangled as they trickled down his body. But the memory was like a shadow on a distant wall, distorted by the flickering of the flame that cast it.

'All my life I have wanted to run. But they wouldn't let you there. You may not enter the events, you see.' Mr Patel was bubbling over. 'You may not enter major games events. Not if you are coloured or black, you see. I am coloured.'

'Yes.'

'All my life I have known that I would run. I wanted to run. And so I came here. With thirty pounds.'

'I didn't know you could.'

'You can't now. Not at all. No. But you could then. And so I did,' Mr Patel continued as he laughed. 'I was a very rash young man, actually, yes. The first time I ran here, in this country. I can still remember it. Do you know? It was a strange situation. I was staying with my uncle in Wolverhampton. He had a house there. It was a nice house, actually. Quite a nice house. In a way. I was walking down this lane, strolling down it, really. And there over this hedge, it was a well-cut hedge; all these people were running. I could see their heads bobbing rhythmically up and down, up and down. They looked quite strange you know. I could see only their heads behind the hedge. Then, suddenly I leapt the hedge and landed in the middle of the track. So I joined in. I just joined in you know. And then when I was finished, the race they were running, the race I had half-finished, and joined into, you see, they came up and embraced me. They called and shouted with joy. They thought it was funny you see. But you can't run there. Not like that really. And then it's not the same you see. They were calling, cattawooping my name. Patel . . . Patel . . .'

'Tell me, do you still run?' enquired Mr Pommerance.

'No,' replied the Asian.

Mr Pommerance had been born in India. But his parents had died needlessly and carelessly in a car accident when he was ten. He had spent the rest of his childhood with a spinster aunt in Hitchin. His peopled world in India had given way to a more isolated one in England and he had cocooned his memories in the way a butterfly cocoons itself for protection during metamorphosis.

'What other experience have you had, Mr Patel?' asked Mr Pommerance.

'I have had a great deal of experience, really,' replied Mr Patel.

'You mean you have had a lot of jobs?'

'It is very difficult.'

'Exactly why is it so difficult?' enquired Mr Pommerance, pressing harder now.

'It was very difficult when I first came, because all I wanted to do was win a medal. I thought then that I might do it. So I did a lot of little jobs, stupid little things, you know. I was working in a slaughterhouse near my uncle's house in Wolverhampton to be near the friends that I had made, and doing – I did a lot of other things too. I worked at night you know, a great deal, so that I could run every day. I became quite exhausted.'

'I expect you did,' said Mr Pommerance. It was obvious that Mr Patel was enthusiastic and charming, but not tenacious.

'However, you are qualified,' continued Mr Pommerance.

'I have a lot of qualifications, that is right.'

'Then why not use these qualifications?'

'I have tried,' said Mr Patel.

'Really?' said Mr Pommerance.

'But I am not so young any more, and it is difficult.'

Neither of the men was so young any more.

Through the vast window Mr Patel saw a place shifting across the wide expanse of sky towards another corner of the world. South Africa maybe.

'What a marvellous view isn't it?' exclaimed Mr Patel. The sun was striking the edges of the surrounding buildings so that they shone gold and glittering.

'It's like Christmas here every afternoon. They shine like the decorations on a Christmas tree,' stated Mr Pommerance, shuffling the papers on his desk. Mr Patel was reminded of the glistening jewels in his sister's hair and skin as she turned her lovely face in the sunlight. He had not seen her for a long time.

'The trouble is, Mr Patel, that there's not much room for promotion in this job.'

'I don't think I would mind, you know. I don't think it would matter really.'

'But there are other jobs, Mr Patel.'

'But I am coloured, you see.'

'This is a free country, Mr Patel, you know. There is no prejudice here.' The Indian crumpled at his words and Mr Pommerance felt obliged to speak. 'I was born in Bombay too, you know,' he said lightly.

'Really,' said Mr Patel.

'My father ran a club for polo players.'

'Yes,' said Mr Patel. He did not know what else to say.

'We used to have this Goan cook. That's about all I can remember. He had two small daughters. I don't remember any of their names. They didn't wear traditional Indian clothes. Being Christians, which they were.'

'Yes,' said Mr Patel again.

'He used to dress them in pink dresses and wide-brimmed white organdie hats.' He paused. 'And he used to slaughter chickens in the yard. We had this yard. Outside the house. The servants lived around this yard. A square yard. He had a cleaver and a wooden chopping board. Oh – and there were monsoons too. Heavy rain. I'm sure you know.'

'Yes,' said Mr Patel, who could remember only South Africa.

'The only memory really – the only thing that jars, that sticks in my mind is that one monsoon day – is that what you'd call it – a day of very heavy rain – and a strange sky – this cook killed a chicken that refused to die – and it ran headless round the yard spurting blood, with these two little girls dancing in their pink dresses behind it. Odd memory, isn't it, to remember this chicken strutting headless for a long time? But it must have been seconds. They can't go on for long. It's nerves you know. Nerves.'

Mr Patel did not know what to say. He sat there. Still. And then, suddenly, encouraged by what he considered to be a confidence, he began to talk.

'I think this is a wonderful country, really. I think this is a wonderful place. I read about it when I was a boy. I read all the books, you know. My father bought them for us. He had known the British in Bombay. I read about Waterloo, and Wellington

218

and Dickens. We read Dickens, you see. We all read Dickens.'

'How nice,' said Mr Pommerance.

'We thought this country wonderful. It must be filled with splendid things and splendid people. That is why I came, you see.'

'Oh,' said Mr Pommerance, who could scarcely credit such naïveté.

'And then, when I got here, I found it was quite different.'

'It is,' said Mr Pommerance. 'The literature to which you are referring is part of history. Factual and literary.'

'The place is smaller, much smaller, than I had thought it would be,' Mr Patel continued, and then paused. 'And all the people are not kind.' Mr Patel paused again. 'And I must tell you, that there is a great deal I cannot care for here.'

Mr Pommerance found this statement arrogant but said nothing.

'I have been surprised. Very surprised, really. It isn't how I thought it would be, how I thought I would find it at all, at all. Do you know? There is one thing that I must say though, that I must tell you. At home, in South Africa where my family is, the streets are wide and the buildings modern. But we can't go there.'

'You mean that certain areas are prohibited to you? In the way that you may not enter games events?' Mr Pommerance was pleased to re-enter the conversation at a less personal level.

'No. It is more than that. Much more. Do you know that I may not enter a government building there? I may not even enter a building like this one. I may not go inside. I may not enter it at all. Do you know? And so you see when I come here to talk to you, I am quite . . . it is quite wonderful to be here, you see. I can never quite forget.' Mr Pommerance had never appreciated prohibition in this sense.

'You see I would like this job,' the Asian continued, gathering courage. 'I need it,' he continued. 'I have a wife and two small boys. They jumped on me before I left this morning. The little one is quite, he is really quite . . . engaging.' Mr Patel laughed. Mr Pommerance caught the expression of affection in

Mr Patel's eyes. 'You see I need it. And I am sure that you can understand the reason. I have a right to ask here.'

Mr Pommerance suddenly felt extremely angry for a reason he did not understand. 'And I have the right to refuse,' he said.

The Asian was confused. 'But I think that you can understand, can't you?' said Mr Patel, 'You must have a wife and children too, a family to care about . . .?'

'No. I don't understand. You see. I have no family. I live quite alone. I live alone.'

Both were silent. Mr Pommerance looked down at his desk and then continued. 'I'm very sorry Mr Patel, but there is no reason, I think, for prolonging this interview. It is my opinion that you are too highly qualified for the job. I do not see how we could place you here.'

'What am I to do?' Mr Patel had applied for many jobs.

Mr Pommerance almost snorted. 'What would you like me to say, Mr Patel?'

'I don't know. I am sorry. Very sorry.' Mr Patel apologized.

'How can I provide your answer, Mr Patel? What am I to say to an Indian draughtsman who wants to be a runner? Tell me that. Can you answer me?'

Mr Patel did not reply.

'You have to provide your own answers, Mr Patel. You have to provide your own.'

But Mr Patel had gone already, bowing, bending, as he moved towards the door. 'Thank you for the interview,' he mumbled. 'But now I have to go. Thank you very much. Thank you. Thank you.' He was backing out of the door. He was backing down the corridor. He descended in the lift and left the building without looking back.

Mr Pommerance rose from his desk and looked out over London. He could see the white glare of the Nash Terraces. It was growing dark. The moon was appearing again, and under it, an echo, was the golden crescent of the new mosque. He could see the post-office tower, blinking, and the frame of the aviary in the zoo.

Mr Pommerance was an experienced personnel officer. He

had done his job for many years. Tomorrow he would see ten more applicants for posts and positions within the structure for which he worked. Mr Patel would be a number in a filing cabinet, a white piece of flimsy paper with comments scrawled upon it, and finally a piece of computer data.

Mr Patel caught the tube immediately. He ran for it. But this time there was no friendly face from Bombay, and no smattering of Gujarati to remind him of other times and places.

He tumbled through the barrier and towards the Central Line. The rush-hour crowds curbed his direction but he shuffled through towards the platform he wanted. Somewhere down one of the dusty passages he could hear snatches of song; fragments of rock music played badly on a battered guitar. Someone, down one of the filthy tunnels, was singing. The voice was louder now. It was hopeful and strong. But the rumbling of the oncoming train dispersed all other sound and Mr Patel was carried forward into the carriage by the weight of the other people who surrounded him. And then the doors closed.

J. NEW

Crossing Demon

'For by the grace of God I am the Reviver of
ADORATION amongst ENGLISHMEN'
(*Jubilate Agno*, Fragment B 332)

These are miserable times. I felt this deeply when at three
o'clock on a morning in March, walking home after a
twelve-hour night shift to make myself a little bit extra, I came
to the crossroads which separates the industrial estate from the
village. A roundabout in the centre. Where four high streetlights, one for each angle of the cross, cast the scene into a sick
orange light at that dark hour, a flood of it, the sides of the grass
shone sick in it and I shone sick in it too, the backs of my hands,
the oil on my boots and trousers.

It was stepping into that gleam made me stop a spell on the
kerb because there was no traffic to stop me, so early, only
force of habit and the glare. Odd birds screamed from the fields
and scrappy woods back of the estate. What kinds I don't know.

It was because worn-out that I stopped to get my breath for a
space over the gutter at the bottom of the embankment where
planners had planned their landscaping effects, and over on the
top of the roundabout too, now high grass and weeds growing. I
don't know what they call the grasses, I don't know what they
call the weeds. And cartons and drinks-cans riptopped and
stubs. And the back off a shirt in the centre that I thought some
couple have stripped in their car and tossed it out the window in
a gallivant. But as I looked longer, stirred by the thought, I saw
it was really a man's back and rising and an old man's pale

long-haired head and his face in the light of the streetlights was an old drinker's.

It seemed to me I had disturbed him at his *kip*. I felt in my pockets wondering would he recognize a penny in the dimness. Cheers I says.

He answered, but in an odd way starting like a scream deep back down in him, a keen sound that at first I thought it was an articulated on the distant bypass, heading for Rickmansworth on an all-night run, but as he rose the sound was louder and more *thick* then rough too from an old big throat then simple gabble (as with kids in the street) and then something that was so clearly rational speech that if I could have recognized his manner I might have been able to understand it (now he was right, stood upright).

But facing away from me too, looking down the London road so I wasn't quite able to catch what he said. I don't know why I stopped. He must have been a tough old bird in this weather.

The other thing is it was a cold night, weeks before Easter, and the smoke tumbled out of my mouth and nostrils just breathing (which isn't *smoke* at all only the warm inside of me touching the cold outside thereby precipitating a transformation as they said to me at school) but this man. This character who was doing a lot of talking himself must have been as cold as the night *inside* because no smoke came from his mouth. That's all.

He turned still talking on the spot until he faced me and then I could understand what he said which was this:

I was under the constant necessity to pray, sir.

Then I was much afflicted and this for a period of years. My mind, as if it had been some small beast, was hunted about by a pack of fears sir.

That my wife would die in the night.

Anna. Maria.

That my two girls would be taken.

Polly. Elizabeth. Four. Six.

That townsmen in the dark would set upon and beat me for my money or out of spite or murder me as I wandered night by night among the streets of the city.

For I was often lost in that city and wandered among its handled stones.

Handled. Touch of hands. Worked of hands. Stones.

Or that I might starve as I have seen stouter men than me do. The heaviest man can starve in these hard times, that's no fancy. Or might take a cancer and waste. Or die drunk.

For I drank from simple fear.

And my family be made paupers and set on the parish and put in the *house* and set to work and beaten there, whipped to it, chained to their tasks and starved at them too to keep them peaceful, until they were all dead, as is the custom nowadays. In my time.

I did not follow him at this point. What house? Which time? Nowadays?

Because these are the rigs of the times that poor humanity is carried from its home and pressed to such use, used to its death, shackled, benched, shedded, ranked with neighbours, tasked, such was not the usage when I was a boy, it was some new spirit born in our towns since.

And I said: *ab hoc daemone terreor*, which is to say: I am terrified by this spirit.

Now I was a reasonable man at that period and could see no unlikelihood that such things might happen to me and mine especially as I was not a *provider*, I will be honest with you, not a provident man.

Because I said: their pleasures are not my pleasures their satisfactions are not my satisfactions their hopes (these people) are not my hopes. Am I then to live and work without pleasure? Without satisfaction? Without hope?

Not a saving nature, not a *saver* at that period.

And as I saw the terrors of debt and labour and helplessness bring others down and more of them day by day and down lower and lower I thought I must take to my knees and pray to the Omnipotent Omniscient Ineffable to keep them from me, reasoning thus: if I do not pay HIM with my praise when I should then such a thing will come upon me.

Or.

If I do not pray to HIM in the correct *manner* then such things will be sent against me, which puzzled me, to know if I prayed at the right time and in the right manner, and this set me on my knees many times more such was my anxiety.

Meantime walking a calm man amongst my fellows, a scholar and fine poet (in the Classical style) by day, a prize-winner, friend to the chief of critics, and at night to *vary* it and sugar my melancholy I went out skirted like a midwife on the stage in London, practising my obstetrics upon the vicious body of that town, displaying its true offspring in the fit company of midgets, dogs, and apes.

God bless Ballard Mango my great monkey.

I say again.

And always falling down in the quiet between discourse, in secret between acts, praying to keep misfortune from us all. And if for company I could not fall down on my knees I would fall down in my mind, to keep it from us.

And was still in fear.

Then took a fever and could in no way regulate what I did and thus an illness stopped me in this *work*. And it was as if the fever burned out all my fears so that on recovering from it I said: you have been a mad man to quarrel with the ALMIGH-TY and begging HIM to keep such misfortunes from you. As if those things you fear had been HIS work.

Look about you again with your working eyes I said, look about.

It is very *plain* who the culprits are, and there is no praying to *them*.

And I prayed no more for a season, only in measure and by custom, and laboured rationally to forget my fears though often sick and dizzy from the memory of them.

Then a lorry came down the London road turning the roundabout with its headlights full-on to my face blinding me for a minute, and when the rattling of its load had died away and I could hear this man's voice again, and I don't know if it was my eyes but his hair seemed darker and his face smoother than they had been before, and as his speech grew intelligible again I recognized that he said this:

I was mad to rejoice.

My need is to be *clear*.

It appeared to me in starts that whatever I might say in praise of this world it would fall too short and that I must therefore be an ingrate and a sour thing on HIS tongue.

I began to reproach myself with this each day saying: try again, try again, for I conjectured that by constantly attempting to speak my fill I must one day succeed and do it.

But since I was forever seeing and hearing and feeling new things in this world (or rather seeing that I saw them, feeling that I felt them, for they were too *quick*), the magnitude of blessings would bring me to my knees again saying: speak, idiot.

You dumb head.

And even while I did this I could see my plight multiplied in all the men and women who forever walked about me in the public places, and I thought how can my speech ever be complete when there is always some part of me held dull and lost in them? It cannot.

And would be ever shouting at them: on yr *knees*! And could never rest from it while these creatures were about me, every hour of the day and night, walking and standing still.

Thus was I crippled. For I could at that time barely take a step without falling down and crying out.

And glad enough when one day friends carried me to an isolate place where I had few fellows to magnify my needs in this way, so that I could cease my shouting and give myself up to prayer alone, which I did, and prayed without ceasing for several hundred years together until the people of that place grew weary of me and put me out.

For though I was small charge on them they had to feed me every day, opening my jaws wide with harping-irons and pushing the food down my throat as if I had been a young bird in the nest.

Because I had forgot my mouth was made for any other *thing* but praise.

Neither would I lay down to sleep there but they wrapped me in a coat and made me do it.

So I distressed them, as I say, and they put me out again among the hosts.

My thought again was the magnitude of people and the magnitude of things would bleed me white for I could not in any way *stop*.

Then friends seeing my predicament brought me to a second house before the chattering of 'ghosts' could destroy me and I was happily for a season *pent*.

Now I took occasion to be clear with myself anyway and said: you have worked with yr mouth through these dark ages and said nothing yet, and it's certain if you continue in these freaks you'll not live long.

And this seemed strange, that HE would have me die in my ingratitude, for so I was still, having never yet spoken my mind.

Then I said: how is this? Yr an educated man? You have talked days at a time. Days? Weeks. Weeks? Years. Yet now considering your case you can in no way remember what it is you have said and what you have left unsaid.

For I thought that this was the heart of my failure, that I always left something unsaid.

And not remembering, it is also certain that you are foolishly repeating yourself, what you have already said.

For I thought this lay at the root of the heart, that I repeated myself and grew tiresome in his ear, like the heathen.

Or.

That my anatomy of the world in praises had still some joints neglected, some articulations missed that left the body of my prayer unsound and limping. And as it, therefore I myself limped. In the mind.

This reasoning brought me to a halt from constant crying and I lay quiet not understanding what I should do. Not understanding what I should do I lay still in my agitation.

Then it seemed to me I should move with method in all my acts and that if I acted with a *plan* I might do it yet, which was to take one element from the multiplicity of existences and set down its *name* with the blessing that was natural to it in a great Catalogue, and next day to set another thing down by name, in its place, and next day another.

Then I would have them stored.

Then I would suffer no anxiety that I had repeated a name for every thing I set down would have its name set down in store, clear to be seen.

Nor fear that I had missed any thing that would leave the Praise unfinished, because I now understood that what could never be given out in the shouting of a moment or a year could be built up slowly through the years, with patience and steadiness in the task whose incompleteness at the end of any day was a sign of its growth, that it approached completeness closer than it had the previous day, and that it would approach still more closely on the next, so that the fears which had almost killed me were now changed into a hope that I might develop through the play of my own effort to that state where I could speak at last. Full and Clear.

So set to work and would enter a name each morning, or no more than three names, and none at any other time for I would not clamour.

I had clamoured enough.

And I said: *huic arte nova conservatus sum*, which is to say: I have been saved by this new science.

And for three years remained steady in the performance though often sick and dizzy from the glory of it.

And this was my *theory*, that praise is not the special but the ordinary state and that without such speaking there can be no thing. And because I understood this I kept the world spinning with my tongue and pen.

The remainder of each day I spent in the garden of that house, or in reading books of material philosophy, cyclopaedias, histories, and newspapers, seeking out examples of the

228

world's variety for at last, I said, I will have all things set down.

And I blessed the friends who brought me there and left me so that this work might be accomplished.

And I blessed King David who was my forebear in his head and in his dance and in his preservation of ISRAEL (and in his madnesses and appetites too) who spoke straighter to HIM than we can now and who was at his work. While I still knelt in the dark, praying and not seeing, calling out and not tasting, kneeling and not lying down.

And I blessed the appearance of every stone and every other thing that receives light, the skin of the world.

And I blessed my hearing, sweet-harped by the multitude of discourse of all creatures.

And I blessed my taste, I taste *salt*.

For rejoicing with me at last my eyes spilled red milky tears.

To nurse me: to nurse, to *nourish* or *sustain*,

That I had not felt since I was a boy.

And I blessed the taste of that world I took as GOD'S GIFT who makes me tears to salt me, oceans to *preserve* me, amen.

Was I supposed to leave this poor soul here? Could I take him back and let him bed down on the floor? Would I have to get in touch with the authorities though on the following day? Would they hold me responsible for his wandering about? I could not solve this one and as I stood in a fix he passed a hand across his face (it was old and broken-up after all) and said this:

Then I was taken from the house again.

Then I had to be a *busy* man.

Then I could not continue my work and had no hope that I might complete it.

Then the world spun down as I had predicted.

Now it has spun down quite.

Then I was in the King's prison for my debts but they would let me into the streets by day but I had to be back and celled again each night for my care.

This was their Rules,

Then I thought I will go to my wife's father in Aylesbury who will pay to set me free.

Then I thought I cannot. For I had only the day's light hours to travel in and no money for my fare.

Then I thought with HIS help can I not reach that town and be back in my cell by nightfall if HE wills it who holds the sun in the palm of HIS hand? Yes.

Then I set off in the morning walking.

Then night came down and I was not even at Aylesbury, I thought this is HIS trick to test me, and praised HIM a little, and went on, and it soon turned day again.

Then went on and could not reach the town, as if I had been led out of my way.

These tricks again I said. This is a demon in my imagination.

Then a second appearance of the night.

In reality, I said, I have been out barely an hour.

He is my STAFF.

And went on.

Then HE imitated nightfall over me a third time but I closed my eyes and went on still.

Then I thought I must rest a while to be fit for the completion of HIS miracle in me.

Then I lay down here.

Then I fell asleep on the blessed grass.

(1722–1771)

Birds on the overhead wires started up, the streetlights cut out, and dawn broke. Some sort of birds. And the odd thing was that though everything was getting brighter the man on the roundabout (quiet now, or only a murmur anyway) became so indistinct that in a few minutes when I was able to see the outline of the new housing estate over the fields above the opposite embankment there didn't seem to be anybody standing between me and it at all.

Then I felt the one side of my face gone wet and cold and the other side dull in a pain because of the early-morning frost because I had my head in the rubbish grass lying face-on to the gutter of the main road. Lucky? I'll say so. Because if I had blanked out a second later it would have been right in the middle of the road and cracked my head on its tarmac at least or a car gone over me in the dark. Lordy lordy I thought. Best get me home.

ROSALIND BELBEN

The Licences to Eat Meat

Helen Atmen's written paper, prelim. Her answer to question 4(e), describe your sensations on eating Emmenthaler cheese.

'It is rubbery, and has a funny smell. I suppose I was six or seven when my mother placed Emmenthaler for the first time on my plate instead of my usual Irish Cheddar. I know now it comes from a valley in the country of Switzerland, probably called the Emmen; and, though it tastes as if a she-goat put her teats into it, it's made by cows who eat nothing but the purest grass and mountain herbage. It tastes of the Alps, and white milk, and frothy wooden buckets, and flowers, and of the cows' big rubbery lips eating the flowers; and where the cheese has large holes in it, that's because the cows have to take large, contented breaths; rather like us, when we eat and feel it's all so delicious it's quite, quite unbearable.'

I marked Helen's Emmenthaler piece with a B−; imaginative, but a little hectic, and doesn't come to grips with subject.

The same examination. Helen could have answered 5(a), describe and compare the lives (nasty, short and brutish) of fourteenth-century swine and contemporary porkers; or 5(b), composition entitled If I were a Bull Calf. Helen took 5(c), describe your emotions on eating a pork chop with apple rings.

'I felt fine, honestly. Oh yes, I remarked to my mother how the pork chop had really been rootling acorns in a shady wood, *in its mind*, while its sweat (hot-house) and shit (powdered food) and piss (OK, clean water) and PIGGINESS, melted into the concrete; it being mucky, because that's what we think pigs are, don't we, so they have to be.

'After it was deaded, it wouldn't have cared if its skin was scalded, would he?'

Very unoriginal. D+.

I wondered what Helen had been reading. There is no *pressure* on these children to take the examination. I advised that a failure in the practical was in the offing. Helen wished to persevere. The desire to continue to eat meat in adulthood is overwhelming, it seems.

To question 3(a), she managed the following.

'Beef, it's smashing. The meat squelches, it tickles the old taste buds, it wraps around the teeth and tongue like it was fresh beech leaves and marshmallow. The Yorkshire's nice.'

Hardly a gift for words. The boys are better. They write macho things about sinews, roasted muscles, bones to chew, and a bit too much on gravy; but with rich colour. Helen has no sense of colour.

Helen's practical prelim was done in the abattoir at Little Molding by the Fosse. All Helen said was, 'Funny, when we were in France, me and my mum, we passed, in the Datsun I mean, a Café de l'Abattoir. How could anyone drink coffee in a . . . They aren't half rum, Frogs.' Then she turned her head away, screamed, and bolted like a frightened sheep.

I failed her.

I advised that there was minimal point in her proceeding to the full practical, parts 1 (poultry) and 2.

I also failed today three out of four boys. Two of them, because, in practical part 2, they both dropped the humane killer and were sick (extra fee to slaughtermen for hose and disinfectant); and one, because he enjoyed himself. To the (impassive) fourth boy I awarded licence.

The Present

Erin Casey was mad. That fact had been well established by the staff at Bellbury General and Erin's mother. Hebephrenic Schizophrenia. That's what it said on his admission papers. Of course, his mother hadn't called it that. 'I simply haven't the vocabulary,' she told them. 'No, I shall leave it to the experts, now. He's out of my hands.'

Erin had been in his mother's hands a long time before she finally committed him. Forty-three years to be exact. He was her only son and she did so want to keep him at home, but it had got so she couldn't cope. 'He does things,' she told the doctors.

His case report was not extensive. The hospital had no recorded medical history to go on and so relied a fair deal on his mother's words.

The patient appears to be suffering a mildly symptomatic personality disorder and will, therefore, be treated for non-organic psychosis and schizophrenia, grp. B. He has not been shown to display any excessively aggressive behaviour. His manner is pleasant though he is prone, at times, to behave in a withdrawn or uncommunicative fashion towards other inmates and the staff.

Erin was not unpopular at the hospital. 'He's one of our cheeriest patients,' Nurse Brown told the visiting specialist on one of his rounds. 'He gives so much of himself.'

Erin liked Nurse Brown more than anyone else on the

hospital staff. Shortly after his arrival he had taken to leaving presents for her under his pillow or in his bed-pan. Locks of his hair, small cellophane packets containing cut fingernails or toenails and occasionally the odd bundle of used handkerchiefs tied neatly and wrapped for her special attention.

Nurse Brown was still in training and did not yet qualify as a full-time, paid member of staff at Bellbury. She did not think it her place, therefore, to report having received the gifts and indeed, was almost embarrassed to do so. Instead she thanked Erin, saying that she truly appreciated the thought behind his gestures, if not the actual items being presented.

She attempted many times to refocus his attentions and discourage Erin from giving her these gifts. On the odd occasion when art therapy had been administered in the ward, Erin had proven himself to be a very able sculptor. Nurse Brown laid special emphasis on this. 'You have lovely hands, Erin. You ought to use them more. People appreciate a craftsman, so it means he can afford to appreciate himself.'

Erin loved it when the nurse spoke to him like that. His eyes crinkled and his face lit up in a huge impish grin. When she complimented his hands he moaned bashfully and hid them under his red woolly pullover, stretching it out and down to cover his flies.

Often, it appeared that Erin had accepted Nurse Brown's advice, for she would see him working in the corner on his knitting which he was being taught by one of the day nurses, or adding more bits to his sculptures. He always showed the results to Nurse Brown who gushed approval, admiring his skill and dexterity. 'I'd give anything to be as creative as you,' she told him. 'My fingers are so clumsy and nervous. I wouldn't know one end of a knitting needle from the other and my artwork's hopeless.'

Once, when Erin had been playing football with some of the other patients from his ward, he cut his knee on the forecourt. Nurse Brown had come rushing out on to the field and swabbed and dressed it for him, expressing great concern over his injury. The wound took a good few days to heal and during this time

Nurse Brown paid Erin special attention, helping him to change the bandage and apply disinfectant to the knee. To the rest of the ward it appeared as though the student nurse was rather overemphasizing the tragedy of the event but Erin seemed visibly affected by Nurse Brown's tender show of care and concern.

On her way home one evening Erin handed Nurse Brown a small package, telling her it was to say thank you for her careful nursing of his knee and to make sure she would not forget how much it had meant to him. She thanked him, fingering the package, which felt soft and padded. Assuming it was one of his attempts at knitting and not wishing to embarrass him by opening it in front of him, she made a great show of tucking the present preciously into her bag, explaining that she would save it to open at home, before bed, as a special treat. Erin's face beamed with pride as he watched her leave from his upstairs window, with her bag on her arm.

Nurse Brown lived with her boyfriend, Ken, who was an auxiliary in the same hospital. Ken worked in a different wing and so he and Nurse Brown often exchanged stories about various patients or events they had encountered in their own sections. Ken knew from Nurse Brown all about Erin and the presents he had left her in the past. In fact, the whole thing quite amused him and he prided himself on having analysed the situation completely.

'It's obviously very Freudian,' he told her. 'The poor bloke's trying to tell you how much he'd like to screw you. 'Course, deep down he knows you don't actually get off on fondling his snot-rags, but short of giving you the old one-two, what choice had he got? He's probably got an anal fixation or something. Obviously never reached sexual maturity.'

Nurse Brown was tickled by Ken's lay psychology and liked to tease him about his theories. 'All right, smarty. What's an "anal fixation" then?'

'It's basic, isn't it?' he told her. 'I read it in one of your books on quacks. It's like, say, when you're little, your mum or someone tokes you up on goodies every time you do a plop.

236

Well, face it, you're bound to grow up thinking that the way to a woman's heart is through your excrement.'

On this particular evening when Nurse Brown came home with the package from Erin, she decided to wait and open it with Ken when he returned back from his late-evening shift.

'Another present from Erin?' he asked her when she showed him. 'How sweet. He's probably cut off his prick for you this time.'

'Don't be horrible,' she scuffed him. 'He's stopped doing that. I think he's knitted me something. The day nurse is teaching him.'

'Let's have a look, then.'

The two of them pulled at the bits of string and sellotape Erin had used to secure the package. The wrapping tore to reveal a mass of small cotton-balls from the hospital surgery. From the middle of the padding fell a small, brown, paper-thin object on to the beige shag carpet in the bedroom.

'Jesus Christ, it's his scab!' Nurse Brown stared in disbelief at the hardened conglomeration of dried blood and dead skin. 'I don't believe it.'

'What a fucking pervert. I'd report this if I were you,' Ken told her. 'Honestly, the guy needs putting away.'

She looked at him pointedly.

'Well, you know what I mean. Being taught a lesson or something. That's disgusting.'

'Perhaps I will say something,' she sighed, 'tomorrow. Ugh God, pick it up and chuck it will you. It's giving me the jeebies.'

The next day in the staff-room Nurse Brown informed Erin's doctor and the senior staff nurse of his gift of the scab the night before. Although the doctor did not seem unduly surprised he did seem to think it was not a matter which should just go ignored. 'He's one of the brighter ones,' he told her. 'He ought to know better.'

The doctor suggested that the ward staff suspend Erin's visiting rights for a month as a way of teaching him the repercussions of such anti-social behaviour. 'As his mother's the only one who ever comes to see him, he's not really going to be losing out then, is he?' The doctor winked and sent Nurse Brown off to impose the sanctions.

Erin did not seem too perturbed at the proposal of the punishment. His mother, however, was livid. When informed she marched straight down to the hospital demanding to know the reasons why she was being kept from her son. The doctor explained about the scab incident and assured her the suspension was only for a month.

'It's nothing to do with seeing me that makes him do these things,' she told them. 'Believe me, I've been the victim of his terrible atrocities myself.' She became tearful and related a story to the doctor and the staff nurse of how Erin had, on her fiftieth birthday, presented her with a sample of his own faeces on a china plate with one burning birthday candle stuck in the middle. She claimed that he had insisted she make a wish on the candle before blowing it out and then had become hurt and upset when she tried to flush the present down the toilet. When the doctor questioned her further about Erin's toilet history, she became even more irate and insisted that he had never had any problems in that area before. 'Even when he was a baby he went in the potty,' she huffed. 'No thanks to anyone but me, I might add. I gave him a sweetie every time he did one.'

As well as having suspended his visiting rights, the staff had decided to provide Erin with extra therapeutic activity to fill his spare hours. At Nurse Brown's suggestion they sent him to do woodwork twice a week in the occupational therapy unit in the left wing, where Ken worked. Erin appeared to enjoy himself immensely at these added sessions and came back to his own ward brimming with tales of how he and the other patients had mended this table leg and that window frame, or added a new bit on to one of the doctor's broken chairs. He described to Nurse Brown the types of tools that he and the other patients were being allowed to use in the workshop. Nurse Brown was horrified to hear how electric drills, circular saws and razor-sharp planes were all given quite freely to the patients to use. 'I suppose that's the way they try to teach them responsibility,' she told Ken later.

She warned Erin how dangerous tools like that could be and begged him to be careful when doing anything with them. Her concern brought back the familiar warm glow to Erin's face and he threw back his shoulders like a hero whenever he mentioned his activities in woodwork.

It had been nearly a month since the doctor had decided to suspend Erin's visiting rights and the Christmas holidays were fast approaching. Nurse Brown encouraged Erin to work on something special that he might be able to give his mother when she came to see him after the long break. He told the nurse that he would far rather make something for her, but she told him not to worry and that she was bound to receive lots of nice Christmas presents anyway.

The patients in Erin's ward had been busily making preparations and decorations for their Christmas party to which visitors and nurses from the ward had been specially invited. Nurse Brown and Ken planned to make a brief appearance at the party before going down to the main Christmas dinner laid on annually for all the doctors and the nurses from the psychiatric wings of the hospital. Erin told Nurse Brown that it was very important that he see her at the party so that he might present her with the Christmas gift he had planned for her. She promised, explaining that she would not be able to stay long, but that she couldn't wait to see what Erin had intended for her.

Mrs Casey came early to the hospital on the day of the party as it was the first day she had been permitted to see her son since the sanctions were imposed a month earlier. She brought with her several packages for Erin from various of his relatives and one special one from herself. She would not let him open any of them until the party, saying that presents were always nicer when one waited for them.

When Nurse Brown arrived at the party with Ken, she found Erin sitting in a corner of the ward with his mother, absorbed in opening the boxes of chocolates and small parcels of socks and handkerchiefs his aunts and uncles had sent for him. She smiled and nudged Ken, suggesting they pop up a bit later after he had had a chance to open his presents and spend time with his mother. Erin saw her leaving just as he was about to open the special package from his mother. He ran out after her and followed her down the hall corridor, begging her to come back as she had not yet seen what he had for her. Erin's mother appeared behind him, holding the package she had brought for her son's Christmas.

She stared angrily at Nurse Brown, 'I'm sorry, I'm sure,' she said, 'but really, if he'd rather spend his time with you . . .'

'Don't be silly,' Nurse Brown interjected. 'Erin only asked me to come and collect my present from him. Ken and I are just about to have dinner with the rest of the staff in any case.'

'Give her her present, Erin. It's obviously all she came for!'

Erin seemed confused by his mother's anger and turned appealingly to Nurse Brown, explaining that he didn't actually have the present yet to give her and that he needed to go to the workshop to get it ready.

Ken explained that the workshop had been locked up according to regulations but, in an effort to erase the puckered look of disappointment from Erin's face, he promised to look for the keys and open it up on his way down to the canteen. 'It is Christmas, after all,' he said. 'What the hell.'

He made Erin promise to do nothing else in the workshop but get the present and return straight back up to the ward. 'Otherwise it'll be my ass,' he warned.

Erin nodded and looked relieved as he followed his mother back to the ward to open the present she had brought for him and to give her the one he had made for her.

'What a horrible couple,' his mother told Erin as she watched him gently pulling the wrapping from a pair of brown and white hand-knitted gloves with the letters E R I N written skilfully in knitted design on their fronts. 'I'm surprised they let people like that work here.'

With gloved hands Erin proudly handed his mother the wrapped parcel he had, at Nurse Brown's urging, eventually intended for her. The package contained a small statuette of praying hands he had sculpted out of wood during his woodworking sessions. The carving was a crude replica of the model of the Praying Hands of Jesus which stood in the hospital chapel next to the burning candles of remembrance.

'Ooh, it's nice,' she cooed. 'Is it hands?' A sugary school-marm inflection crept into her voice. 'And what are they doing? Praying? Well, they're very good in any case. You copied them, I suppose. Do they teach you religion here?'

After Erin had shown the gloves round a few of the other patients and visitors, and after Mrs Casey had stuffed the praying hands into her John Lewis carrier-bag next to some wads of used Christmas paper she had salvaged for future wrapping, one of the supervising ward sisters suggested a party game.

'Blind man's bluff!' she called out, trying hard to imbue some enthusiasm into the gathering. She moved energetically over towards Erin and began to tie a large white handkerchief around his head to cover his eyes.

Taking her cue, Mrs Casey patted the nurse on the arm and whispered, 'That's it, I'll be off now. Got my sister coming round in a bit. Bye bye, Erin. Happy Christmas, dear.'

When his mother had left and Erin had dutifully played a few rounds of the game, he excused himself from the party saying that he had something special to do before Nurse Brown returned.

In the staff-room, Ken was helping one of the porters carve the turkey while Nurse Brown sat talking with some of the staff, telling those who hadn't heard the story of Erin's scab. 'But honestly,' she insisted, 'he's been so much better since he's been allowed to do the woodwork.'

'Christ, that reminds me,' Ken wheeled round quickly, the knife in his hand dripping with gravy. 'The bloody workshop'll still be open. I completely forgot.' He put down the knife and told the porter he would be only a moment as he had better go and lock up the workroom just in case anybody unauthorized should happen to wander in.

Erin was in the workshop when Ken arrived. His large body lay slumped on a bench. Across his face was spread a serene smile of accomplishment as on the table in front of him lay the present he had so carefully planned for Nurse Brown. Both his hands had been sawn off at the wrists and lay limp by the circular saw which was still humming round on the workbench table. By the side, carefully folded and completely unsoiled, were the gloves his mother had knitted him.

At home, on Mrs Casey's mantelpiece, stood the small wooden statue Erin had made for her. 'It's not the real thing, mind,' she told her sister. But at least it was a proper present. Clean and acceptable.

GABRIEL JOSIPOVICI

Children's Games

What we should do is invent a game.

What sort of game?

I don't know. There must be lots of games.

We've played all the games.

That's what I mean. We need to invent a new one.

What about that game with the letters and the blindfold?

No. We must invent a game. A completely new game.

Do you mean a game with a ball or with paper and pencils?

It could be that. Or it could be different.

How can we invent a game? We're not clever enough.

You don't have to be clever. You just need to stop and think for a bit about what you would really like.

Well you stop and think. We'll watch you.

No, he's right. We just need to stop a bit and think about what we really want to play.

I don't mind. I don't mind what I play.

But some games are better than others, aren't they? Why should we just play the games other people have invented? Simon's right. They may not be the ones we really want to play. Not really.

How can we know what we really want to play? Do you know what you really want to play?

Oh, shut up all of you. Either we concentrate and think of a new game or we give up and play one of the boring old ones.

I don't want to play anything at all.

Why not?

I just don't.

You can't just not want to like that. There must be a reason.
Why should there be a reason?
Hey! You know what?
What?
What?
I think there's someone at the door, listening to us.
Oh? Are you sure?
Wait. Listen.
I can't hear anything.
Can't you? Listen.
Do you know who it is?
Of course I know.
Is it him?
Who else?
He's standing there behind the door. He's stooping down and putting his ear against the wood.
Has he got sandals on?
Of course he has. He always wears sandals. When it's cold he puts on socks, but he always wears sandals.
How else is he dressed?
He's got his white pullover on that always looks dirty and his trousers hang down because he doesn't wear a belt. What else do you want to know?
Do you think he realized we were talking for his benefit at the start?
Are you talking for his benefit now?
No. For ours.
Why ours?
Work it out.
Haven't we had enough of him? Couldn't we think of something else?
You mean because there's no one outside the door?
Of course there's no one. Who would want to listen to us?
Well, who would?
No one. Isn't that so, Jojo?
Well, Jojo, we're waiting for you to reply.
Jojo doesn't want to speak today.

But Jojo must speak today. Mustn't he?

Oh yes. Jojo must speak today. It's essential that Jojo speak today.

Even if he doesn't want to?

Even if he doesn't want to.

Perhaps Jojo's listening to him out there, in his sandals, snooping about behind the door. Perhaps Jojo has ears only for him.

Is that what you're doing, Jojo? Are you straining your ears to catch a sound outside the door?

Jojo doesn't want to have anything to do with us. Look at him putting his hands up to his ears.

But we want to have something to do with Jojo, don't we? When he won't talk to us we stick little pins into his arms and legs, don't we?

Even if he turns his back to us and puts his hands over his ears. We stick little pins into him all the same.

Give me the pins. I know exactly where to stick them.

You and Jeremy can do it this time.

Why does he open and close his mouth like that and not say anything?

That's his way. His way of pretending he can't speak at all.

But we know better, don't we? We know he can speak if he wants to.

Of course he can. As soon as we're gone he starts to speak. Isn't that so, Jojo?

He's turned his face to the wall.

That's all right Jojo. You just stay there like that. We'll sit behind you where you needn't see us. And every now and again Lynn and Jerry will stick pins into your arms and legs.

Not very often.

Just once in a while.

Just to let you know we're there.

Hey! You know what I think?

What?

I think he's still outside, listening. Holding his breath and listening.

In his sandals?

In his sandals.

Are you sure, Mary?

He's standing there in his sandals and his dirty old white pullover, with his unshaven face and his greasy hair, stooping and holding his breath and pressing his ear to the door. He thinks there's someone called Jojo in the room.

Do you think he's really as silly as that?

He's not silly. He just believes his ears.

You know what I think?

No. What do you think?

I think he doesn't realize it's he who's in the room and and we who're outside, behind the door, listening to him.

Listening to him stirring on the bed, breathing.

Listening to him straining his ears to catch what we're saying. Sitting up in bed, his eyes closed for greater concentration, turning his head slowly from side to side, trying not to make a noise, trying to hear.

But all he hears is his own heart. The blood pounding in his temples.

One moment he hears, the next not. One moment he could swear we were there. The next not.

Now we'll all be silent. Now we'll all stop talking. We'll hold our breath and listen. We'll wait for him to act.

Yes. When Simon gives the word, everybody stop talking.

Now. Everybody. Silence.